ATLANTIS

THE LOST CHRONICLES

CORIN THISTLEWOOD

Also by Corin Thistlewood

Chants of Power - Songs of Spirit

Introduction to Celtic Shamanism

Spirit Quest - The Hero's Journey

The Touchwood Chronicles trilogy

The Sun & the Moon

The Velum Scroll

Blue Moon Rising

For my friends who had the patience to Beta read countless versions of my manuscript.

Preface

Although classed as a fictional/ fantasy book, the concept for this work, (as with most of my books), is to follow the ancient druid tradition of telling a good story, yet woven within it is much sacred lore and knowledge of the metaphysical world.

Within this work, I explore age old fundamental life questions. Questions about the nature of reality, existence, and the universe. It delves into topics such as the nature of objects, time, space, causality, and possibility.

In the modern world, where the unexplainable is dismissed or exploited. What if the UFO sightings gripping humanity's imagination aren't alien at all—but ancient? What if the fairy tales of old contained some truth? What if the Tuatha de Danann, a hyper human race, reported in the Celtic myth and legends where actually memories of actual events long ago?

Today, natural disasters, strange lights in the sky, and unearthly encounters disrupt lives across the globe, leaving only whispers of conspiracy in their wake. But what if, beneath the surface, a chilling revelation is hidden in plain sight?

In recent years the veil of deception begins to lift, championed by reporters such as Graham Hancock, Dr Robert Schoch, Randall Carlson and Terence

McKenna, who explore alternative theories about ancient civilisations and human history. Humanity's understanding of the past and the supernatural is being shaken to its core.

As a druid, I have spent a lifetime researching these topics and have engaged in much practical work using ritual, shamanic path-workings and hypnotherapy. This includes past life regression techniques with the aid of trance work and psychedelic journey work, in a structured and intentional way to explore consciousness, gain self-knowledge, and promote personal growth.

These techniques have allowed me to explore realms that go beyond the physical and observable universe, encompassing concepts that are abstract, spiritual, or supernatural. Including beliefs about the soul, the afterlife, spiritual beings, and other dimensions of existence.

And for me, this work has answered questions about existence, reality, and the nature of our being that cannot be explained solely by physical science.

Yet much of what I experienced in this work has been experienced by others too and documented by anthropologists studying shamanic cultures. Shamanic cultures from vastly different parts of the globe and often millennia apart.

Irish mythology and legends are rich with fascinating stories and characters that have been passed down through generations, and with my Irish ancestry, are particularly close to my heart.

The Mythological Cycle focuses on the so called 'supernatural' first inhabitants of Ireland, known as the Tuatha Dé Danann. I say 'so called' because in recent years there is growing evidence, which is becoming overwhelming, that there once existed a hyper-human race prior to the Younger Dryas event (approximately 12,000 years ago).

This pre-diluvian race appeared to have been highly spiritually evolved, had advanced psychic powers and intimate knowledge of nature's life force energy. Across the globe, there are myth and legend stories about such a race. I firmly believe that the stories about the Tuatha de Danann, referred to in Irish myth and legend, are deeply ingrained memories of such a race. Another well-known story related by the ancient Greek philosopher Plato in his dialogues, referred to a highly advanced pre-diluvian race and called them Atlantean. The name has stuck.

I have woven into my story many of these elements, together with breaking scientific developments, which support metaphysical beliefs and the existence of an advanced pre-diluvian race. Thus, creating a metaphysical journey through time, myth, and the power of the ancient world, which echoes the plight of our modern era.

In short, this book is for lovers of epic tales brimming with mythic quests and metaphysical insights. This novel is a profound exploration of how ancient wisdom can illuminate our future paths. It's a must-read for aficionados of Celtic myths, visionary epics, and anyone who yearns for a story that bridges the gap between science and spirit.

Corin Thistlewood
SW England 2025

Chapter 1

Victoria

1

At first light, Victoria had snuck out into the herb garden. She had already picked several leafy herbs using a small sickle-shaped knife her grandfather had made for her. Now she carefully placed some collected roots she had dug with her bare hands into the tote bag she had slung over one shoulder. She loved the sensuous feeling it gave her, digging into the rich loam with her bare hands.

Satisfied with her haul, she walked down to the end of the garden. This was her favourite vantage point where she could see through the willow trees down onto the vista below. At this time of the day, just as the sun was rising, a carpet of mist stretched as far as the eye could see, in all directions below.

The rising sun, low in the sky, casts a magnificent golden light over the entire scene. The effect created what seemed to be a sea of red and gold, billowing and rolling below her. Ah, she thought, surely this was the fairest view in all the archipelago of islands where she lived.

At sixteen, Victoria had a natural beauty all her own. Her long blond hair tied at the back. But several scraggly bits had escaped and were trailing down her young adult face, which, after digging for roots, was smeared a little with the rich loamy soil.

She wore a funky woollen hat that had a long tail and a small woollen tassel at the end. Made with many shades of natural wool; browns, russets, and oranges - every manner of autumnal colours.

Her grass-green eyes looked through her blond tresses. She wore her usual baggy, blue denim dungarees. Just the other day, her grandfather, Touchwood, had laughingly told her she was too skinny by far and looked more like an elf in that hat. But he had also often told her that her yellow hair and beautiful smile lit up the room whenever she came to see him. The thought made her blush, which somehow only made her look more adorable and cuter than ever.

Her teenage angst suddenly made her look back towards the house in case anyone was looking, but she was alone. All was silent, except for the faint hum of the wind turbine on its tower beside the house.

The self sufficient community where she lived had been called Rath Grain by her Grandfather who had founded this place before she was even born. Solar panels adorned the roof of the main house. The community relied on these things for light in the dark evenings. Over the years, the main house had been extended in all directions possible. There were also two stone barns, which had been converted to living accommodation. Her grandfather had often told her that as the community grew, several small eco-dwellings had sprouted up around the main house. Touchwood had proudly told her that they were a testament to the ingenuity and green morality of the New-ager mindset.

Victoria had visited them all: there were several canvas tepees, a bender with a stovepipe sticking out of it, a few mud brick dwellings, and a small straw-bale house. Someone had even experimented with building a small dwelling made of slabs of turf!

Long before Victoria had arrived at her grandfather's island home, as a refugee from England, the community had shifted and changed over the years. It had grown and shrunk in size but had now settled down to about twenty people. Victoria could not remember it being any other way.

Her eyes wandered back to the billowing mists below. With the rising sun, the morning mist gradually started to disperse, revealing smaller islands. After some minutes, the mist was gone, and she could once again see the familiar shallow sea below.

She had been told that once there had been land down there, a wetland that connected all the hills and mountains together into one land - called Ireland. But that was many years ago; before the climate crisis and the great oil wars had ravaged the world.

From what her Grandpapa -Touchwood, had told her about the people in those days, they seemed to be a race of wizards and sorcerers. Apparently, those people had marvellous machines that could fly through the air like magic. Some of them, he had told her, had even flown to the moon and walked on it, but that, she was sure, was a tall story, the result of her Grandpapa taking too much of his favourite Potcheen.

There were many other communities dotted about her mountain island. She had heard amazing stories about the 'before times' from some of the old people, who still remembered this marvellous race. Some had told her that they carried in their pockets magic black mirrors that could see people in far-off lands and even talk to them through those mirrors. And that those same black mirrors gave them access to all the knowledge mankind had gathered over the centuries.

One old woman, from a community close by, had even told her that as a child she remembered that all her mother needed to do was poke at the magic mirror with her finger a few times, and food, from all across the world would magically arrive at their very own doorstep. That race did not need to dig and toil and grow their food like we had to do. Truly, they did seem like a very fortunate race of wizards and sorcerers.

But her Grandpapa had told her also that in their achievements, they had become arrogant. In their hubris, they had neglected the very natural world that they relied upon—and had caused catastrophic changes in the earth's climate, ravaging and destroying the great civilisation they had built. Over the years, the great ice lands to the north had started to melt, causing sea levels to rise.

In dismay, they had built barriers to protect the land. But the sea levels had continued to rise. Ultimately, it had swarmed over the coastal barriers and swamped the wetlands of Ireland. The magical mountain of Sliabh an Iarainn, Victoria's home, had become an island in a shallow sea—one of an archipelago of islands that now spanned the north-western area of what was once

Ireland.

Then the Great Oil Wars began.

Victoria's grandfather had told her the story often. He had told her that it had all seemed to happen so quickly, like a house of cards collapsing into a heap. All of a sudden, he had said, the modern civilisation he had once known had ceased to exist!

Victoria gave a shiver. That particular story always made her squirm. She could never understand how that very fortunate race of wizards and sorcerers could let it all fall apart like that.

Shrugging her young shoulders, she turned back to the house. Remembering that she had signed up for the early morning shift on the kitchen rota and had to prepare breakfast for the rest of the community.

2

Dafydd awoke. It was so gloomy he could barely see, but what he could see seemed to swim before his eyes. He tried screwing them up, to focus them. Then he tried to move. That was a big mistake! The movement caused his head to throb violently, causing an involuntary retching, he vomited on to the straw beside him. His head ached. In fact, he realised his whole body ached. Dafydd put a comforting hand to his forehead and found there was sticky blood there. There was blood on his arms and legs too, and his fine clothes were all in tatters. Slowly, his eyes began to come into focus and he looked around him. And found he was lying on filthy straw, in a corner of a gloomy stone cell. And what was that smell?

Looking over to the far corner where the foul smell was coming from, he could just see a pile of steaming manure. Dafydd involuntarily put his hand over his nose. But on closer inspection, it didn't look like it was a horse that was responsible.

"Sorry about that," said a voice out of the gloom. "They won't let us out of the cell to relieve ourselves."

Dafydd strained his eyes looking about in the gloom, trying to see where the voice came from. Over by the barred door was a dirty pile of rags. Two bright eyes stared out from the filthy heap.

"Who are you? Where are we?" asked Dafydd, trying to comprehend what was happening to him.

The body in the dirty pile of rags remained lying down, but said, "My name is Rumanadil. We are prisoners in the dungeons of the dark elves. From what I can gather, something has happened to the king and the whole of the dark elf realm is on high alert. You wouldn't know anything about that, would you?"

Dafydd tried to think. His usually sharp mind was clouded. Vague memories of a magical spear and the Lord of Chaos came to him. But he stayed quiet. If he was a prisoner in the dungeons of the dark elves, he didn't know who he could trust. This pile of rags could be a dark elf operative trying to trick him into revealing information.

So instead he asked, "We are in the Otherworld, are we not? How come I can feel pain and bleed. And clearly we can produce waste matter too," Dafydd involuntarily glanced over at the manure in the corner. "Those things are a consequence of physical bodies, are they not?"

Rumanadil sat up in his corner, suddenly interested and said, "The 'Otherworld' you call it. You must be of human descent, for residence here call this land Tír na nÓg. But there are many realms here. We are imprisoned in the dark elves realm, which we call Tech Duinn." Rumanadil painfully stretched out his arm, rubbing it. His ragged clothes were stained with blood. Grimacing, he said, "Oh, did you not know we can be injured here in Tír na nÓg and feel pain and bleed. My people enjoy a good jousting tournament and hand-to-hand combat in a mock fight, but we heal quickly too and can not die here. But the dark elves are a sly race and pass evil spells over their prisoners so that they experience the misery of physical existence. Now we hunger for food, pass waste and our wounds do not heal." He coughed suddenly and spat blood on the floor.

Dafydd screwed his face up in disgust. Then said, "You look to be a dark elf yourself. How come you are here in prison?"

Rumanadil shot him a black look saying, "I am no dark elf sir, I am high elf. Although I admit I am a little shorter than most. Which is why I was picked and sent here spying and in disguise as a dark elf; till they captured me. Who are you anyway? You who have many questions but no answers. Do you work for your masters, the dark elves?"

"Why would I be imprisoned here and bleeding if I did?" said Dafydd indignantly. He still wondered if he could trust this fellow. But he needed to win his trust in order to gain as much knowledge as he could about this place; if he was ever going to escape from this miserable cell.

"My name is Dafydd ap Gwilym. I am human," Dafydd continued. "As you say, living in the physical realm. Some call me an alchemist, but I prefer the name

Dyn Hysbys, for it has wider meaning. I was here in this realm on… other business."

"Why so secretive Dafydd? If you were here spying on that abominable Fomorian King Indech, they all know it and imprisoned you here. So why not tell me?"

Dafydd could not argue with the logic of this fellow. He may as well admit why he had come. The dark elves all knew it, anyway.

"Yes, I suppose you are right. But I am no spy. I came to put an end to that treacherous Lord of chaos, King Indech."

"How so? I thought in Tír na nÓg we could not die."

"And so you are right - to a point. But I had discovered a way to do it." Dafydd didn't want to reveal to anyone anything about the hoard of Tuatha treasures that he and Touchwood had found. He had spent most of his long life looking for the four magical treasures of the Tuatha de Danann. The ones they had left behind in the physical realm after they transcended to the otherworld.

And it had been a long life indeed, for Dafydd was an 'Emrys', one of the few yet remaining in Wales. He was of an old fay blood line, one that the druids of old had sought to maintain and keep pure. They were called the 'Bluebloods', as their lineage could be traced back to the original Tuatha de Danann. In such families with that fay blood, the seventh daughter would be 'gifted' as a healer and would have special powers. She would be designated the name and title 'Rosetta'. And that a similar thing happens when the seventh child is a son, in those fay blood families. He would be designated the name and title 'Merlin'.

But most secret of all were the ancient druid rituals,

held under very special circumstances in a megalithic circle. When the seventh daughter a 'Rosetta', couples with the seventh son a 'Merlin'. The child born of this union causes a very strange genetic thing to happen. They seemed to almost revert back to the original Fae race. Not only do they have special powers, but they become almost immortal; their designated title was 'Emrys'. And so Dafydd did not want to reveal his lineage either; this secret should never fall into the wrong hands.

However, Dafydd decided to go bold and declared, "So it was I who killed King Indech. It was a suicide mission from the start. I knew it. And so here I am imprisoned."

"Well played, sir. Though I would dearly like to know how you did it?" was Rumanadil's answer.

Dafydd wasn't going to answer that question either. But he was starting to think this ragged fellow was genuine, so as a distraction asked, "Do you know any possible way out of here?"

"If I had, sir, I would be gone already. But perhaps with the two of us working together, it may be possible."

Chapter 2

The Temple of

the Moon

1

Star was suddenly awoken by the bright morning sunshine blazing through her east-facing window. Opening her eyes, she could see the gentle rays flickering above the ocean horizon. She smiled and gave silent thanks to Surya the Sun God for the blessings of a new day.

Star immediately rose from her bed, the light covers sliding from her, she loved summer, for it was so warm on her island home. She had been born in July a mere sixteen summers ago, and had lived in the house of maidens since she was ten summers old; it had become her home.

She pranced over to the window like a panther, enjoying the first rays of a new day on her youthful body. The blue tattoo on her shoulder depicted the moon phases, and made her skin look even whiter than it was. Her bronze hair flowing to her shoulders in tight ringlets framed her handsome face. Her amber eyes scanned the city below.

'Ah Murias', she thought, 'surely the fairest city in all of Y's'.

Instinctively, she touched the blue crescent moon on her forehead, that declared she was a priestess of the moon; to reassure herself that she was no longer in a dream.

Her home in the house of maidens was nestled against the mountainside, high above the sea. Turning away from the blue waters, she looked above to see the familiar temple of the moon, standing majestically on a mound, looking down on the city below.

Almost certain now she was back in her true body, she checked her toes. The nails weren't just painted, but someone had also painted half of each toe an aqua green. Examining her long nimble fingers, each was half painted the same aqua green, but that was not all. Along her artist's fingers were blue tattoos, strange hieroglyphics she knew to be spells of protection. On those same fingers were also simple bands of white gold, silver and red gold from some faraway land. There was also one ring made of an unusual metal called Orichalcum.

Now she was certain she had returned to her true body. For her dreams of late had been so powerful and so realistic that she truly felt she had become that 'other girl'. The one she somehow knew lived in a far-off land, and stranger yet, she instinctively knew existed in another time altogether, millennia in the future.

Star gave herself a vigorous shake, her whole body now franticly dancing and shaking, as she had been taught to do, to remove any remnants of energy left from spirit walking or powerful dreams.

Now she once more looked out the window, taking in breaths deep into her lungs. Looking up once more at the temple of the moon, perched majestically on the mountainside. Once an ancient druid from the Sun temple had taught her that the mountain was actually an extinct volcano, which had formed and risen above the sea millions of years ago. As had the other islands in the archipelago, the group of islands that were the homeland of the nation of the Y's.

In the far distant haze, she could just see the forms of the four other islands in the group: Falias, Finias, Gorias and the capital city Spyridon, which stood on the island of Atlantis.

The Temple of the Sun, she couldn't quite see now, but she knew it was down in the centre of the city where most of the townfolk could visit readily.

Her own temple, however, was a secret place, closed to the public and only allowed neophytes and temple priestesses within its walls. It was said to house the mystical cauldron of Cyrridfen. She hadn't been allowed to see it yet, but she would only be permitted into the inner sanctum of the cauldron once she achieved her seventh degree. There were nine degrees in all and although she had risen through the early grades quickly, she knew the higher you climbed, the harder it was to rise.

Her present partner Blaze, was a seventh-degree Acolyte, he had left earlier, before dawn in fact, so he could prepare for the sunrise rituals. He was training at the 'Temple of the Sacred Flame', which reminded her she must stop daydreaming and get dressed and start her day.

2

The scented garden behind the house of maidens had been laid before anyone could remember. It was for the use of the young priestesses who resided in the house of maidens. Star walked down the stone pathways, breathing in the perfumed air. Her priestess robes were gossamer thin, billowing in the warm wind. Although in daylight the robes appeared white, they had been dyed with a particular mixture of herbs and sea creatures that was a secret of the moon temple, which made them glow with a silver phosphorescence in the moonlight.

At the end of the garden was a pile of building stones that some builder of the walled garden had forgotten. But it was here, amongst the rubble of stones, that Star had found a few herbs growing; when she had first moved to the house of maidens as a neophyte.

From as early as she could remember, she had been drawn to those particular plants that humans could use to provide a healthier and more enriched life - the family of herbs. So Star had made it her mission to develop that small rocky patch at the end of the garden and had created an herb garden of her very own.

Now she sat on the low wooden seat that some thoughtful person had installed and closed her eyes in meditation. Turning inward, she became conscious of her breathing, each breath gradually becoming deeper. Until she felt ready to begin the exercise. Taking as deep a breath in as she could through her nose, she held it to a count one, two, three and four. Then, gradually exhaled through her mouth, to the same count of four; till her lungs felt emptied. Now, she held it again to the four count. Then breathing in again through her nose, repeating as before. Over and over she continued this exercise, feeling herself rising and increasing her vibrational frequency.

She continued in this way, till she felt ready for the next step in the exercise. Slowly, she expanded her consciousness beyond her own body, a short distance at first, then gradually extending till it filled the perfumed garden. Then, she stretched her awareness beyond the walls of the garden, till it encompassed the whole of the island.

As she did this, she became aware of the sounds of the new day. The sounds of the city awakening. A dog barking on some outlying farm; the chink of horse brass, as a farmer's boy placed a harness on the Draft horse, readying her for the plough. And nearer, the sound of clanging bread pans, as the baker's boy scrubbed the still-warm pans, after the newly baked bread had been removed and packed into the awaiting wicker baskets.

Now Star brought her expanded consciousness back to her herb garden beside her. With her eyes still closed, she looked with her mind's eye at the flourishing herbs. Searching among them for that telltale glow on the plant. One that her human eye could not see, as it was beyond normal human vision. But insects, and her mind's eye, could see that ultraviolet fluorescent glow; when a plant was ready to harvest.

Star rose to her feet, and still with her eyes closed, guided only by her mind's eye, made her way to the glowing leaves. She reached down to her small sickle-shaped knife that hung from a cord about her waist. One by one, she collected the leaves that indicated to her they were ready to work with humans.

At last, her work was done; only then, opening her eyes. Smiling down at the leaves in her hands, she had Sage, Chamomile, Valerian and Turmeric. She knew that several of these herbs were imbued with magical powers and could be used to ward off negative energy and protect against disease.

With a deep sigh of satisfaction, she placed her hoard in the little crane bag which hung from the cord about her waist. These cords that the priestesses wore, indicated by colours and combinations of colours, their grade within the temple.

But now, it was time for her to attend the moon temple. Returning to her room, she donned her saffron cloak and pinned a knot worked, gold brooch into its folds. Ready to leave the house of maidens, she proceeded along the stone cobbles of the street, up the hill, towards the temple of the moon.

The majestic temple of the Moon was on a mound looking down on the city below. Several tall towers adorned the temple, and it had onion-shaped domes, gilded with the sacred metal Orichalcum, that shimmered in the early morning sunlight. Above the arched entrance was a large silver crescent moon; the symbol of the temple.

As she walked through the arched entrance, the sensual smell of incense hit her. The sweet-smelling smoke created a peaceful atmosphere within the temple walls. She had come to love that particular fragrance. It was mystical, yet invigorating, cleansing, and healing all at once. She felt at peace here. It was a place where she belonged.

The open hall of the Mandapa was a gathering place for devotees, but today it was busier than usual. Neophytes and priestesses bustled about, and several elders were there, surrounded by excited neophytes, all asking questions, which created an expectant buzz of voices within the Mandapa.

Star, puzzled by the air of excitement and unusual crowds of people, stopped dead in her tracks. Usually, when she came to the temple, it was a place of peace and devotion. She felt it was somehow tainted by this invasion of talkative people. Looking about the hall, she noticed several of her friends were gathered about the notice board, hung on a far wall.

She made her way over to them. They all seemed very intent on examining the daily rota. As she approached, her friend River turned her head and greeted her excitedly with, "Star, you have been chosen to teach one day a week at the neophytes training hall."

It was like a blow to the chest. The last thing she had expected. She just stared at River, disbelieving. Then suddenly realising her mouth was agape, she snapped it shut. "That's impossible. I'm working at the apothecary and..."

"Have you forgotten its inauguration day?" River interrupted.

She had forgotten. Or perhaps she had not been interested in the first place, and pushed all awareness of it from her mind. Her work at the apothecary had become her whole life... well, except for Blaze, whose ability to pleasure her was extraordinary. The thought brought a thrill of excitement that raced through her body, ending in her young womb. A satisfied smile came to her lips as she thought of the last time, only a few hours before.

"What are you smiling about? I thought you said you never wanted to teach the neophytes. Ah! I recognise that look. You're thinking of Blaze, aren't you?" River teased, elbowing her in the ribs.

Star felt her face flushing red, and she knew it made her freckles stand out even more. She threw her hands over her face to try to hide it. But River, her friend, was merciless, and took delight in eliciting emotional responses in her. As sixth-degree priestesses, their training emphasised carrying themselves with decorum and mystery, silently gliding along and not displaying any emotion.

River, encouraged by Star's response, blurted, "And guess what? You start today. The rota says you are to be there at the training hall at noon."

Startled and disbelieving, Star pushed her friend out of the way, and bustled to the front, to consult the work rota. But it was true. Her name was there chalked on the board in the neat hand of Ignis, one of the temple elders:

Star sixth-degree priestess of the moon, to attend the school of neophytes today at noon, for orientation training. This is an ongoing position, of one day a week till further notice.
Decreed by the temple elders.

Star was floored. How could Ignis do this to her? She turned to River and exclaimed, "Surely, Ignis is aware of the important work that I am doing in the apothecary!"

But River's logic was inscrutable as she echoed,

"Surely, you knew that all sixth-degree priestesses are required to teach at least one day a week, at the school of neophytes. Poor Raven was required to give two days a week, for neophyte training."

Star felt betrayed, but kept her cool. She silently turned, striding without another word, across the hall of the Mandapa. She must go to the temple apothecary and inform her tutor and, of course, begin preparing her precious herbs.

3

Of all the temple duties that she was required to perform, her work with herbs was her joy. Star was never so at home, as when she was within the sanctuary of the temple apothecary.

It was a small room at the back of the Temple; well away from the bustle and hubbub of the Mandapa. Star spent much of her time here, creating the various herbal medicines, tinctures, teas, and salves used in the ancient art of herbal healing. As she opened the door, the intoxicating smell of herbs hit her, it was a very particular smell that she loved, and it didn't seem to matter which herbs were being boiled, seeped or what decoctions were being made, it was always the same.

And there was dear Selen, one of the temple elders, who was in charge of the apothecary and Star's tutor and mentor. The middle-aged woman was bent over, her back to the door, preparing a batch of salve; probably for the Marius hospital. Many of the Temples on Marius had their own apothecary, which not only supplied the temple's needs for ritual incense and Dreamtime elixirs, but had regular orders to fulfil from the hospital.

Selen was a kindly, well-rounded woman, who seemed to embody her name, for in their language it meant 'embodiment of the full moon.' Selen was luminous, graceful and influential within the temple. However, she was no woman to cross, and Star was so very glad Selen had taken her under her wing, so to speak.

Early on, Selen had told her that she could see that Star had a quick and retentive mind, that soaked up every bit of learning, as quickly as it was put before her. This was because, Selen had said, that Star was one of the 'old ones' that were born and reborn again and again; learning more each lifetime. Such a one, only needed reminding of what she had learnt from a past life.

As Star entered the room, Selen turned her head and beamed at her protégé. Her face seemed to radiate a silver glow, which was highlighted by her long, brown robes. The temple key that hung around her neck swung as she turned.

"How are you, my lovely girl," she said? "What have you brought me today?"

Star's eyes were momentarily drawn to the Orichalcum key. These keys, along with the brown robes, symbolised Selen's high rank as highly placed Adept, and rewarded for her dedicated service, by being placed as a guardian of a sacred temple space. The key reminded Star of her own aspirations of attaining, one day, a green robe, which would declare her apprentice to a master herbalist.

With the question, Star's hand instinctively went to her crane pouch at her waist. Opening it, she reverently produced the leaves and flowers of Sage, Chamomile,

Valerian, and Turmeric.

"Ah! Some of my favourites here. Well done," Selen remarked. "But we usually use the roots of valerian and turmeric. So next time, go for the roots. But I happen to know," Selen said with a wink, "of the ritual use of Valerian and Turmeric leaves, so I will keep those for temple use. Now, be a dear and tincture them straight away, in the brandy alcohol. There should be enough in that enormous vase in the corner. Remind me to order some more from the distillery, would you? There are plenty of corked jugs in the storeroom. Now you know to wash and cut them up finely to get the most absorption, and don't forget to always label your tincture with the herb used. And be a dear, and put them in the darkroom before you go, my lovely."

With that, Selen immediately bustled off to finish her Salve making. Star, smiling and shaking her head at the storm of commands from Selen, dutifully proceeded to tincture her herbs. She should have enough time, she thought to herself, before she had to present herself at the school for neophytes.

Chapter 3

Rath Grain

1

The snow was beginning to melt off the sacred mountain, swelling the frozen streams with pristine meltwater. Snowdrops, too, were beginning to poke their heads above the fertile earth in those sheltered valleys.

Further down, on a level plateau of limestone, stood a farmstead surrounded by neat rows of vegetable gardens. Several poly-tunnels housed a riot of green growths. Beyond those are several animal pens, with chickens, ducks and geese wandering freely.

The roof of the main house was lined with arrays of solar panels, reflecting the brilliant sunshine off their glassy surfaces. Several wind turbines hum happily, fed by the persistent winds. Dotted about the surrounding land were various eco-dwellings: a couple of canvas tipis; a bender with a stove-pipe sticking out; one mud brick dwelling; a small straw-bale house and even a dwelling made of slabs of turf! A veritable haven of self-sufficiency for those twenty individuals who dwelt there.

Besides the burning bright wood stove, Touchwood sat at his writing desk, ledger book open, looking out over the apple orchard, and sighed. Ah! It was so good, he thought, to be back in his own little self-sufficient community on the magical mountain of Sliabh an Iarainn.

His long silver locks, tied at the back with a leather cord, fell down the tan leather waistcoat he wore over a warm, woolly jumper. During the winter months, he had taken to wearing several other layers under that, in a bid to keep warm. Touchwood was looking forward to the heat of summer.

After the initial ravages of climate change, the local climate had settled down leaving the summers considerably warmer, and the winters milder than before.

As was his habit, he stroked his long silver beard while thinking. Touchwood thought about his recent long and convoluted quest to find the missing Syrinx. With the help of his granddaughter Victoria, he had finally completed the mission and returned the mystical instrument to its rightful owner, the God of nature and the wild animals. It had been an unforgettable encounter meeting with the Great God Pan. And Victoria had excelled herself, at the last, playing a crucial role.

Then, at last, Pan had played his Earth Song once again.

Touchwood was still trying to get his head around the significance of this. He knew it had something to do with 'The Lost Chord,' which coordinates everything in nature. It was like some sort of 'Music of the Spheres' which was channelled by Pan through his Panpipes, which he called the Syrinx.

The music had caused all the animals of the forest to leap and cavort in an ecstatic dance for what seemed like hours. Afterwards, Pan walked off into the forest with all the animals following him. Victoria too had wanted to follow, but he had grabbed her by her arm to stop her. She seemed to be in some sort of trance and took quite a lot of persuasion to keep her in the stone circle. Touchwood had used the very last of his magical energy to teleport them both back to their island home, on the magical mountain of Sliabh an Iarainn.

Exhausted from the ordeal, and after months of over-stretching his magical energy, he had gone to his bed, and left Victoria to explain their mysterious absence to the other community members, however she would. He was past caring, but had gone to bed that night with a glad heart, and with a deep sense of fulfilment washing over him. Now at last he could rest.

Touchwood had stayed in bed and slept and dreamed for a full two days; so exhausted was he. On waking, Victoria, bless her, had brought him food from the community kitchen. He found he was absolutely ravenous. He had estimated that he would need at least a full two months' rest from all magical work; to recuperate.

So, all that winter, he had rested and replenished his energy. He ate well and did little. And was starting to enjoy a sort of retirement at long last. And he had even started recording the entire adventure in his ledger book journal once again.

2

As he looked out over the apple orchard, sat at his writing desk, pen in hand, he sighed again. Oh, it was good to be back home. However, that night, a mere six months after Pan had played his earth song, his sleep was interrupted by a most unexpected source.

He was fast asleep on his platform bed, built up in the slope of the roof, above the wood-burning stove. He was having pleasant dreams about milking goats early in the morning. It was one of his favourite farming jobs. When suddenly, the goat started talking to him, "Touchwood?" it said in a very nanny goat sort of way. "Is that you Touchwood? Look, we need to talk."

Before he knew what was happening, the goat's face slowly morphed into a human face, one he hadn't seen in a long time.

"Morgana," he asked, stupefied?

"Yes, it's me, you fool. Did you think the goat had suddenly developed a voice of its own?"

"But this is my dream," he whimpered, quite taken aback by being reprimanded by a talking goat!

"Well, yes, point taken. Anyway, we need to talk. It's Adge, he's in trouble." The voice was more like Morgana's now, but he was still trying to come to terms, with his dream being interrupted by a talking goat - with Morgana's head!

"Remember, Adge. Your friend?"

"Why are you a goat?"

"Oh, this is intolerable. I knew it was a mistake to try to contact you. But the Oak King gave you a very good recommendation."

Touchwood remembered now how ill-tempered

Morgana could be. The first time his friend Adge had introduced her to him, she had hurled a tirade of abuse…

…There she stood, a tall, willowy woman, handsome in an ageless way. Her mane of hair was a dark red, almost bronze coloured, and flowed down past her shoulders in waves. Her green eyes regarded Touchwood with a humorous glint. He couldn't see the tops of her ears, but later he would confirm they came to a point, like all Noble high elves. But her lobes were adorned with large golden hoops. The dress she wore was a deep green and looked medieval in style, made with baggy lower sleeves. But it was made of some impossibly sheer, tight-fitting material accentuating her voluptuous curves. The cut of her dress revealed extensive areas of her belly and her ample breasts. Around her neck hung a chunky gold chain, with a medallion bearing strange runes that he hadn't seen before.

Morgana had looked at him with utter contempt, then burst into her tirade.

"Oh human, the earth does not belong to you. Since your very creation, humans have betrayed everything they hold dear." She gave an enormous sigh. "And all we did was watch. We expected that you would understand that the earth is not yours human. The earth does not belong to you! The Fey Queen and I have debated long and hard; would the earth be a better place without humans? Are human beings always the destroyer? Always the betrayer? You cannot seem to co-exist with other life. Or is there still some hope for us along the way?'

It had been a bitter reprimand of his species, but at

the time he could think of nothing to contradict her.

But now she was attempting to contact him through his dreams and had said that his friend Adge was in trouble. So, trying to push aside his confusion, he asked, "Morgana, what has happened to Adge? Can I help?"

"Ah, human, you have finally come to your senses. We must talk. But not like this. How can you take me seriously dressed as a goat? You must awaken and I will come to you as a shade."

Suddenly, Touchwood found himself awake in his bed. It was still dark outside, but he could see a crescent moon through the skylight in the roof. He put on his dressing gown and padded downstairs to the stove, opened the stove door and found it was still alight and warm, so threw in a couple more logs and opened the damper. Then he sat in his comfortable chair, warming his hands on the stove, awaiting Morgana's appearance.

He didn't have to wait long. Despite the wood stove burning away, the room suddenly felt very cold. His vision blurred and his head swam a little. He could feel a churning in his gut. But then, right before him, a blurred cloud of light seemed to form, hovering in the air. The more he stared at it, the more he could discern some sort of entity within it.

There was some sort of human shape within the light cloud. It seemed to take on the form of an ancient crone, bent almost double, all dressed in black. But those eyes! Those eyes had an intensity that left him in no doubt they could turn him to stone on a whim.

Then, quite suddenly, the crone transformed into Morgana, the tall, willowy, young woman, incredibly handsome and seductive, like when he had first met her. She seemed to shake herself like a dog shaking off water and started to brush herself off. For a moment, he detected a look of embarrassment, but then that handsome Nordic face beamed at him, and those cold eyes cast a warning—not to mention that, for a moment, he had seen her true form.

"Touchwood, so good to meet you again", she crooned as she extended her hand for him to kiss. But once again, as before, he refused the invitation. Just lightly taking her hand to shake.

"I never got to thank you for freeing Pan from his imprisonment in that tree," he began. "We have you to thank for saving my world. We are all very grateful."

Morgana glowered with the praise but answered, "Not at all. But it is that, I wish to speak to you about."

"How is Adge? I haven't seen him since that time. Unfortunately, I was so exhausted from my efforts that I have been resting most of the time."

"Yes... Yes, well, I know where he is, so no need to be concerned. But he is… a little indisposed."

"Oh! So he is not in any immediate danger, then?"

"Er… not exactly. You see, unfortunately, he got in the way."

"What do you mean, 'got in the way'?"

"Well, as you are aware, your friend Adge transcended to the Otherworld and has been… assisting me with my work…"

"He said he was your apprentice."

"Yes. Yes, something like that. But you see, while I was conjuring the spell to free Pan from the tree; which, as you know, was incredibly vital to all our plans. Oh...

how can I explain… You see, according to the laws of magic, I wasn't able to completely destroy someone else's spell. One has to create another one, on top, so to speak. I couldn't just remove Pan from the tree. I had to replace him with another object. There was a nearby boulder I had my eye on to use as a substitute, you see. But during the conjuring, I was so wrapped up in the magic that I hadn't noticed poor Adge had been sitting on that boulder to rest." She paused a moment and eyed Touchwood sideways to see if he was still following. Touchwood, still sitting, had folded his arms across his chest, eyeing her mistrustfully.

Morgana continued nonplussed, "Well… n… now that I had finally released Pan from his entombment, you see, we were both… yes both of us were so excited and… and I was concerned with bringing Pan up to date with the next part of the plan, you see, which was to reunite him with his beloved Syrinx. So… neither of us noticed that Adge was missing." She paused again and gave me that sly sideways look before continuing.

"And of course, it needed the combined magic of both Pan and myself to return Pan to his rightful place on the earthly plain. We… yes, we both of us, you see, were so very keen to remove ourselves from the miserable domain of the dark elves… b… before we were discovered. So it wasn't until long after that I realised Adge was missing - and what must have befallen him." This last, she said, trying her best to sound like a lost little girl.

Touchwood angrily stood up and blurted, forgetting himself for a moment, "Wait a minute. Are you telling me that you're not quite sure what has befallen him?"

The look Morgana shot him left him under no misconception that he should guard his tongue in her presence. But then she composed herself, casting a sickly grin his way.

"Of course 'human'. You have no way of knowing that my kind can relive from memory all that I have seen. Yes, I am sure of his fate. Just as I am sure that the dark elves are now on high alert after your… your 'magical mentor' Dafydd ap Gwilym, saw fit to murder Indech, king of the Fomorian and leader of the dark elves!"

"What! Dafydd killed Indech? But how? I thought elves were immortal in the Otherworld."

"Never mind how. Your idiot mentor, decided to kill the dark elves' leader, just as I was secretly in their realm and vulnerable. They could have come down on me before I rescued Pan from entombment, ruining all our plans and the fate of the physical realm. I am not best pleased with your mentor, I can tell you. I could have been captured and suffered the same fate as Pan!"

"Ye Gods, this is terrible! What are we going to do about Adge? And Uncle Dafydd, what news of him?"

But Morgana wasn't listening, she was still caught up in her own self-pity. "If it wasn't for the fact that the dark elves had captured him, I would have turned him to stone by now."

"Uncle Dafydd! Do you mean the dark elves have captured him? What will happen to him? Is he still alive?"

"The realm of the dark elves is squirming about like a disturbed termite nest. Or is it a headless chicken? I can never remember which it is that you humans say. But I need to lie low now. I can't possibly go anywhere near the dark elves' realm. In fact, I need to keep my head down, even in my own realm. Which is why I have come here to you. Through Adge, we have established a tenuous link between us, so I can haunt your house. The longer I stay here, the safer I will be."

Touchwood just stared at her disbelieving, his mouth dropping open. Then managed to utter, "W... what!"

Chapter 4

Neophytes

1

The sun was shining brightly on the yellow stone buildings of Murias and lay like topaz on the gilded sea below. On her way to the school of neophytes, Star had taken the steep and winding narrow lanes down to the harbour. The road, with its many steps, was lined with cobbles. As she approached the bottom, the air was full of the sound of gulls and the acrid tang of brine wafted on the gentle breeze. The harbour was her favourite part of the city, such a bustling place, full of interesting people from all parts of the world.

And oh, the ships!

Ships of every shape and size lay lifting and jostling to the swell of the incoming tide. As a small child, her father, a sailor, had brought her here often. He had once told her that as a lad he had been dared to run from one side of the harbour to the other, across all the ships tied together. He had proudly told her he had won the bet.

Some of the ocean-going boats were over two-hundred feet long. The shaped cedar planks were stitched together using twisted branches of yew and willow. Tall masts were rising to the sky, and yard arms that could hold ten men standing.

All around the wharves, the many merchants had set up their stalls early and were now crying out their wares in a cacophony of voices. In the crowded markets, priests in luminous colours, farming landowners and ragamuffin boys, all crowded together, equally enthralled by the vast array of wares. Baskets full of colourful spices sat beside vegetables of every shape and size. It was a feast for the senses.

As a sixth-degree priestess, Star had been taught to carry herself with decorum and mystery, at all times, silently gliding along, not displaying any emotion. As she walked past some ancient fishermen mending their nets, she was aware, using her peripheral vision of one old salt leering at her, showing his black teeth. But he was too superstitious to call out abuse to a priestess of the moon temple.

Further along, there were rows of lobster pots stacked up high and more fishermen mending nets. Star decided it best to cut up a side street to avoid them, making her way to the square of Poseidon where the school of the neophytes resided.

At the end of the street, workmen were renovating the old amphitheatre. Even though the volcano at the centre of the island was no longer active, there were often earthquakes here and the old amphitheatre had been damaged. The workmen were replacing large sections of the outer walls with enormous blocks of stone, some of them weighing several tons. Star was fascinated to see that they were using psychic priests from the Temple of the Mystical Portal to move the megalithic stones. Her tutor had told her that these gifted individuals used the power of Psychokinesis to teleport the megaliths from the ground up to the top of the wall they were building. Star had never seen it done before, but she remembered from a lecture she had attended that it had something to do with changing the frequency of vibration. Star knew, of course, as every priestess was taught, that everything was energy and each object was vibrating at its own particular frequency. And that the frequency of vibration was proportional to its mass. Star knew also from her own botanical studies that plants transform sun light into matter and that therefore that matter was frozen light. But she didn't quite understand the reverse process, whereby the psychic priests transformed the energy of the blocks of stone into pure light, thus they became weightless. In the same way, the massive stone blocks could be effortlessly shaped to fit in with the other stones, so that barely a sheet of parchment could be fitted between them.

Watching these psychic priests working, Star lost in fascination, saw the massive stones suddenly burst into blinding light and guided by the priests' hands start to rise above the ground. Slowly, the priest walked up a ramp, guiding the glowing stone along the way and eventually to its place in the wall.

But then suddenly remembering her appointment, Star looked up at the Sun and realises it was almost midday, so rushes off to the school of neophytes not far away.

2

The square of Poseidon, was a large formal square, with many of the civic buildings of Murias placed around the perimeter. And there, on the far side, stood the school of the neophytes. In fact, it was more of a public meeting hall and it was by far the largest building on the island. With its thirteen wide steps leading up to the raised plaza and five tall columns at the top of that. Above the columns was a frieze of intricate mouldings and topping that was the triangular gable containing the emblem of the neophytes moulded in stone. A circle of nine hazel nuts accompanied by their leaves.

As Star approached the imposing building, she looked up to the emblem, and remembered that she had been taught on her very first orientation day that those hazel nuts represented the Otherworld hazel nuts of all knowledge, which were contained within them. And it was where the expression 'in a nutshell' came from.

The large hall within the school of the neophytes was used for public meetings and announcements. If it was a particularly important announcement, the whole of Poseidon square would be filled with people and the announcements made on the raised plaza at the top of the steps.

But today, being the end of August, she would just be greeting the annual intake of aspirant neophytes and teaching the orientation class. Although she had been reluctant to use her precious time teaching neophytes, she was a priestess of the moon and knew her duty was to serve the people of Y's in whatever way was decreed by the elders. Besides, she could remember how nervous she was on her first orientation day not that long ago, and wanted to help the young hopefuls to orientate to their new life in the temples.

As Star entered the foyer, she could hear the babble of many excited voices coming from the main hall. Before entering, she composed herself, remembering all her priestess training. To these people, she was representing the Moon Temple. She needed to carry herself with decorum and mystery, not displaying any emotion. Suddenly it dawned on her, and she realised what an important role this was. It was an honour to be the chosen representative of the Temple. And now realised the wisdom of the elder who had chosen her, above all the other priestesses, to host the very first day of neophyte training. The thought humbled her.

Star now silently stood in the elaborate doorway of the large hall within the school of the neophytes. Her eyes closed, concentrating, radiating the power of the moon; the power of the Goddess throughout the hall.

Gradually she could hear the babble of excited voices, diminish, then eventually fall to silence, as the people in the hall noticed she was there. Now she knew she had their attention. She opened her piercing amber eyes to a sea of awed faces, all looking at her.

She was very pale, her chiselled features white as new cream, her long bronze hair flowing down to her shoulders. The saffron cloak, her priestess robes, phosphorescent white in the dim light of the hall, all made her look like a Goddess standing there.

Taking all this in, with an inner smile to herself, she stepped forward, remembering to walk the priestess's walk she had been taught to do; fast, brief steps that didn't billow her long robes that hid her feet, so she appeared to be silently gliding along, like magic. The people in the hall parted as she made her way to the front and the speaker's plinth.

Most of the people in the hall were relatives of the selected neophytes. It was a big occasion for any family to give a daughter or son to the Temples. Often it could be years before neophytes would see any of them again. So mothers and fathers, aunts and uncles, brothers and sisters all would be there to send them off.

3

Afterwards, Star could hardly remember what she had said while addressing the crowds of people in the public meeting hall. She just knew that she had channelled her higher self. The Goddess within her had spoken. Then she had bid them all goodbye and a safe journey to their respective homes and had ushered the neophytes into a small classroom off the main hall.

There were in fact only twenty actual neophytes, a mixture of boys and girls and a range of ages from seven to ten summers.

Once her class had settled down and benches allocated, Star began.

"Greetings class. And welcome to the hall of the Neophytes. I will be your teacher for today. You may call me Mistress Star or simply Mistress. I am a sixth-degree priestess of the moon temple.

"I am sure you have been told or are aware by now that people in other parts of the world fear our great nation. They fear us, because many of our people have been given special 'gifts', and that gift is magic; a power that you have inherited. You all must be very excited about being chosen to enter the temple. You are here because you have displayed certain signs that you have one of those 'gifts'. The latent talents of clairvoyance or psychic abilities. In our culture, as you are probably aware, we call people with such gifts 'blue bloods'. That's people like me and people such as yourselves.

"As you may know, your first year will be basic training. We will be introducing you to how the temples work, all the different branches, and what each branch focuses on. You will learn basic ritual techniques. Each of you will spend a little time within all nine of the branches, where you will be assessed to see where your natural talents or gifts lie.

"We do indeed observe certain family houses more than others, as they tend to produce psychic talents regularly. For example, the House of the Lion or the House of the Unicorn are exemplary when it comes to psychic talent. But please, don't be intimidated if you were not born into one of these noble houses. For it is well known that these talents from time to time, do pop up in lesser-known houses, and often your talent needs to shine brighter, to be noticed. But more on that later.

"The temple memory goes back a long way. It was many millennia ago, even before the 'Great Ice' that we lived in the land called Eriu. It was there, on that isolated island, on the very furthest outreaches of Europa, that our race first started to recognise that there were people among us who could spontaneously enter the spirit realm.

"Of course, our tribes back then didn't know this. They just knew that certain people would often fall to the ground, writhing about violently and babbling incomprehensible things. Most of the tribe's people got used to this and ignored them. For after a short while, they seemed to recover, seemingly unaffected by their apoplexy.

"But our wise elders began to take an interest in what these people, usually women, felt and saw during these spontaneous bouts or fits. After many years, the wise elders began to discover that during these fits, the victims sometimes received visions that turned out to be prophetic; what they saw in their visions somehow came true.

"Consequently, the elders became more interested in these poor unfortunates and called them prophets or prophetesses. The elders wondered if they could somehow harness or refine the power of these visions. Suppose they could somehow utilise it for the benefit of the tribe?

"But as it turned out, it was a breeder of hunting dogs, a man named Zola, who first suggested the use of selective breeding for these 'prophets'. Zola knew that it was possible to use selective breeding to select and enhance desirable traits in his hunting dogs. Giving the hounds longer legs, or modifying temperaments etc. Zola suggested that the wise elders could enhance the natural powers of these prophets, using his knowledge of selective breeding. So this was the beginning, the ancient history of the reprogenetics program, that we still use today; albeit in a much more refined way.

"Today, of course, we have refined and perfected this

program and have divided the many special psychic powers into spiritual groups that we call branches, like those of a tree. Divided, but all part of the same tree, the great nation of Y's.

"Now, class, can any of you tell me how many spiritual branches there are? Yes, Lila." The little girl in the front row of the class with her hand up proudly pronounced, "There are nine branches of psychic abilities housed within the temples."

"Absolutely correct Lila. Now, group, tell me what the nine branches are. Yes, Nia."

"Seership branch, mistress."

"Yes, well done. Anyone else? Zane."

"Telepaths, Mistress Star."

"Good one Zane. Another?"

"Medium-ship branch mistress."

"Excellent Ria. Another."

"Healer?" asked a little girl of only eight summers.

"Yes, of course Lana. Your family are well-known healer's."

"Geomancy miss?"

"No Leo, that now comes under the Seership branch. And we didn't have those back in Eriu. The art of Geomancy didn't develop till we arrived here in Y's. Come on group, there are several more we haven't mentioned yet. Go on Reed"

"Astral projectionist."

"Excellent Reed. Some more. Anyone?"

There was quiet in the classroom for a few moments then, "Teleporter mistress."

"Well done Elfie. I believe you have some family in the Teleporter branch. Come on, group, we are nearly there."

"Is a Mindbender in a branch mistress?"

"Yes, of course Cora. Mindbenders are a branch that includes shapeshifters and illusionists, who can place a 'glamour' on someone and make them believe they are something completely different. Now, group we have named seven. Just two more. Yes River."

Little River very shyly held up her hand. She was only seven summers old. "Elementalist mistress?"

"Absolutely correct River. But how could you forget till now that your own father is in the Temple of the sacred flame and an Elementalist?"

This remark brought laughter from the whole class. But Mistress Star interjected, "But there are a total of nine branches. What's missing anyone?"

The laughter quickly died away and was followed by an embarrassed silence. Star looked about the entire group. There were twenty children in all, covering a range of ages from seven to ten summers. But nobody was forthcoming with an answer.

"I can see that I'm going to have to tell you," remarked Star. "We must never forget the Draoi branch. For this is where all our great leaders and tribal elders ultimately ascend to.

"But not always. Occasionally, someone is born with exceptional skills or perhaps great wisdom as well; because of many previous incarnations. They may have natural skills in several of the branches. These very talented people, we call them 'Ascended Master.' They will often decide to reside in the Sun temple of the Draoi branch.

"Or, as is sometimes the case, someone within the

temple has the ability to learn very quickly and rise rapidly; right up to the ninth degree. We call these wise people 'a sage.' Both types of talented people may become a Great Magician, or 'Arch Draoi'. They usually reside in the Sun temple along with the other tribal elders.

"Ok, class well done. We got there in the end. Now, talented children can enter the temples between seven and ten summers, depending on the development of their particular talent. I must stress that there is no stigma attached to how early or late your talents develop. We do not tolerate any teasing, bullying, or elitism within the temples. I myself was a late developer. My talent didn't develop till I was ten summers old."

"What is your gift, mistress," asked a girl whose blond hair had many tight braids against her skull and an adorable red tartan dress?

"Thank you Cora." But instead of answering, Star just pointed to the blue crescent moon on her forehead that declared she was a priestess of the moon.

But a tall boy at the back of the class blurted out, "That blue crescent means you're a priestess of the moon temple, mistress."

"Yes, absolutely correct Oak." But she turned to Cora, looked directly into her eyes, like she was reading something there, and smiled, then said, "I think what Cora meant was as a seer, what was my particular gift? Isn't that right, Cora?"

The little girl with the many tight braids just blushed delightfully, lowered her eyes and nodded her head.

"My gift lies in communication with plants. I only

need to place my hand on a plant, and I will know many things about it. Whether we can eat the plant for nourishment, whether it is poisonous, whether it can be used as a teacher plant. Or if it can be used to make dyes for clothes or the inking of our skin."

Star paused and looked around the class. She had their full attention now, so continued.

"In the temples, we are taught how to take control of our gifts and utilise them properly, when we want to use them. So they don't control us. For when we are young, those gifts can be like a team of horses, pulling a wagon when the reins have been lost. We are taught how to be in control of those powerful forces. Any questions?"

The tall boy at the back of the class, Oak, blurted out, "Do we stay in mixed classes, mistress? Know what I mean?"

The entire class erupted into jeers and laughter. Star was expecting this at some point, so let the laughter and rib-digging subside, keeping silent and not biting the bait. When all was silent, she answered.

"No, only the first few inaugural classes are mixed. After that, you will be assigned time in each of the temples under the tutelage of the relevant priest or priestess, and you will be walking your own path. However, at fourteen summers, we are encouraged to find a sex partner within the temples.

"Most of us don't need much encouragement, however. At that age, I was very keen to seek out a handsome boy. But I must stress here and you will hear it again and again during your training, that it is vitally important that we keep your blue blood pure and only bond with another blue blood.

"We have been following this technique for millennia, since Zola's time back in our motherland of Eriu. This has made our nation strong and powerful. It has allowed us to build the magnificent temples, you see in all our cities. And has given us the edge when trading with other lands to the east and those lands within the Internal Sea. As some of you may know, we sometimes trade with those far-off lands to the west, across the Great Western Ocean. As I said before, some people in other lands fear our 'gifts,' fear our great nation. In fact, across the Great Western Ocean, because of our gifts, they believe us to be Gods. All because of our special gifts and talents that we have nurtured and developed over the millennia.

"At fourteen summers, however, nobody will be forcing you to take a sex partner if you don't feel you're ready. But if you do take a sex partner, you will have learned enough herbal lore to create your own birth control medicines. We discourage pregnancy until you have reached your third degree. But by the time you have reached your third degree and are fourteen summers or over, you will be eligible to attend the Beltane revelries within the sacred stones upon the hill. For one month before Beltane, participants will need to discard using their birth control methods, because we want to see a goodly amount of pregnancies after the rituals."

Suddenly a Sistrum was ringing in the hall outside.

"Now class," continued Star. "We will now have a short break. You can get fresh fruit and well water in the refractory. When you hear the temple bell ringing, please return to this classroom and we will continue with your training."

Chapter 5

Nature's Dance

1

All during her childhood, Victoria had felt a strong attraction towards the animals in the smallholding and thoroughly enjoyed spending time with them. Over the years, she had learned about their ways and became by far the most experienced person in the small holding when it came to animals.

However, since she had started her moon time, bleeding with the rhythms of the moon, she had noticed that she seemed to have all sorts of other 'gifts' naturally. She was pleased to find that not only did she 'have a way with animals,' as her Grandpapa had put it, but she also seemed to intuitively understand their individual behaviour. And by this, know when an animal was out of sorts, and found she could send them some sort of healing energy.

As if this wasn't enough. One day, while she was cuddling a duck, she found she could go inside its head and know what it was thinking. Not in words you understand, but in feelings like happy, sad, pain, or hunger. She had also tried this with a chicken, but she wouldn't do that again.

Then recently she had gone into the head of a cat. It was Titan, her grandpa's cat, and she was very surprised to find her Grandpapa in there as well.

Afterwards, he had said this 'gift' was called 'mind-melding,' but at the time he was furious with her and told her that meddling with this sort of thing without training could be very dangerous.

But he had relented afterwards and said that now he knew she had 'gifts' naturally, he would begin her magical training. Since then she had had to send her Grandpapa healing energy often, as he had been very tired after using up all his magical energy, travelling to all those lovely stone circle 'thingies'.

Victoria had at last got her own way, and had accompanied her Grandpapa through the ley matrix to a stone circle, on a mission to return the magical pan pipes to their rightful owner, the Great God Pan. It had been the most wonderful experience of her young life, when at last, she had seen that the Great God was, in fact, the man from her dreams, the one who had been helping her heal the sick animals.

In the end, her Grandpapa had been taken ill, and she had had to take the Syrinx pipes herself and give them to the wonderful Pan - the giant of a God. She would always remember the moment when Pan, bent low and smiling at her, carefully took the glowing Syrinx from her hand.

The moment Pan touched the pipes as she held them, something strangely erotic and mystical passed between them. Time stood still for a moment. Then suddenly came rushing at her like an express train. Through the flowing mists of time, she saw images of past events that raced past her: terrible wars with massive machines destroying people's homes; soldiers fighting, wielding swords and wearing metal armour. Then she saw men in long flowing brown robes, with hoods marching throughout the land in pilgrimage, telling stories of wondrous deeds in the east.

A small part of Victoria's mind realised she was seeing time going backwards, but it was all happening too fast for her to contemplate. Relentlessly, it all came rushing towards her; now, Roman soldiers all marching together like clockwork in groups of a hundred at a time. Back time raced, now slaves were building great pyramids in a sandy Egypt overseen by God-like rulers; back in her own land of Ireland, she saw men building great megalithic structures, stone circles and burial mounds like New-grange, all over the country.

Time began to race past even faster. Now she could barely see women and men laying the first seeds of agriculture; great ships bearing a raven crest arriving off the west coast of Ireland; now in horror, Victoria watched as a great comet, soaring snakelike through the earth's atmosphere above an archipelago of islands. Suddenly, in a horrific, blinding explosion, it rained down death and destruction on the terrified people below.

Then suddenly it all stopped.

The express train of time was over. The mist cleared and she could see the face of a young girl with a blue crescent moon on her forehead, her hair bound at her brow by a thong of birch bark. She was looking down at her through the waters of a well and she knew somehow that the girl was seeing her also, for her face suddenly showed recognition.

Something that Victoria could not quite understand passed between them. But what she did know was that ever since that momentary touch of Pan's hand, she had seen the same girl's face in her dreams often.

Suddenly, the vision was gone, and she was back in the stone circle. Pan was playing his panpipes, and the animals were all dancing about her, and she was dancing with them, following them; the vision forgotten.

Then, before she knew what was happening, Pan and the animals with him had wandered off, and her Grandpapa was urging her back to the stone circle. And suddenly she was back on her island home, back in her small community, to a sea of worried faces and a thousand questions.

Ever since her encounter with the great nature God Pan, Victoria had taken to walking up the mountain track, to clear her head and think. Today, on her walk, Victoria had been contemplating all these things. She had walked all the way up to the old Dolmen on a flat ridge, the one her Grandpapa had taken her to and told her about the mysterious matrix of leys that stretched across the countryside.

Sitting on the rocky ground beside the Dolmen, she looked down below at the shallow sea and the other islands that could be seen from here. She thought about the young priestess in her dreams. For priestess she was, with her blue crescent tattoo and white glowing robes. She had told Victoria so too, and that she lived in a country called Y's. And that her name was Star, and that she lived long, long ago.

How this could come about, and how Star knew those things, Victoria did not know. All she knew was that in her dreams, they had taken to talking about herbs. Star wanted to teach her all she knew about those plants that she called 'teacher plants'. And all the properties that they had that could help us in the human world.

Star also talked about the Mineral Kingdom, the Plant Kingdom and the Animal Kingdom. And all this talk with Star in her dreams seemed to somehow imbue her with a wide knowledge of not only herbs, but the workings of the natural world as well. Victoria sat contemplating all this for a long time, but then realised that dusk was approaching, and she needed to make her way back down the mountain track.

2

She was nearly home, when, as she walked towards the Singing Tree, she noticed a large gathering of starlings roosting in its branches. The large sycamore tree had become known by the residents of her community as the 'Singing tree,' because at dusk, birds often gathered here. And, as today, they were all singing together, making a cacophony of screeching excitement.

As Victoria walked under the tree, the noise became almost deafening, but it always made her smile at the sheer audacity and wonder of all those birds gathered together, making so much noise. But Victoria knew that when this happened, it was a prelude to something else. So knowing this, she made her way to the end of the vegetable garden and waited.

Suddenly, the sky explodes with a black cloud of living creatures. Thousands of starlings swoop and glide, all together in perfect synchronism. A symphony of motion, producing strange and impossible organic shapes. In the fading light, Victoria watched in awe, transfixed by the murmuration. A living constellation— sweeping across the canvas of the sunset sky.

A tilt of wing spun mid-flight, causing the whole single organism to fly overhead. A frenzied swirling rush, then the soft murmur of wings. Each bird a note in a grand composition of grace and urgency. A single pulsing, cosmic heartbeat, a living organism, navigating the currents of time and space. Each follows the dynamics of Morphic fields. All in synergy, pure joy in motion, performing nature's dance.

Victoria watched all this in awe. It didn't matter how many times she had seen this spectacle of nature performing at sunset, she still was entranced and overcome with the wonder and mystery of nature. It made her more determined than ever to know more about the workings of nature. And she vowed to herself that she would ask her Grandpapa to teach her more about his magic.

But now she needed to return to the community kitchen. People would be gathering for the evening meal.

3

Dafydd and Rumanadil lying in their filthy prison had been talking for some time. It was clear that the dark elves felt them securely detained, so had left them alone. The guards seldom showed themselves, they knew that their prisoners needed no food or water, although their spells had made them thirsty and hungry.

Dafydd was keen to get as much information about their prison and their guards as he could from Rumanadil. Besides, he had nothing better to do with his time, now that he was detained in prison. His sharp mind was beginning to clear. Although the guards had beaten and mistreated him, nothing too serious was wrong with him. Eventually, he asked Rumanadil what he had discovered while spying.

"Perhaps you may know," revealed Rumanadil, "that we high elves have been intelligence gathering within the human realm for millennia. But what you may not know is that there are factions within the Elven realm that we call, in our own tongue, the Druchii."

Rumanadil paused a moment, thinking, perhaps not sure of how much to say, but then, "Human, you know them as Dark Elves. They are more akin to humans as they have moved over to the dark side and joined the destructive forces. They are upsetting the delicate balance of the Otherworld."

Dafydd winced at this damning opinion of the human race, but answered, "Yes, I am aware of the dark elves' malignancy toward the human realm. And the massive upheavals that they have instigated within our realm. But now I am interested in what they are doing in this realm of Tír na nÓg. What have you discovered of them here, Rumanadil?"

Rumanadil was silent for some time, staring at his cell-mate as if trying to establish a melding link with Dafydd's mind. Dafydd could feel the invasion and fought hard against it, closing his mind as he had been taught.

Rumanadil eventually answered, "I am not sure how much you will understand, human, of all the things I have seen. But for many of your centuries now, ever-increasing numbers of Elven kind have grown weary of the otherworld, and wished they could walk the physical realm again; as they once did as the Tuatha de Danann. They crave to have children again as we cannot do here.

"But the Druchii are obsessed with this wish, no more so than King Indech himself. With him as their leader, the Druchii have taken grave measures to bring this about."

Rumanadil paused, looking about to see if anyone else listened. Then crawled nearer to Dafydd. In his tattered and filthy clothes and crawling on the floor, he looked like a mad thing, as his eyes darted from side to side. He crouched over Dafydd, his stinking hot breath breathing in his face, Dafydd shrank back against the wall in disgust.

"But let me tell you," Rumanadil continued in hushed tones. "That the Druchii have somehow been utilising technology from your realm and blended it with their own magical abilities, creating hybrid machines combining science with magic. We high elves find this very distasteful." He peered about him again, searching for unseen listeners.

"I have seen a strange craft being used, a giant ball that flies across the dimensions. They can transport spirit beings from this realm into the human realm for indefinite periods. It somehow generates a power that maintains the spirit being without depleting their own magical energy."

"This is terrifying indeed, Rumanadil," exclaimed

Dafydd. "But also very interesting. If we could somehow escape from our cell, we could perhaps use this craft to escape from Tír na nÓg and back to the human realm. Do you think you could fly one of these crafts?"

"Quite possibly," Stated Rumanadil. But after thinking a moment, " I would imagine that they use elf magic to fly the thing. That I could do. But there is more I need to tell you. I have seen vast nurseries, filled with something they call incubators. Inside them are foul creatures; hybrids of human and elf." Rumanadil spat a great gob of blood to the floor, then continued, "They are breeding an army, Dafydd, of tiny hybrids. Hybrids that will swiftly grow and can inhabit the human realm. I know not how they have done this Dafydd. But they intend to wipe humans from the face of the world and replace them with these hybrids. They call it the 'Genesis Project.'"

Dafydd turned pale at this and was horrified. It confirmed his worst fears. "I can believe what you say is true, Rumanadil. By their meddling with the earth's climate, they have already reduced our numbers to a fraction of what it was. Now I can see why."

Dafydd was quiet for a moment, contemplating the horror of the situation. Then, he replied hopefully, "But surely, with their king now lying dead, they will not continue with this crazy notion."

"It will certainly slow them down for a while," admitted Rumanadil. "At the moment, they are on high alert, running around like headless chickens. But the dark elves are nothing but a resilient and persistent race. In time, they will recover and elect a new leader. It remains to be seen what they will do then."

"So. If I read you correctly, we have a reprieve, a brief space of time, to act against them." Dafydd paused, thinking. Then exclaimed urgently, "Rumanadil! We both must escape from here, and soon. We must return to the physical realm and warn my people of what the dark elves are planning. It's vitally important. We must find a way. But what else have you discovered that we may be able to use?"

"My espionage has uncovered many things, as I told you. But the most promising thing I have discovered and may be of help to us. It is this craft I told you about. It is made with a strange mixture of quantum physics and high magic. I don't pretend to understand how they did it, but it could be used as a way to escape from the dark elves. If only we had someone on the outside to help us."

"But surely you have friends within the high elf's realm that could help us," said Dafydd. "What about the ones who sent you here?"

"That would be impossible, for it was the Fay Queen herself who sent me. She could not risk a rescue mission, for it would be a diplomatic nightmare. It would be an open admission that she had been spying on the dark elves."

Chapter 6

Morgana

1

Touchwood found this new situation very strange indeed. After all he had gone through, hearing about the dark elfs from his spirit guide, the Oak King; visiting the Otherworld and meeting his druid brother Adge, who had 'transcended' to the spirit world. Then there was the gruelling search for the missing syrinx, which meant he had had to teleport through the ley matrix many times searching for it. And then there had been that terrifying encounter with the Great God Pan! Poor Touchwood now felt he was entitled to a quieter life and some peace from the pressures of the spirit world.

But it was not meant to be; now he had the inconvenience of this irritable shade sharing his rooms. Morgana was not the easiest of entities to be around at the best of times. As a high elf, she lorded over whoever she was with. And expected Touchwood to apply himself as her servant.

If Touchwood showed the slightest reluctance towards her commands, she would start to throw things about the room, creating loud noises that Touchwood was afraid might alert other residents, in the self-sufficient community he lived in.

He really did not want anyone else in the community to know that he had a 'shade' residing in his room; what on earth would they think? They would surely freak out if they discovered what was behind the noises. Most people there already thought he was a strange individual, doing mysterious rituals up on the mountain and disappearing for days on end without a word. Most were convinced he was some sort of wizard.

He had tentatively talked to Morgana about this. And asked her if she intended to stay, then the least she could do was to dematerialise when someone came into his room to talk to him. But Morgana typically was very grumpy about this 'inconvenience' to her.

In the past, Touchwood had sort of got used to his fellow druid, Adge coming occasionally to visit as a shade. But it seemed that Adge wasn't able to build up enough energy to maintain the link for long. He had told him that non-corporeal beings could only remain in our realm for short periods.

But in any case, he had only materialised a couple of times. After that, they were engaged in the quest looking for the lost syrinx and had met in a dolmen or a barrow away from the house.

But it seemed that Morgana, being a High Elf, had enough magical energy to maintain the link for much longer. Which was problematic, to say the least, for Touchwood.

He had tactfully suggested that she stay close to the dolmen up on the mountain so that she could tap into its energy and remain longer. Morgana had very reluctantly accepted this suggestion,   occasionally vanishing from his rooms; and at last giving him some peace and quiet.

2

But this 'vanishing from his rooms' became a problem in itself. For when Victoria had very kindly brought him some food on a tray, and stayed to talk to her Grandpapa for a while, about all the strange noises people had heard coming from his room. Poor Touchwood was torn between lying to his lovely granddaughter and trying to explain the situation without causing alarm.

Then, just as he was trying to explain things to Victoria, Morgana materialised right in front of them both.

"And who is this?" Morgana asked imperiously.

Touchwood's jaw dropped in surprise, and then he just slumped into his chair, putting his hands over his head; momentarily giving up.

Victoria too was momentarily taken aback, but recovered quickly, saying, "Hello my name is Victoria. Touchwood is my grandfather."

Then, after taking in Morgana's fine clothes, realised that she must be someone important and asked, "And who might I have the honour of addressing?"

Morgana, pleased with her reverential address, declared, "You may call me Morgana la Fay. I am high elf and former companion to Myrddin Wyllt. You may have heard of him.

Victoria nodded. As a child, she had read a book from Touchwoods library on the Arthurian legends. But then Morgana held out her hand for Victoria to kiss; however, Victoria did the strangest thing. Instead of kissing the hand, she did a funny little curtsey with one leg bent and her hands at her sides held out like a duck's wings.

Morgana seemed satisfied with this response. Then Victoria, looking at Morgana with wide eyes, asked, "Are you a witch?"

"No child. But I will admit to being an enchantress."

Then, turning to Victoria's grandfather slumped in his chair, commanded, "Touchwood! Are you not going to find our guest a chair?"

Poor Touchwood leapt out of his armchair, but had a hard time trying to find anything that the wrath of Morgana hadn't smashed. But eventually, he found, under the bench, a small three-legged milking stool he had made many years ago. Laying it gently by the stove, he offered it to Victoria, who very daintily squatted on it, in the most lady-like way. Touchwood had never seen Victoria behaving like this, but it seemed to have a calming effect on Morgana, so didn't question it for a minute.

Touchwood slumped back into his chair, feeling like he could not cope anymore. Things seemed to be getting out of his power to control. He had tried hard to protect Victoria from the perils of magic and the otherworld. But it seemed to be leaking into his own kitchen now, which had always seemed a sanctuary to him. He closed his eyes, deep in thought, his mind wandering to how he could rescue his friend Adge from his fate in the otherworld.

Meanwhile, Victoria seemed to be fascinated with this imperious visitor that was dressed so finely. Morgana, too, seemed fascinated with Victoria and seemed to talk with her as if she were her equal.

"Are you the Morgan le Fay from the tales I have read about?" asked Victoria.

"I'm afraid so. But you can't believe all that you hear you know; so many conflicting stories there are."

Morgana lowered herself to the floor beside Victoria so they were face to face. Her tone changed to that of a bard reciting the sacred tales. "Originally I lived here on the earth plain, I was of the Danann race. This, perhaps, you know, was many thousands of your years ago. My ancestors came from the great nation of the Y's. But understand, you humans only know of it as Atlantis."

Victoria's eyes lit up in recognition, for she had heard of Y's. Star, the young priestess from her dreams, had said she lived in a country called Y's and that she lived long, long ago. But she didn't want to interrupt Morgana's story. So stayed quiet.

"But a great catastrophe occurred. The waters rose and our nation was submerged beneath the waves. However, many prophetesses predicted the end times. The priestesses and all those confidants of them knew and were prepared. Before the final days, many had boarded ships and followed the trading routes to other lands that we traded with. West, east and south we went. Some even came north to the colder climes. My ancestors were part of that group.

"So of course I wasn't born in the nation of the Y's. I was part of the new births that came when we evacuated to Ireland. The 'new dawn generation' they called us. When we all felt we had found our new home, and the call was to procreate as much as possible to increase our numbers, after the disastrous losses incurred when our nation was destroyed. But away from our homeland, for some unknown reason, there were very few successful pregnancies and even fewer grew into adulthood.

"But of course we were forbidden to mate with the indigenous population - it was a tabu. In any case, they considered us to be Demi Gods. They feared us, because our people had special 'gifts,' telepathy and other psychic powers. They considered us a race of sorcerers and wizards.

"Everybody agreed it was important to keep our blue blood pure. Just as we had done in our homeland of Y's. We did not want to water it down with the blood of the natives. But now we were only very few, so even at the cost of mating with our own mothers or siblings, we continued to follow the Tabu.

"This, of course, was the cause of our second downfall. Although at the time nobody realised it. It was only much later that we came to realise our mistake. This in-breeding instead of keeping our blood pure and strong - only weakened us.

"For many years, the wise ones debated what should be done about this. Some of our young rebelled and took it upon themselves to mate with the indigenous population. And it was feared that we, as a great nation, would soon be lost by integrating into the indigenous population.

"So it was, that the elders decided that the entire

Tuatha race should transcend permanently to Tír na nÓg, via the gateways of the stone circles. And so it came to pass. When all the Tuatha race had at last transcended to Tír na nÓg, they left the two of us behind. They had chosen us as 'sacrifice'; myself and Merlin.

"You see, the ritual to transcend required the help of people on the earthly plain. When all others had gone, they left us behind; it was meant to be a noble sacrifice. Merlin and I were married, and the elders thought we could sustain each other during what time we had left. As you may be aware, on the earthly plain we were long lived, but not immortal.

"During the long years, we tried to amuse ourselves, interfering with the lives of indigenous humans. Together we wandered all across the isles of Brigid. But eventually we wearied of each other and drifted apart. Merlin went his way, and I went my own,"

Morgana sighed,"I hid myself away on an unassailable island surrounded by lakes and marshland. It was there I surrounded myself with young women, for in them I could see possibilities for the indigenous race. I taught them all I could in the ways of magic.

"However, Merlin seemed to get quite attached to the squabbling humans and tried to unite them; but it proved quite impossible. In desperation, he quested to find Claíomh Solais, one of the treasures left behind by the Danann's. You would call it the 'sword of Light.' It belonged to our king, Nuada; the sword makes the keeper insuperable and impossible to defeat.

"Merlin eventually found the sword and renamed it Excalibur. Using his magic, Merlin buried it into a megalithic stone, only allowing his protégé, Arthur, to remove it."

Her eyes had a faraway look as she told her story, as if she could travel back in time to those ancient times. "Of course, the magic of the sword worked, and Arthur was impossible to defeat, and the foolish humans united under him; for a time. But as is the way with humans and magic, there was a kickback and as time passed, things started to go badly wrong."

"Poor Merlin," she said sarcastically, "Became very disillusioned with his 'pet humans' and reclaiming the sword, returned to me on my island of Avalon. To the locals, I became known as 'The Lady of the lake,' and there were many stories told by wandering bards about us; garbled and exaggerated versions of the truth."

She paused again, contemplating. Then, "And so we remained on my sacred island for many years."

She took another great sigh, then continued, "But as we grew older and close to death, I grew weary of the human realm and begged Merlin to help me to transcend to Tír na nÓg. In the end, Merlin sacrificed himself for me, and remain behind."

This version of the familiar tale completely enchanted Victoria, hardly believing she was listening to the true story from the original Morgana la fay.

"We found his body, you know," said Touchwood sleepily, his eyes still closed. Clearly, he had been half listening to Morgana's tale all along.

"Where," Morgana asked softly?

Touchwood now opened his eyes and looked at Morgana. Was that a trace of a tear in her eye? "It was in a Crystal Cave where we found the missing Syrinx. At a darkened end of the cave, we found his mummified remains. He was wearing around his neck a druid's golden lunula. He must have come to die in the Crystal Cave. Clutched across his chest in his bony arms was a magnificent sword. We thought it must be the legendary Excalibur, Núada's Sword of Light."

"So he did finally die beside his humans, that he loved so well," Morgana said softly. "I often wondered if he had found a way to transcend by himself. And kept it secret from me."

Victoria was trying her best to understand the situation, but enthused, "Tír na nÓg sounds like a wonderful place to me. If you transcended there, why are you here in our house?"

Touchwood looked sharply at Victoria for being so rude to Morgana. He expected her to react badly to the question, but she answered calmly.

"Once I had freed Pan from imprisonment in a tree. And the King of the Dark elves had been killed. The Dark elves were searching high and low for any conspirators. I felt it wise to lie low for a while."

Victoria took a sudden intake of breath at this mention of 'Dark elves'. Her eyes widened as she asked, "Dark elves! What are they?"

Touchwood visibly cringed. He had tried his best to protect Victoria from the darker side of the magical world. But Morgana was in a mood to reveal all; no bars held. He slumped back into his chair again, putting his hands over his head, lost in his own misery.

"Victoria," Morgana said softly, "You must be aware that in nature there are two forces at play. That which 'creates', and that which 'destroys'. It is the eternal cycle; it is the natural order of things. And so, what is true for the physical realm, is also true for the spirit realms. The High Elves are the most handsome of the two types of elves. We are a tall, slender race. Graceful and agile of movement, yet strong. We are pale-skinned and aesthetically beautiful. Naturally white hair, but we can appear anyway we choose, on the earth plain; you could even mistake us for high-born human. We have a love of elegant and finely crafted things. All elves work magic, but we high elves work with the elements creatively. We have even been known to aid humans; when it suits us." She finished with an ironic smile as she softly slid her hand down Victoria's long, blond hair.

"You know Victoria, you could make a fine elf yourself."

Victoria lowered her eyes, perhaps not knowing quite what to make of Morgana. Then asked, "But what about the dark elves?"

"The Dark Elves, or the Druchii, as they call themselves. Are similar in looks to High Elves, but shorter, and dark of skin. Dark Elves stay in the shadows. They are sadistic destroyers, working with rot and decay, seeking nothing more than to despoil a world. Be warned, they watch your dying world with malevolent eyes, wishing to claim it for themselves.

"They have spawned a race of deformed servants. The 'Greys' are lighter of skin; somewhat grey in appearance. Their hair has been shaved and they are not allowed to wear the exotic clothes of the dark elves, and forced to go naked. They have no ears, very wide-spaced eyes that wrap round the sides of their heads and have no reproductive parts, being spawned in a laboratory."

Victoria had gone very pale after hearing this and sat

up very straight and stiff. Morgana, seeing her terrified reaction, took her head and laid it to her chest, placing her hand comfortingly on her head. Victoria threw her arms about Morgana, nuzzling in like a lost child. Morgan waved a curious hand movement over Victoria's head; before long, she was fast asleep.

.

Chapter 7

Delia's Herb Garden

1

Touchwood had been gardening this patch of ground for years and years. Sometimes it seemed to him too long. Yet although he had grown older; nowhere near as old as his years on earth. He had seen young people come to Rath Grain. Watched them work and grow old and eventually die. Yet he lived on.

He put this down to his magical work and his many visits to the Otherworld, where time didn't seem to work in the same way as it did in the physical world. He suspected too that the Oak King, his spirit guide, had some influence with this? For he was fairly certain that the Oak King had protected their little corner of the world from the ravages of climate change that had destroyed the modern civilisation he had once known. And since the waters had risen and the climate crisis had settled down, their little island home had enjoyed a mild Mediterranean climate.

2

Far from being a mere myth and legend story, the Oak King and the Holly King are as old as time itself, certainly as old as the human realm. They are part of the pantheon of 'Old Gods.' So it is, with many other Gods, such as the Horned God - Cernunnos, and Ogma. Perhaps the oldest of all is Anu, for she is the mother of the Gods; but in later years, she was called Danu. Other cultures over the millennia have given these 'Old Gods' other names, such as Pan, Dionysus, and Gaia.

But to get back to the two brothers, the Oak King and The Holly King. They represent the battle of opposing forces in the world. The Oak King governs fecundity, light and the creative forces of nature. Whereas the Holly King governs the darker energies of rot and decay, he is a destroyer of established order.

But let us not concern ourselves overly with the Old Gods, for they have agendas that are far beyond human comprehension. It is the relative newcomers to the otherworld that we are concern with here. The hyper-human race of the Tuatha De Danann, who transcended from the physical plane to the otherworldly realm, millennia ago. A mere flash in the pan compared to the agelessness of the old Gods.

Even though some people call them elves or fairies, or even believe them to be Gods, for they do have magical powers. These 'Elven kind' are as far from the Old Gods as a human is from, say, a slug slithering in your garden. In reality, these 'Elven kind' are more akin to humans and some of them have moved over to the dark side and joined the destructive forces.

3

As for what the other community members of Rath Grain thought about Touchwood? They knew that he was the longest running member of the community. He had been there longer than anyone could remember. In fact, Victoria had proudly told them that her grandfather had founded the community before the waters had risen.

If this could be believed, that would make Touchwood very old indeed, perhaps even over a hundred years old; yet he certainly didn't look it. This prospect made some members a little uneasy at the thought. Which wasn't helped by the fact that in recent years, there were often 'strange looking' visitors arriving late at night, seen entering his rooms.

In addition, Touchwood had a habit of suddenly rushing off. 'Just going for a little walk up the mountain,' he would say. But in fact, had gone missing for days, sometimes weeks, at a time. Then, suddenly, out of the blue, arriving in the community kitchen as though returning from a leisurely Sunday afternoon stroll.

When pressed for a reason for his absence, he became evasive and retired to his rooms with no explanation. Then there were all those times when Touchwood had been overheard talking to, 'someone,' in his rooms, when everyone was accounted for and all were sitting together having dinner in the refectory.

A rumour had been spread by one of the young adults who reported that when she was making a batch of bread one evening, Touchwood, who was sitting in a corner eating his supper, had suddenly seemed to become 'possessed'; his whole body jolting and speaking out in a strange voice.

But worst of all, was just recently, people could hear loud bangs and crashes coming from his rooms. It sounded like the furniture was being smashed. People became very curious about this latest activity, and poor Victoria had been pressed several times to explain what was going on. Unfortunately, she didn't know either, and couldn't enlighten them.

But now Victoria had begun to see what was behind these rumours about her grandfather. She had 'so to speak' entered into the inner circle of knowledge about those magical activities. Morgana had enlightened her about the wicked plans of the dark elves. And even though it frightened her, she wanted to know more about this strange new world she had entered. But for the moment, she needed to continue with her everyday tasks about the community.

4

Brad was an ex-Irish soldier who had deserted their main base in the Wicklow mountains after it had been all but destroyed during the oil wars. He had, in fact, been one of the soldiers on the Irish navy boats that had once visited Touchwoods island with supplies. So he knew there were survivors on those far-off islands.

After his base was destroyed, very few were left alive. So Brad had stolen an army motor launch and made his way to the island. Unfortunately, the launch had run out of fuel before he got there. But he had drifted for days, eventually landing on the far side of Sliabh an Iarainn island. He was found on the shore dehydrated and half-dead. But he was inherently strong and quickly recovered, staying with the community that had found him for a couple of years. But then had moved to Rath Grain three years ago and had become a very useful member of the community.

Brad was tall and dark with deep blue eyes and was very fit. He had experience with building and working with wood. One day, he had decided to reorganise the old workshop. Victoria had been assigned to help with the clearing out.

Brad wanted to reorganise it and build shelves and strong benches. The original's had been built many years ago by Touchwood and Adge when they were running their woodworking business, 'Tree Wheel Crafts'. There was still lots of bog oak and many other bits of wood that had been collected from every type of tree imaginable. There was a great pile of it in one corner.

As Victoria was clearing away the old woodpile, she found a shaped piece of wood that had a lovely grain to it. She picked it up and was admiring the grain, when Brad came over and asked, "What have you got there Vicky?"

"I don't know. I just love the grain."

"Looks like someone was making a pipe bowl out of a root ball. I reckon that's bramble. I've dug up enough of those in the backfield. If you clean it up, you could use it; it just needs a stem. Here, look, there's some bamboo in the pile you could use."

5

During her dream sleep later that night, Victoria had told Star about the pipe she had found, and asked her what she use it for.

Star had informed her that, "Many herbs can be

smoked for beneficial effects using a pipe. In fact, in the Temples, we often use smoking herbs as a way to relax which helps us go into deep meditation. An herb we call 'old woman's broom' is smoked before the Beltane revelries, but I believe around the inland sea, they call it Damiana. Mugwort and Blue Water Lily are smoked to help us enter the otherworld, where we can learn a lot about the natural world."

Star had also advised her, as part of her education on herb lore, that she should look for two particular herbs that needed to be smoked together and use them to enter the otherworld. One was Mugwort and the other was one she called 'Ma'.

"I think I have been to the otherworld before," replied Victoria. "It was really beautiful there."

"Really? How did you get there?"

"I went with my grandfather. It was an accident really," confessed Victoria. "I was sending him some healing energy and the next thing I knew; we were in this euphoric paradise with fruit trees and…"

"OK, that is good that you have had some experience. But it seems like you didn't go there using your own power. That's where these herbs I spoke of will help you. That will be your next assignment to find those herbs that will lend you their power. You will also be able to gather even more power if you perform your ritual at a place where the earth's dragon power is strong."

6

Now Victoria stood in the herb garden. Victoria's Grandpapa, Touchwood, had told her that long ago a wonderful gardener friend of his called Delia, had laid out their herb garden. She planted every type of herb that they could find at the time, and some of them were more suited to warmer climates and could only be grown under glass.

However, her Grandpapa had told her that since the great ice fields to the north had melted many years ago, and the waters had risen, the local climate had become warmer. It was almost Mediterranean; he had said with a wry smile.

In time, the herbs had become the only form of medicine that they had. So they had always tried to maintain somebody that knew the herbal lore that Delia had passed on. Recently, it had passed to Victoria to become the local herbalist. Victoria had soaked up any knowledge the other community members knew about herbs. And with the help of Star, the young priestess from her dreams, she had become quite adept in herb lore.

Now Victoria placed her hand down to her belt where the little sickle-shaped knife her grandfather had made for her lay securely in its little holster. The handle had been made using bog oak and had been lovingly carved with spirals and Celtic knots. The holster was made of leather. She had found the Mugwort plant that Star had suggested she collect, but she had called it by the name 'Dreamers Herb.' She had had to describe it to Victoria in detail. But Victoria was still not confident about which one it was, as several other plants in the garden looked like it as well. In the end, she had consulted Ruby.

Ruby was in her late forties and was a very down-to-earth and calm individual. She had trained as a midwife and enjoyed cooking, both of which required a knowledge of herbs. Ruby was a great asset to the community. She had called the mystery herb 'Gypsy Tobacco' and told Victoria exactly where to find it in the garden.

Ruby had said it was a herb greatly revered by Ayurveda and Chinese medicine, and also by the ancient Greeks who named it after Artemis; Goddess of the Moon. Ruby had told her that when Western medicines had become hard to obtain during the Oil wars, she had used them as incense. The aromatic smoke helped to calm her 'mother's' during childbirth.

So, in a roundabout way, Victoria had managed to find mugwort in the herb garden, even though Star had called it by a different name. But now she needed to find the herb, 'Ma,' based on the descriptions Star had given her. However, Victoria had searched high and low, through the whole herb garden for it, but could find no trace of it.

7

So when she found the time, Victoria decided to go out looking for herbs in the wild areas surrounding the community. In one particular area, not far away, there was an old ruin. The walls had crumbled long ago, but the stone flag floor still lay on the ground, covered in moss and weeds. It was a place she rarely went to. The gardeners said there were too many stones there to make into a garden. But she found wild hops growing as a vine all over a low hawthorn bush. She also recognised some mistletoe growing on the same hawthorn tree. And over there, it looked like someone in the past had been hedge-laying hazel trees, and on the south-facing hedge were what looked to be some tomatoes growing wild, climbing up the hedge.

This area, Victoria thought, looked like somebody had been living there and had been working a small garden. She sat down on the low wall a moment, and then, low and behold, she spotted something that looked very like the description Star had given her for the herb 'Ma'.

The plant had leaves which were stipulate and opposite, with seven unequal, elongated and spiny segments with toothed margins. Star had also said they had quite a pungent smell, which these had. So she decided to collect some leaves and check with Ruby, the head cook.

Victoria was just entering the refectory door when she met her grandfather coming out with a plate of fresh bread, cheese, and olives for his breakfast.

"Oh hello, my lovely," greeted Touchwood.

"I see you have got yourself some breakfast Grandpapa. Is some of that for Morgana too," Victoria asked?

But Touchwood hadn't heard her. His mind had been somewhere else as he said, "You know Victoria, those olive trees Delia planted all those years ago are producing some delicious olives."

"Thats nice but I've been meaning to ask you, Grandpapa, if I could build a little shed specifically for procuring herbs. I've been using the kitchen, but Chef is saying there are too many herbs hanging up cluttering the place. After all, it is our main source of medicine."

"Ah, Delia," a small tear came to Touchwood's eye as he entered a reverie about the past. "She had the foresight to see that the climate here was turning towards a Mediterranean one…" Then he stopped mid-sentence, for he had noticed what Victoria was carrying.

"What is that?" he asked, pointing to one of the herbs Victoria had collected.

"Oh, just some wild herbs I've collected. I'm trying to expand the herb garden…"

"Yes, but that one there. Do you know what it is?"

"Yes, it is one called 'Ma'. My spirit guide asked me to collect it."

"Your… spirit guide!" Touchwood nearly choked on the words. "I didn't know… But… but that's a cannabis plant! Where on earth did you find it?"

"It was up the track a bit, over by the old ruin; not far away."

"That's where Adge's caravan was. We cannibalised it long ago. But there must have been some seeds and…"

"So can I build my shed?" Victoria pesisted plaintively.

"But that's… that's cannabis. It's illegal, you know."

"Illegal? What's that? We don't have any authorities on this island to declare it illegal."

"Yes… Yes… I suppose you are right," he said, shrugging his shoulders. "But be careful with that one," he said, pointing at the Cannabis leaves.

Touchwood went away shaking his head and muttering something about Adge still making his presence felt after all these years.

Chapter 8

Beltain Lectures

1

Star had only recently attained her sixth degree as a priestess of the moon, so she hadn't yet realised that with attainment, in the hierarchy of the temples, came added responsibility. One of those responsibilities had been teaching the new intake of neophytes. At first, she had reluctantly accepted this responsibility. But as the months went by, she realised she was a natural teacher and loved conveying her knowledge to the younger people. After all, it was only one day a week.

Throughout the mild winter, Star spent the rest of her time dedicated to the study of herb lore. She had attended many of the lectures intended for apprentice healers. And spent some time in the apothecary under practical instructions from Selen. She even went to the libraries in the Sun temple and listened to the philosophical discussions between sages and Draoi Masters. These wise elders seemed to embrace every subject, but Star was especially interested in discussions that enquired about the very nature of healing both bodily, mentally, and spiritually.

But as the year turned and spring flowers started to blossom, thoughts turned to the up-and-coming Beltane rites. At last year's rites, Star had coupled with Blaze. It was quite unusual, but they had stayed sex partners for the remainder of the year. Several of the other junior priestesses had been teasing her about this unusual practice. Star enjoyed being with Blaze, but because of this teasing, she was seriously considering choosing someone else this Beltane.

Within the temples, it was considered the duty of each boy and girl to work with the tantric teachings that they had been taught in a practical way. This involved developing a wide experience of sexual relations.

Star entered the open hall of the Moon temple, Mandapa, to consult the daily rota chalked on the notice board, which was hung on a far wall. As usual, the hall was peaceful and almost deserted, but there were a few of her fellow priestesses gathered about the rota board. As she approached her friends, she could hear their whispered voices and an occasional stifled giggle.

"Hello, what am I missing?" she said as she joined the excited group. Both Zilla and River turned, trying to stifle their excited chattering.

"The Beltane lectures are beginning this week. We are all invited to attend," Zilla whispered before returning to her fits of giggling.

Star, amused by the immaturity of her friends, declared, "Yes, I went to them last year. So see you all there. But right now, I am needed at the apothecary."

2

"The plainest girl will be beautiful if she rises early on Mayday and bathes her face in the morning dew at sunrise," declared the head lecturer at the Beltane lectures. Fiamma Bhagasana was a high-ranking middle-aged Adept at the Nathair Temple. A lithe, sensuous woman, that moved about the platform with a dancer's grace.

Star, along with several of her friends and fellow junior priestesses, had agreed to attend the Beltane revelries this year. If so, it was mandatory to attend these preparatory lectures. However, it was made clear to all junior priestesses and priests that it wasn't mandatory to attend the Beltane revelries. If a person felt their path was one of chastity, remaining a virgin, then this was highly thought of within the Temples. This path of dedication brought its own rewards and specific roles within temple life.

"Washing one's hands and walking barefoot in the morning dew, bring many positive benefits for both sexes," Fiamma continued with animated gestures, making intimate eye contact with those foolish enough to sit in the front rows.

"So the special day begins with the dewy dawn," Fiamma continued. "I would recommend stripping Skyclad and rolling in the dewy grass, as a perfect way to cleanse and purify before the main rituals of the day. We then dress ourselves in the white gossamer robes that all priestesses wear for the Beltane rituals, regardless of temple branch or rank. However, priestesses may also adorn themselves with exquisite jewellery of their choice and distinctive headwear, like the diadem.

Although, be aware that too elaborate a diadem, could get tangled in the maypole ropes and cause no end of problems for all concerned." Fiamma paused again, gracing everyone with a sardonic grin.

"Meanwhile, the young novice temple priests go out into the wild woods seeking the flowering may blossom. They return… eventually. And present the may blossom to the awaiting young priestesses, who by now should be all dew-washed and dressed in their ritual robes. Class, it is important to remember that at this interchange, there is to be no touching or any contact with the males whatsoever. We must be building the tantric power from the very beginning.

"The young novice priests then go off to prepare for the mayday games and competitions. The most accomplished is decided, and becomes the winner of the games: the King Stag. Meanwhile, we priestesses take the green boughs and flowering branches to the stone circle and decorate the entire area. This, of course, symbolises the renewal of life and the flourishing of nature, which is the dominant theme of Beltane. We also set up the maypole in the centre and the long ropes for the dancing — Now, does anyone know the symbolism of the maypole?"

"Fertility and Rebirth," called a dark-haired girl from the back of the hall.

"Well, yes, that's what the festival is all about, but what specifically does the central pole represent," Fiamma asked?

"A representation of the God's phallic energy mistress," giggled a rather large girl in the front row.

"Yes, excellent," Fiamma complimented. "The long

central pole represents the male principle. The holy lingam of the horned God. Birch is the traditional wood used for the Maypole. Remembering that Birch is associated with renewal, new life, new beginnings, casting out of the old self or making a clean sweep of it.

"Now, you may have noticed that on top of the pole is mounted a willow hoop. The circle and the tree 'Willow' represent the female principal, the sacred Yoni. This hoop is adorned with leaves and flowers, and the fine dancing ropes are connected to it.

"The tantric symbolism is clear, the phallic Maypole properly pierces the circular hoop and thus conforms with the lingam and yoni co-joined. Now we come to the Maypole dance. Initially, all the dancers will stand in a circle around the maypole, boy-girl, boy-girl, all the way round, each holding one of the thin ropes. Class, does anyone know the symbolism of the dance," Fiamma asked as she beamed expectantly about the hall?

"The intertwining of human connections," called River, who was sitting next to her friend Star.

"Yes, you could put it that way. As we dance, the ropes of each boy and girl are all twisted together into a single pattern, symbolising that we are all part of life's tapestry or pattern. We are all linked to each other and individually contribute to the whole pattern. Thus, the Maypole encompasses themes of unity and the cyclical nature of life. However," she said with relish, almost licking her lips. "The sexual energy created by all those young... young bodies jostling... yes jostling around each other as they dance, intertwining with each other," she paused a moment, panting, seemingly out of breath. Then continued, "creates an energetic cone of power, which the Draoi Master and his adepts utilise and directs to ensure the fecundity of the earth, thus creating abundant crops."

Fiamma Bhagasana, looking quite flustered now, paused, and picking up a small fan began to flutter her face franticly. She took a moment to recover, then continued, a little out of breath. "Additionally, as the dancers pull… yes, pull on the ropes, the inevitable jostling… yes jostling, up… up and down of the willow hoop. Which as we remember is pierced…" The fan was fluttering frantically now, "B… by the phallic maypole, is the hidden imagery of the God and the Goddess celebrating life's sweet union. Class, I think it is time for a break now." This last, Fiamma Bhagasana uttered breathlessly as she, frantically fluttering her fan, ran off the platform without another word.

3

Dafydd was brooding, lying in the corner of his cell. The conversation with Rumanadil had run dry, and all was quiet. Occasionally, Dafydd saw a Grey elf running past their cell; they were clearly searching for other intruders. Those 'Greys' made Dafydd's blood run cold. When Dafydd first saw one, Rumanadil had explained that the Grey Elves were the result of early experiments in genetic engineering, by the dark elves. They had become a lower cast, a slave race, under the leadership of the dark elves.

Rumanadil had told Dafydd that the Grey elves were born deformed, with no visible ears, and enormous eyes that wrapped around the sides of their heads. They were much shorter than the dark elves and had lighter skin - a grey appearance. They were also born with piebald hair all over their body, which was distasteful to the eyes of the dark elves. So they insisted their hair be shaved all over, and for them to go naked - not allowed to wear the exotic clothes of the dark elves.

Rumanadil explained that these 'Greys' were the ones most often sent to the human realm, to kidnap humans and perform sadistic experiments on them, before letting them go. The experiments were part of the 'Genesis project'; the dark elves attempt to produce a human-elf, hybrid race.

Now, as Dafydd lay brooding in the corner of his cell, he couldn't believe that things had somehow become worse than he had thought possible. This 'Genesis project' of the dark elves spelt the death knell for the human race. It was imperative they escape and warn the remaining survivors of the human race.

Dafydd had drifted off into a fitful sleep. He had used his dreams to try to contact other Drui Masters that he knew of in the physical realm. But the dark elf's sly spells had robbed him of that ability. He had even tried to contact Touchwood, in Rath Grain, but to no avail.

Lurid dreams haunted him. Disturbing visions of grey elves, looking down on him with their big slanted eyes, holding strange instruments that they inserted into his body. As he struggled in terror, he found he could not move, and panic ran through him. As one Grey moved towards him with a sharp knife, it then opened up his body and mercilessly poked about inside him…

Then suddenly all that vanished, and the face of Goibniu, the metalsmith of the Tuatha de Danann, appeared before him, in his sleep.

'Dafydd, I have been trying to contact you,' he said. 'But at last, as you slept, I could break through. I do not have much time. The dark elves are in turmoil. When I heard that the Lord of Chaos, King Indech himself, had been murdered. I knew it must have been you who had done it.'

Goibniu was Dafydd's spirit guide. He was the blacksmith and alchemist for the Tuatha de Danann. Unknown to Touchwood, Dafydd and his spirit guide had been planning this assassination of King Indech for a very long time. Together, they had worked through every scenario that they could think of, to free Pan from his entombment in an oak tree. But each time, if the dark elves' evil plan was foiled, and Pan freed again, each scenario revealed that the dark elves would rise again, and perhaps this time, set in motion a more permanent eradication of the God Pan.

Millennia ago, Goibniu himself had crafted the magical weapons for the Tuatha tribe. Among them was the Spear of Assail, which he had made for Lugh, the Lord of shining Light; the Irish God of nobility. This was a powerful weapon and wielded magical properties so that 'none could stand against it.' This included mythical creatures and other spirit beings.

Indech, King of the Fomorians and leader of the dark elves, had spent many years searching for this magical weapon so that he could destroy the God Pan. Knowing this, Goibniu had charged Dafydd with the task of searching for this magical spear, before the dark elves could wield it.

Dafydd had spent much of his long life searching for

those sacred treasures of the Danu race. In the end, he had unearthed an ancient document, held in the forgotten archives of the St. Johns Hospitallers; it was a poem called 'The Song of Merlin'. Dafydd and Touchwood together had unravelled the riddle in the poem, and by it, discovered the location of the missing treasures of the Tuatha de Danann. It was the mythical 'Crystal Cave,' where Merlin was said to have spent his last days on earth.

At last, after many years of searching, Dafydd and Touchwood had stood in the Crystal Cave, and had found what they had been looking for. Dafydd, holding the Spear of Assail in one hand and a shimmering, silvery invisibility cloak, the 'Mantle of Arthur' across his other arm, had formed his plan. His ultimate goal was to rid the world of the Lord of Chaos, for all time. However, he didn't want to distract Touchwood by revealing what he himself was about to do. For he knew Touchwood's task was to return the missing Syrinx to the Great God Pan: the fate of the earth depended on it. Dafydd's task was extremely dangerous, and his life could be in great danger. Which is why he had kept this secret, even from those involved in the search for the missing Syrinx.

When Dafydd had at last found the Crystal Cave, and the magical spear, he had kept it secret, even from his own spirit guide, whose face now invaded his dreams.

'Goibniu!' Dafydd thought in his dreams. 'Thank all the Gods. I didn't expect to see you here. But believe me, I am so glad to see you. Yes, you are right. I did kill Indech, and I found the Crystal Cave with the Danann treasures. I do apologise for not informing you, but everything was moving so fast. And I didn't even want to think too much about it, in case the dark elves read my mind. I thought the less anyone knew about it, the better'.

'Dafydd old friend, I quite understand your dilemma. But we must get you out of this prison straight away.'

'You won't find any arguments from me. But can you help us? Do you have a plan?'

'I managed to retrieve the cloak of invisibility. It was left discarded on the floor of the throne room. But the magical spear of Assail that killed Indech, has been locked away within the palace vaults.

'I can use the cloak to steal the key from the guards and release you. But I don't know how you can escape from the realm of the dark elves. They are on high alert, and there are grey guards everywhere.'

'Don't worry about that,' exclaimed Dafydd. 'I think I know a way around that.'

Chapter 9

May morn'

1

On May morning, Star rose early, just as first light graced the eastern horizon. She walked with the other neophytes and priestesses in a processional line from the house of maidens. They wore only the white gossamer robes that were provided to all the priestesses who wished to attend the Beltane rituals.

At the allotted place, a grove of ancient oak trees, the women paused reverently at the clearing edge. At the centre of the grove stood a tall, pointed finger of greyish-blue stone that pointed skyward. The menhir was covered in green and yellow lichens. The stone lifted from the forest floor and looked to be part of it, but was, in fact, very much older. It was part of something mysterious and secret, almost forgotten.

Stags gathered here, in springtime, and scraped the velvet off their antlers against that stone. They would graze here, wild goats and sheep too, causing the grass in the clearing to be cropped short like a lawn.

After permissions were asked of the grove guardians, prayers were offered. Girls and women alike proceeded into the Grove, stripping their robes, standing naked in the early morning light. Then they did bathe in the dewy grass. Some girls coyly bathed only their faces, whilst the more adventurous priestess lay in the moist folds of the grass, rolling in pure sensual joy, with gay abandon.

After some little time, they dressed again in their white robes, and awaited the arrival of the young men. They didn't have to wait long, for the young priests appeared quickly with branches of flowering May blossom; hoping, perhaps, to catch the young women still naked.

The young aspirants stood in awe before the young priestesses, their bodies still wet beneath their almost see-through robes. Their hair, loose and tousled, was sprinkled with grass and leaves. The young men solemnly delivered their May blossom with barely repressed sexual tension. Then, with lingering looks, the novice priests departed to prepare for the mayday games and competitions.

Star, as a sixth-degree priestess, could delegate the task of decorating the stone circle to the younger girls and lower ranks; these all willingly ran off to the stones, excitedly chattering and chirping like a flock of starlings. However, Star returned to the house of maidens to get ready for the coming rites.

Before an old bronze mirror, Star worked a carved horn comb through the tangles in her hair, frowning at the freckles on her skin. However, her mind wandered as it often did… In the Temple culture, women bore children in freedom to such fathers as they chose. And counted their lineage sensibly, through the mother line. She had heard those tales from the sea traders, that some of the little dark tribesmen, at the far eastern part of the internal sea, counted their lineage through the male line, which was ridiculous, how could any man know precisely who had fathered a woman's child. She had also heard that these strange people were ruled by a warrior class of men, who treated their women like slaves. But she could hardly believe that to be true; probably some fisherman's tale to scare naïve cabin boys.

She picked up some little silver rings and placed them on her slender fingers. They had been given to her by her mentor Selen, whose fingers had now grown too large for them. Selen had said they had come all the way from the skilful tribesmen who lived in the rain forests, across the great ocean to the southwest. Her mind wandered to what Fiamma Bhagasana had said in the Beltane lectures... 'That a daughter of the temples must do what is best for her people. But she who often works silently and alone, may at certain times and certain rites, find that she cannot work her magic, without the courage and strength of He who runs with the deer. He who is of the sun and helps to draw forth life from her womb. This is at the very heart of nature.'

Fiamma also said, 'that the temple priestesses were not harlots, as some of the lower castes in Y's thought. In the sacred rituals, we give our bodies to the priests, under conditions far more strict and meaningful, than ordinary folk; the vast majority of the population who were low-skilled craft-workers and farmers. However, we must not take away from the poor country folk, the simple awareness of a goddess who cared for their fields and crops and the fertility of their breasts and their wombs.'

Star finished painting kohl around her eyes to make them look larger. Then put on a necklace of amber beads, some of which had small flying insects entombed within them. She was now ready for the day's rituals.

2

Victoria had built her shed. It was on the very spot where she had found the Cannabis plants. With the help of Brad, they had cleared the old stone flag floor of the ruin, only to discover that the area was quite large; the size of two rooms of a small cottage. Under the hedgerow and mounds of reeds, they had found the original walls of the cottage, which were reasonably intact up to thigh height. On seeing this, Brad had suggested that they could build a small dwelling place here.

Until now, Victoria had been sharing a room with one of the other women, but she was of an age where more and more she was seeking her independence; and the idea of an individual living space appealed to her significantly. With Brad's suggestion, her eyes lit up and sparkled; her vision of a small apothecary turned into a living space with two rooms.

It had taken months of hard work, but with the help of one or two others from the community, they had created a waist-height stone wall with a timber frame above it. The little cottage had a verandah that spanned the length of the front wall; with views over the shallow sea to the south.

Victoria had even managed to persuade Forge, the blacksmith's boy, who lived with his family on the far side of the island, to build her a wood-burning stove, out of an old Calor Gas bottle. It was a thing of beauty, with a small door on the front and a hotplate on top, which could accommodate a kettle for hot water. It also had beautiful ornamental legs, which looked to be cast iron. Forge had said that they came from an old iron bathtub he had found.

Victoria had turned her dream of an apothecary shed into a wonderful dwelling for herself. Ruby, the chief chef, was very relieved that Victoria was finally moving all her bottles of dried herbs, tinctures, and the like from the kitchen shelves. This would at last give her the much needed extra space she had asked for; as she had been told, another extension to the kitchen wasn't going to happen anytime soon.

But it wasn't until Victoria was clearing her very few belongings from the shared bedroom to the new dwelling that she discovered her smoking pipe again. The one she had found while rearranging the workshop with Brad. She had almost forgotten about it, for it had been several weeks since Star had appeared in her dreams. The last assignment she had set for her had been to find those two particular herbs that would lend their power, enabling her to enter the otherworld. They needed to be smoked together in her pipe. Now, what were those herbs? So much had been happening in the last few months, while she had been building her new dwelling, that she had had to put her herbal studies to one side. Ah yes, now she remembered. One was mugwort, and the other Star had called 'Ma'. Her grandpapa had recognised it and called it Cannabis. He had seemed quite upset that she had found it growing wild, but she couldn't think why. Star had made it quite clear that she needed to gather as much power as possible together if she wanted to enter the otherworld.

Since the episode where she and her grandpapa had met the Great God Pan, her Grandpapa had been teaching her some of the basics of magic and had explained about Circadian Rhythms. These were the natural physical, mental, and behavioural changes that follow the Sun's daily cycle, and how this can affect both plants and animals. There was a Circadian Rhythm following the yearly seasons, too.

He also mentioned the Circalunar Rhythms that align with the phases of the moon, and they too affect the behaviour of animals and plants. The full moon is a particularly powerful time, he had explained, and that magicians knew about and utilised both these natural rhythms.

As part of her magical teaching, her Grandpapa had taken her all the way up to the old Dolmen, on a flat ridge high on the mountain, and told her about the mysterious matrix of leys that stretched across the countryside. He had called them 'dragon lines,' and along those lines flowed the earth's 'dragon energies,' which had their own power cycles, which ebbed and waned with the cycles of the moon and the sun.

So it was, that Victoria had decided to venture up to the old Dolmen, on the next full moon; which was only a few days away. And it was there, she would smoke her pipe of Mugwort and Ma.

3

Star arrived at the stone circle just in time to see the May Queen being crowned; a pretty young girl with long flowing blond hair and stunningly blue eyes. Star remembered fondly that she had been chosen as May Queen the very first year she had attended the Beltane revelries, at the time she was a mere fourteen summers old.

She had been a late developer, her 'gifts' not showing till she was ten summers old. It was only then that she had entered the temples. But she had risen through the grades quickly, becoming third degree on her fourteenth birthday. Even though it was a temple rule, she had barely qualified to attend the revelries - for it was quite uncommon for a girl so young to attain third degree .

As a prelude to the ritual, the young priestesses decided on who was to be the May Queen from amongst their ranks; all under the guidance and supervision of several temple elders. The accolade of May Queen goes to her, who is deemed most talented and beautiful; a prize that is never won twice.

Meanwhile, the young priests compete in the tournaments field to decide their own champion. Competitors go through a series of tournaments including hand-to-hand combat, contests of strength, accuracy with bow and spear and, finally, a general mêlée. The most accomplished is decided, and becomes the winner of the games: the King Stag.

At midday, a feast is held outside the stones. Tables and benches having been laid out beforehand. The head table is reserved for the May Queen and King Stag, who sit together and are adorned with flowers of every hue. They are waited on by cumals who bring them the best food and wine.

Now a bevy of priestesses were deciding the best place to sit. Star, among them, wanting to sit next to her friends. Suddenly, Blaze seemed to come out of nowhere plonking down on a bench, and pulled her down beside her with a bump. However, everyone was in good spirits and laughter at this comical stunt broke out within the group. Star, good-naturedly, punched him on his muscular shoulder. However, it had been her intention to try to avoid him, for she had decided that this Beltane, she wanted to find a new partner. Her friends often teasing her that she had been with Blaze far too long and needed to branch out with other boys.

But it seemed like Blaze had other ideas. For he picked up a cold chicken leg from a nearby platter and, taking a bite from it, held it to her mouth for her to bite too. Should she take a bite or not? Star suddenly had that otherworldly feeling of Daja vue. Her priestess training recognising this was a pivotal point in time. If she bit into the proffered chicken leg, blaze would certainly take it as a commitment from her to partner in the coming Beltane revelries.

Yet if she refused it, appearing to snub him. Would he be offended? She could not only lose him as a sex partner, but as a close friend, too. She didn't want to contemplate that he might become a jealous ex-lover and possibly an enemy.

She realised now that she should have talked to him when they were alone, beforehand, about her intention to find another partner, this Beltane. Talked to him calmly, kindly but firmly, making him understand.

Instead, she had been weak and put it off.

Now, at this critical moment, if she snubbed him in front of all his friends, he would feel humiliated, perhaps becoming angry, in order to save face.

She was a healer. And as a healer, she needed to work not only with the physical body, but with the mind as well. But even that wasn't enough! Healers needed to take a holistic view of the person and heal their soul and spirit also.

Avoiding a difficult confrontation because of her weakness resulted in her now dealing with an even more difficult situation. She could not exacerbate the situation by refusing him now. She needed to realise her mistake and swallow her pride. But for her own sake, she would need to commit to confronting him in a few days' time after the revelries were over.

Chapter 10

Coming Together

1

The silver Goddess moon hung high in a clear sky, like a great lantern, pregnant with light, casting a silver pathway onto the rippling shallow sea below. A warm wind wafted across the mountainside, and the sound of crickets filled the air, as Victoria made her way up to the lonely dolmen. As she approached, the moon's serene light lit up the ancient stones. For a moment Victoria was sure she could see carved spirals upon the surface of one of the monoliths; but then it was gone, a trick of the shadows.

With the aid of the rowan tree that grew beside the dolmen, she managed to climb onto the giant slab which formed the roof. It was here she sat and from her tote bag that she had slung over one shoulder, produced the carved pipe. The bowl of the pipe was a shaped piece of wood that had a lovely grain to it and had polished up beautifully with beeswax. Brad had said the wood was a bramble root ball, and someone had carved a strange sigil on the side, but she didn't know what it meant.

Victoria had long ago learnt to make fire using her fire-starter kit. It was in a small leather pouch that hung from her waist belt. In it were dry wood-shavings, lint and a fire starter -- flint stick and steel scraper. Her grandfather had bought up hundreds of these kits when the waters had first started to rise. He had a hunch that one day he would need them, and had kept them stashed away in a secret place; only to be used when no other fire was available. But he had given one to Victoria, which she now used to light a small fire on the dolmen slab.

Once the fire was underway, she started her ritual. Removing the roll of soft deerskin from her tote bag, she unrolled it before her, revealing the dried herbs that Star had advised her to use. As she filled her pipe, she thanked the spirit of the sacred herbs for their sacrifice and prayed that they would teach her the way to the otherworld.

She had also brought some wooden spills that Brad had made in the workshop, which she used to light her pipe. Sucking in the aromatic smoke which curled and twisted from the wooden bowl. She found that it didn't taste that good, and it made her cough. But she continued to draw the smoke deep into her lungs, as Star had instructed her.

After a short while of smoking, she began to feel lightheaded, and then, she gradually noticed that everything about her somehow seemed like a dream, or a waking dream. She started to experience lucid colours in the natural world around her. Looking up at the moon, hanging high in the clear sky, she thought it had never looked so beautiful for she could clearly see the craters on its surface; the ones that her grandfather had told her about, but hadn't seen before.

Now she was drawn to the shimmering silver pathway that the moon cast onto the rippling sea; it was really amazing. That shimmering drew her, she felt she could get lost in its splendour. But as she drew her eyes away, it was like she was seeing everything through rippling water, and along with it came a wonderful sense of euphoria.

Then suddenly it seemed to Victoria that everything grew still. All around her, everything seemed to distort and shift like it was very far away. Everything seemed all at once distant and small, yet somehow looming over her. Yet, at the same time, she seemed to see a shimmering image of a forest through the gap in a copse of willow trees.

She realised that she must have been walking for some time, for she had grown up on this mountain island and knew every inch of it like her own hand. But she had never seen trees like these before; great gnarled oaks and yews, thicker than five men huddled together.

A mist lay thick here, but this was often the case on the mountain, so she continued further through the ancient forest. After a while of walking, a clearing appeared before her and a circle of hazel trees. As she approached, gradually she could see a wondrous sight. Shimmering before her, a crystal-clear pool of water surrounded by nine hazel trees. As she stood transfixed, a salmon leapt out of the water, its scales glistening in the ethereal light, creating rainbows across its body.

An icy shiver ran down her back. Where

in heaven's name, was she? She felt sure she had not seen or heard of such a place on her mountain island. Then, upon the softly flowing perfumed wind, she could hear the haunting sounds of Irish pipe music. A wild lament filled with the cries of seabirds and crashing waves. The haunting sounds of the seals on the rocks, and the ethereal sound of those larger mammals, who inhabited the deep oceans her Grandpapa had told her about.

Suddenly she noticed, there, beside the flowering branches of a hawthorn tree, stood a young man. His back was to her, and he seemed to be engaged in some activity regarding the tree. She could see an otherworldly wind blowing his long white hair. But it seemed to move too slowly, like he was underwater. But even more surprising was the fact that he seemed to have branching horns on his head like a young stag.

As Victoria approached, he turned swiftly, seeming to know she was there by some instinct. In his hands, he bore a branch of the flowering may blossom.

"Welcome to my realm Victoria; we have been expecting you."

Victoria gasped at the sudden movement. But no less at the beautiful face of the handsome young man. His eyes were the colour of storm clouds and their patterns twice as complex. He looked at her with such intensity; it took her breath away. He was tall and slender and graceful of movement. His pale-skinned face seemed to glow, radiating a light of its own. He wore a silken white shirt, with a cut that revealed his sculpted pectoral muscles and smooth, glistening skin.

Victoria felt her eyes involuntarily drawn to his

muscular chest and knew her eyes had widened all by themselves. The young man noticed her gaze and knowingly smiled, which made her blush and turn her eyes away. Suddenly she found she had difficulty breathing, her head swimming. But the young man stepped forward, placing a gentle hand on her shoulder and said, "Here, I picked these for you," as he offered her the flowering branch of May blossom.

His touch instantly energised her, and she looked up into his wide-spaced eyes and for the first time noticed his pointed ears.

"Are you an Elf?" she asked.

"Your kind sometimes call us that. But I am of the Danann race. We once lived on the earthly plane, as you do. But many thousands of years ago, we transcended to this... Otherworld realm." His tone indicated that he was not over-happy with his being there.

But then he moved his hand to caress her hair, saying, "But if all in your realm are as fair as you, I wish I were there again."

And he pressed forward towards her. Victoria instinctually moved her hands to slow his advance, but pricked her finger on the spiny Hawthorn branch. Victoria yelped and sprung back, holding up her hand to examine her bleeding finger. Small droplets of blood falling to the earth.

The young Elf, seeing what had happened, tossed the branch to the ground and advanced towards her again. Taking her wounded hand in his own, he placed the bleeding finger in his warm mouth; then slowly started sucking away the blood.

The warm, sensuous feeling of her finger inside his

seductive mouth had an extraordinary effect on her. Interesting feelings started to stir in her young woman's body. Delightful sensations flowed down to her womb, tickling and enticing. She felt her knees go weak, and she started to fall. But the young elf boy swooped her up into his muscular arms and carried her towards a nearby cave, which seemed to have appeared out of nowhere. As he walked, his hair blew awry with the otherworldly wind. Victoria looked up into his dazzling face and saw something in his eyes, the touch of the non-human. Then he lowered his face to hers. She could not resist.

2

Star had bitten the bullet and bit into that chicken leg, and had been rewarded with a loving reaction from Blaze. After the midday feast, all the participants had rested under the trees for a siesta. It wasn't so much of a feast, more of a light lunch of sweet breads and cheeses, olives and cold meats washed down with plenty of cider or small beer.

Under the trees, Star lay with her head resting on Blaze's chest. Dreamily, Star's mind wandered back to when Blaze, had attempted to explain to her some of the things he had learned about ritual sex, in the Temple of the Sacred Flame. He had told her about the life force or vital energy that was in each of us. The priests called it 'Nwyfre', which literally meant 'sky energy' or 'energy of the Gods'. Nwyfre is the energy that binds all life together. It is the force that we feel coursing through us when we are in nature, or feeling great joy. Nywfre is the spark of life, that which separates an inanimate thing from an animate being. Therefore, to work with this Nywfre, high-level priests and priestesses, must develop control, over the bodies more complex nervous and involuntary reactions.

Blaze had also told her that as a seventh degree priest, he must practice these with a woman who has advanced psychic powers. One who knew how to receive and give the energetic flows within their bodies.

The priest, Blaze has said, only became adept when this mastery was complete. However, the adepts competence in this energy control worked like a catalytic force that could awaken latent forces in a woman's body. Awakening clairvoyant powers of mind and body that were previously unknown, except in dream sleep.

'So', Star thought, 'it was clear that a man could not advance further without the help of a woman. And that advancement by the man awakened latent powers in the woman. Perhaps', Star thought, 'this is why Blaze had the extraordinary ability to pleasure her so well'. This thought brought a thrill of excitement and tingling all through her body, which was focused and strongest in her womb.

Blaze had said something else too that confused her. He had said, that during ritual acts of sex magic, that the adepts practiced. The Priestess's practiced imbibing Luna energy, and that of the Sea Goddess, to bring about her transformation, as a receptacle of the Goddess. While the Priest, must imbibe the essence of the horned God, the Lord of the animals, allowing that power, to flow through him.

'Perhaps', Star thought, 'she had been too hasty in thinking she should cast Blaze away.' She consoled herself that she would commit to the Beltane ritual with Blaze and see how she felt afterwards.

3

Gradualy Star became aware of beautiful harp music wafting through the trees. She knew this to be the signal for all Beltane revellers to end the afternoon siesta and to gather in the stones about the maypole.

They stood in two circles about the maypole, girls in the inner ring and boys in the outer circle, each taking a rope ready for the dance. Star noticed that musicians had gathered in a group in the eastern quarter. All the while, the beautiful harp music played.

The musicians were priests, all of them young, from the Sun Temple. They held curious stringed instruments, rattles and great gongs. For this festive occasion, they wore short kilts, their upper bodies bare except for the intricately fashioned amulets they wore around their necks. From their ranks came a soft piping, a whisper of flutes and the softest echo of a gong.

Meanwhile, the older adepts broke into a subtle chanting of incantations. This continued for several minutes. Then, one adept raised his arm high, his hand arranged in a curious gesture, that Star knew to be connected with the horned God. This caused the subtle music to change. The flutes and gongs broke suddenly into discordant and harsh chords, somewhat like an orchestra tuning. But the tempo increased along with the volume. Faster and faster. Louder and louder.

As the curious music reach a crescendo, the Draoi Magician Helios Arkonephus, from the sun temple, now stepped forward to the front, and raised his arms high in salutation, calling out the sacred names of the horned God. His trained and powerful voice reverberated off the stones of the circle. When he had finished his invocation, he slowly lowered his arms; as he did, the music halted. All was now in silent anticipation.

Gently at first, the leaves on all the trees of the grove started stirring in a wind. But then there was a rushing of sudden winds, causing the tree branches to creak and sway. An icy shiver ran down Star's back, and then she saw him. A dark shadow at the edge of the grove, the silhouette of a crown of horns.

"He has come!" proclaimed the Draoi Magician, smiling, as he raised his arms in welcome.

There, standing at the edge of the clearing, was a colossal figure. The giant creature stood twice as tall as a man. The horned God had a muscular body like a man's, but his legs had the pelt of an animal. From his head grew a crown of horns. Somewhat like a stag's. His face was masculine and weathered, his long hair was thick and wiry, and his eyes! His eyes had an animalistic quality, which softened as he surveyed the revellers who had come to honour him. The enormous mouth now gave a wide smile that matched the humorous glint of his deep brown eyes.

Now he slowly walked forwards, careful of the lowly humans below him, and paraded round the circle of stones, pronouncing his blessing up on the happy revellers. His voice carried the distant resonance of autumn thunder, or the forceful rush of a mighty waterfall.

After completing a full circle around the stones, he went and stood at the edge of the clearing again. He watched as joyful music started playing and the Maypole dance began. The dancers weaving in and out of each other, the coloured ropes forming a complex pattern as the joyful dance continued through the afternoon.

As twilight embraced the land, fires were ignited outside the stone circle using an ancient fire lighting ceremony. The ritual fires incorporated the nine sacred woods, and their crackling tongues of flames leaped from the aged logs, joining both earth and sky. These need-fires where ignited to ritually cleanse and purify the happy couples, who, joining hands, would quickly go between the fires. The two lovers then went a-Maying merrily into the forest, to feel the earth's pulse, and let Beltane's flames ignite their spirit.

4

In another world and time, deep beneath the earth in a cave, an elven man with branching horns and a beauteous young maiden, whose name was Victoria, embraced and kissed again and again before sinking to the floor of the cave. They came together in ecstatic joy and bliss, making bountiful love, on thick layers of fur. The seed of the God planted firmly into the fertile womb of the Earth Goddess. Root and stone and water and earth. The seed in the furrow, the beast in the hole. The fire in the sky strikes the new leaf on the tree.

5

Blaze took Star into his arms, man to woman. As they slowly sunk to the waiting earth, their bodies seemed to melt into each other. No longer priest and priestess; it seemed to her that time had stopped. His kiss was like fire and ice on her lips. It was as if she no longer had nerve and bone and sinew; but only pure spirit.

And She was pure force and energy and therefore pure delight. The God became the crashing of the waves upon the yearning shore. And she was overflowing with pure joy. She was pure, white, light, in a world without time and space. And the fire of the God moved upon the fluid body of the Goddess. God and Goddess co-joined as one, creating life from pure light. Let there be new light in the world and She laughed and there was new light and life.

Chapter 11

The prisoner

in the Oak

1

Pools of fetid marshland and murky water stretched in all directions as far as the eye could see. Above, the sky was plagued by multiple layers of blue-black clouds scudding past at an alarming rate, and blocking what little light there was, making the landscape below gloomy and oppressive.

Here and there, yellow patches of sulphurous mist lie low and clung to the land. Stunted bushes and trees seemed to leer out of the misty gloom, their gnarled and twisted branches presented distorted cruel shapes.

The otherworld dominion of the dark elves was a fetid and miserable place. Rising within a wide expanse of bulrushes is a small conical hill, resembling an island in the marsh. On the mound stands a massive oak tree. Its leafless branches distorted and twisted in a parody of agony and desolation. Yet within the gnarled swollen growths and burls, one could discern a face. It had a rounded shaved head, and a long, reddish brown, bushy beard with two silver beads inscribed with runes. In the centre, below the piercing blue eyes, is a large flattish nose that looked to have been broken some years ago.

Poor Adge was trying to come to terms with what had happened to him.

He could remember that he had been travelling through the gloomy realm of the dark elves with his mentor, Morgana. She was a sorceress and high elf. He knew they had been on a secret mission to free the Great God Pan from his entombment in an oak tree. Adge remembered he was so excited and proud of himself for being part of the grand plan to save the human realm. But it had been exhausting, traipsing through the fetid marshland, and all those stunted bushes, which seemed alive, and reached out wickedly to snag his clothing, scratching his arms to shreds.

At last, they had found the place where Pan was entombed. So he thought he would rest awhile on a convenient boulder near the tree. He had sat rubbing his wounds, which in this oppressive realm didn't seem to heal.

Then suddenly he couldn't move a muscle. Morgana and Pan had gone, and he was left all alone. In the Otherworld, time didn't seem to mean anything. It could have been weeks, months, or even years since he had been turned into a tree.

It somehow seemed ironic to him that he had become a tree; something which he and Touchwood, his druid brother, had all but worshipped. Now he had time to think about that previous life, in the human realm, before the waters had risen and changed everything.

He had been happy then, living in his little caravan on Touchwood's farm. That was before Touchwood had even adopted that name. He had been called Corin back then. Corin and he were friends, druid brothers who loved working wood and creating crafts for sale at the weekend markets in Galway. They both had a strong interest in the Ogham - the Celtic Tree Alphabet, some people called it. They used to carve people's names in Ogham on bog oak pendants. The tourists loved them.

Later, they had together created a small woodworking business called 'Tree-Wheel Crafts'. The workshop had become a busy place, as they had crafted many wooden staffs, wands, Ogham divination sets, pendants, and talismans. All were crafted from the magical 'Elf wood,' or Bog Oak, which they imbued with the magical properties taught to them by their guides from the otherworld. Those had been good times, Adge thought miserably and a small tear formed in his woody eye.

But then, his spirit guide, Morgana had taught him how to transcend into the otherworld, enabling him to remaining there permanently, just as the Tuatha de Danann had done, millennia ago. It had been a hard thing to arrange, but he had been born with a dogged determination, if nothing else.

And so he had become Morgana's apprentice in the otherworld. It was there he had discovered the horrible truth. The Dark Elves were planning to rid the physical world of humans. With their magic, they had manipulated the forces of nature to exacerbate the already escalating climate change. The face of the human world had become so hazardous that all countries warred with every other country. Between the wars and climate change, the effects on human populations had been disastrous.

But as if that was not enough, the dark elves had entombed Pan in an oak tree. Now unable to play the earth song that coordinated the natural world, it had descended all of nature into chaos.

So here he was, somehow he had been substituted for the God Pan and now he was entombed instead.

But where was his mentor, Morgana?

2

In the very heart of the dark elves' realm, which they called 'Tech Duinn', stood a mighty castle surrounded by pools of fetid marshland and murky water. Blue-black clouds formed grotesque shapes as they scudded across the oppressive sky. The castle itself, made of black basalt, seemed to have been formed from melting lava that had suddenly cooled while dripping down its sides. An illusion that was only enhanced by the melancholy lights that shone from many of its windows.

Within the throne room of King Indech, beside the massive golden throne, lay the dead body of the Lord of Chaos; King Indech. Surrounding the body was a group of his councillors, dark elves all. Several pulled their long beards deep in thought.

Suddenly one of them bemoaned, "But we have never had one of us dead before! What do we do with the body?"

"Never mind that, Shadowflame Advisor," sneered an exquisitely dressed courtier, who had a pompous air of authority. "We have at last secured the Gae Assail, one of the four sacred treasures. Do you not realise this is the original spear that belonged to Lugh of the Long Arm?"

"Yes, yes, Right Honourable Nightheart, we all know what it is," countered another of the king's councillors. "But it is secure now in the palace vaults. The fundamental question, if I may be so bold, is what are we going to do with it now that Pan has escaped from imprisonment in the tree?"

"We must capture whoever freed him immediately," demanded a rather ancient dark elf with a beard and hair down to his waist. "Once we find out who it was, that is. I have sent every 'Grey' we have searching the palace for the traitor, and the whole of Tech Duinn if we must. "

"But I say again Sir Gloomwhisper, what do we do with the body? And surely we must punish this 'human' that we have captured for his Regicide."

"No!" countered a rich, loud voice. "We must question him. There may be others. We must use every torture we know to find out what he knows."

"Leave him to rot in the cells for a while, I say. That should loosen his tongue. Sauron Darkweaver has spelt him to intensify his misery."

The vigorous arguing between the councillors continued for some time. They seemed to be completely lost without their king and leader. They fired orders at the Grey guards, one after the other. One councillor often contradicting another.

It was not until some days later that one of them realised a most significant consequence. "But surely, if one 'human' has invaded our realm to kill our king, there must be others. They must have discovered our plans to invade the human realm."

"You mean they know of the Genesis Project?"

"Isn't it obvious? When they come to murder our king. The humans are trying to sabotage all our plans."

"I agree. Therefore, it is imperative that we step up our plans and begin the invasion immediately."

"But the hybrid children are not grown yet."

"I will consult with Dr Feanor Darkbrood immediately. The project is his brainchild, after all. Maybe there is a way to speed up the process."

Chapter 12

Void Craft

1

There was not a breath of air as Victoria stepped outside into the night. The full moon high in the sky gave off such light that everything in the community garden seemed to be glowing with a silver light.

She walked in wonder through the garden. The clouds, too, seemed to have a mystical quality and were lined with a silver outline. The night was cool after the heat of the day. A gentle breeze coursed through the willow trees and brushed feather light across her skin. Somewhere in the trees, an owl screeched as it hunted. Hedgehogs rustled in the hedgerow, and in the distance, a dog fox made a kill. The familiar night sounds comforted her.

Victoria had, of course, told Star about her encounter with the young Elfen boy in the otherworld. Star had smiled knowingly and congratulated Victoria on her conquest.

"Yes, those young high elves know how to treat a girl

right," both girls giggled together. But Victoria had been secretly embarrassed, for she was not as forthright as Star was.

But afterwards, Star had told her that those elves, both boys and girls, can sometimes get besotted with a human and come into our realm searching for us. So you would be well advised to prepare some psychic protection, which should keep away any unwanted spirits. She had advised to make preparations using the herbs Hypericum and Nimba. But when Victoria told her that she had not heard of them and didn't know what they were. Star somehow managed to send an image of the plants to Victoria's mind in her dream sleep. The first herb she instantly recognised as St. John's Wort, for Ruby had shown her how to prepare it as she had often used it for her 'Mothers', as she called them, those women she had been a midwife for. Because sometimes they would suffer from a 'blue malady' after the birth, and St. John's Wort helped with that. And more recently, Ruby had used it herself to relieve her Menopausal Symptoms.

But the other herb, Nimba, was a problem, for neither Victoria nor Ruby knew about it. So this is why Victoria was out tonight looking for a Nimba tree. Star had told Victoria that it was a small tree that liked a hot climate. So Victoria didn't hold much hope of finding it in the community herb garden.

But this night she had used her intuition and looked through the greenhouses. With a stroke of luck, she had found a small Nimba tree growing in a large pot in one of the poly tunnels. Yes, it was definitely Nimba. The vibrant green leaves were smooth and glossy, with sharp, serrated edges. There were many individual leaves on a stem, something like an ash tree. And like the ash, the elongated oval leaves were about four inches long.

As it was a full moon, she immediately collected some of the leaves. Then she went outside again to the herb garden to collect the St. John's wort.

Victoria, sickle knife in hand, was just bending to pick the leaves of the St. John's Wort plant, when she saw out of the corner of her eye a quick movement in the sky. Thinking it a shooting star, she looked up, ready to wish upon it. But this shooting star seemed very different, for now it remained steady in the sky and did not burn out quickly as shooting starts usually did. Instead, the tiny pinpoint of light moved steadily across the sky. At the moment, it was above the peak of the mountain, but as she watched, it moved slowly towards her. Then she realised, it must be one of those wonderful 'fairy lights' in the sky, that her Grandpapa had told her about. 'What did he call them? Oh yes, UFO's I think'.

Fascinated, she watched as it traversed across the sky. But was it her imagination? Did it seem to be getting bigger? And now she thought that it looked much lower in the sky. It seemed to be moving towards her.

Unexpectedly, a shiver ran down her back, and with it a sense of foreboding. For surely it had grown much larger now. It was nearly over her head. She could see that it was round like an apple and had a metallic silvery glow. Eerily, it was completely silent as it started to descend. It grew larger and larger, till it was hovering just a few feet above the community garden. Just hanging there like a balloon bobbing in the breeze. Victoria just stared, hypnotised by the wondrous sight.

Suddenly there appeared a smaller ball of light just

beside it, or had it emerged from the larger sphere? The smaller ball of light gradually descended till it touched the earth of the garden. This caused a silent explosion of light, radiating in all directions; then it was gone. But the light explosion had temporarily blinded her eyes. Gradually, however, she could discern in its place a shadowy form. The moon high in the sky was behind the dark form, making it silhouetted, and very hard to see just exactly what it was. Another shiver ran down her spine. Instinct told her she should run and alert the others? But if she did, she may miss seeing this wondrous sight; and she really wanted to see it.

The dark form started to move towards her. The young adult mustered all her willpower and bravery to remain where she stood. However, she felt an involuntary scream welling in her throat, wanting to get out, but she bravely held it back as the shadowy form moved closer yet. As it did, she could just make out a human shape within the shadow.

Panic once again surged up inside her, but she stood her ground.

"Victoria?" A strange voice called her name.

That was just too much for her. Her hands became limp and dropped her small copper sickle to the ground. The herbs too fell back to the earth. She immediately turned tail and bolted back to the safety of the community kitchen.

It was late in the day, and the community refectory was deserted. In Rath Grain, residents usually went to bed early as they were up with the sun - tending to the animals and managing the gardens. But Ruby was there in the kitchen just putting the last of the loaves into the special proofing box for the overnight final rising of the bread.

The proofing box had been an innovation designed by Touchwood, Victoria's grandfather. There had been many versions and re-designs over the years. With this one, he had used an old fridge that had been abandoned years ago. It had two halogen light bulbs, and a fan controlled by a thermostat and control circuit keeping the area inside the fridge to a constant temperature of around twenty-seven degrees C; the optimum for proofing bread.

Ruby enjoyed the peace and quiet of the kitchen late at night, so she often volunteered to take on the last shift of bread making. Just as Ruby was putting the last bead tin's into the proofer, she heard a loud crash shattering the silence. Somebody burst through the refectory door. Ruby nearly jumped out of her skin, involuntarily exclaiming, "What the…?"

Victoria heard this and, seeing the seating area deserted, rushed into the kitchen.

"Ruby! Thank the Goddess. I thought everyone was in bed. I was out in the garden collecting Hypericum…"

"Hypericum? We don't use that in the kitchen…"

"No, no, but there was one of those wonderful fairy lights in the sky that Grandpapa had told me about and…"

"Fairy lights? What on earth are you…"

"But there are strange silver ball 'thingies', hovering outside and…"

"Look, calm down Victoria. You're making no sense. Take some deep breaths, will you? Look, follow me. Come on taking deeeep breaths and hold. One, two, three and…"

But Victoria wasn't having any of this, so blurted out, "But there is a really spooky man in the garden and…"

"A strange man in the garden? Why didn't you say so girl? We will see about that." Without another word, Ruby marched out of the refectory door on a mission. Poor Victoria stood alone, wondering whether to follow or not. Then, on the spur of the moment, she decided the best thing to do was to call her Grandpapa out of bed.

2

Touchwood and Victoria stood in the little cottage doorway leading outside from Touchwood's rooms. As they held hands, they both stared in wonder at the enormous silver ball hovering above the garden.

There was no sound coming from it, no smell either could be detected from it. The silvery surface seemed to reflect everything around it, but was strangely distorted by the curvature of the sphere. There was no sense of energy or anything that Touchwood could discern.

"See Grandpapa. It's what I told you, this must be one of those 'fairy light thingies' you told me about - but now one has landed in our garden."

Touchwood, still a little sleepy after being woken so suddenly, shook his head, "Hum, I'm not so sure. I have never seen anything like it before."

Scratching his long beard, he started to move toward the strange phenomena. As he got to the edge of the garden, he nearly bumped into Ruby in the darkness. She stood, stock still, staring blankly.

"Are you all right Ruby?" Touchwood asked as he put a comforting hand on her shoulder. Now he could feel that she was shivering all over. He looked at her staring face. She looked like she had been turned to stone. He was not even quite sure if she had even heard him. But then, she slowly raised an arm, pointing into the darkness. Touchwood turned in the direction she indicated and squinted until his eyes adjusted.

There, standing in the garden, was a dark shadowy form. Touchwood was trying to make out what it was. He knew every inch of this garden and nothing should be there.

But then, gradually, he could just make out a human shape within the shadow.

"Touchwood old chap. I was beginning to think I'd come to the wrong place. So good to see you again," it said in a rich Welsh accent.

Touchwood's eyes widened in surprise. "D... Dafydd? Is... is that you?" he stuttered as he stepped forward to meet the strange figure striding towards him. At last, their hands met and Touchwood found his being shaken, by the firm handshake he knew so well.

"By all the Gods, it is you, Dafydd. I hardly recognised you in those clothes. I heard the dark elves had captured you."

"Ah well! It's a long story," Dafydd said, brushing him off. "But perhaps," he said, eyeing up the two women who were now standing together witnessing the conversation. "We should not be talking about this here. Let us retire to your rooms."

Touchwood looked around at Ruby and Victoria, who were standing, mouths open in astonishment. Then he looked back towards the strange silver ball hovering above the garden. "I think we have gone well beyond 'discretion' if that silver ball is anything connected to you. Did you bring it here?"

Dafydd turned back to the silver sphere and grimaced. Then remarked, "Er… yes. Quite, I see what you mean."

He rubbed his hands together, suddenly enjoying everyone's consternation. "Well, in for a penny, in for a pound. I might as well introduce you to my pilot."

Dafydd walked back a little way towards the large silver ball, then called out, "Rumanadil, come and meet the other community members. It's OK, it's safe here."

In answer, the silver craft wobbled a little, then slowly descended. Then it slid sideways, neatly tucking itself under the trees on the right of the garden. Once there, in the shadows, the silver surface reflecting the surrounding environment, you really wouldn't know it was there at all.

But then suddenly a glowing cloud appeared beside it, which slowly lowered towards the earth. When it touched, a blinding light radiated in all directions - in a silent explosion- then was gone.

As their eyes adjusted again, they could see another dark figure walking towards them. It was much taller than Dafydd. As the figure approached, Touchwood could see it was a tall, humanoid figure. But then his blood ran cold. Now he could recognise what stood before him. The imposing being was nearly seven feet tall. His tunic was a dark midnight blue but had a lustre like a stormy sky. There were leather belts across his chest with intricate knot-work tooled into it. About his shoulders was a collar of thick grey wolf fur. His mane of long auburn hair twisted into rough braids and he had a warrior's topknot. He had a thick drooping moustache, his stern face inked with blue-green symbols and stripes.

But most terrifying of all were the pointed ears sticking out of his hair. This was a Dark Elf!

3

Touchwood drew back a pace and found that Victoria and Ruby were hiding behind him, like frightened rabbits.

Dafydd marched forward and extended his hand toward the tall being. Who clasped his forearm and shook it in a warriors handshake.

"Welcome to Rath Grain and the human realm. Rumanadil is a friend of mine," explained Dafydd, as he looked back over his shoulder towards the others, but no one was there.

Puzzled, Dafydd turned and led Rumanadil towards the main house, where he found Touchwood looking very dubiously at Rumanadil, and Victoria and Ruby cowering behind him.

"Ahh... Do forgive me Touchwood," said Dafydd. " I should have explained before I brought him out. Rumanadil is a friend of mine. He helped me escape the dark elves."

But Touchwood didn't seem convinced. Then Dafydd realised it must be the dark elf clothing Rumanadil was wearing, that made them so cautious.

"Rumanadil is a high elf," he pleaded. "He is on our side and wants to help. He and I were imprisoned together by the dark elves. But with his help, we escaped. We found this dark elf clothing in the Void Craft," Dafydd stretched an arm back towards the silver ball.

Then Dafydd looked about him anxiously at the

gathering crowd of community members.

"Look, I will explain everything. I promise we mean you no harm. But I think perhaps, we should retire to your rooms Touchwood."

Victoria seemed to have recovered her initial fear and had bravely moved beside her grandfather, looking curiously now at the two visitors. Reassured, Touchwood glanced again at Dafydd's earnest face, then up towards the gathering clouds and nodded, "I think you're right Dafydd, it's about to rain."

Chapter 13

Touchwood's Kitchen

1

The soft, quiet sound of rain on the windowpane, and the gentle trickle of water running along drains, puddling on paths outside, was a symphony that added to the warm smells of turf burning in the wood stove. On the hot plate, a large kettle gently sizzles as it simmers on the boil.

Now a gentle wind moans across the chimney above. The wood stove spews forth a rich peaty smoke, which floats up to the wooden beams of dark oak in the four-hundred-year-old cottage. The smoke wafting past horse brasses, old jugs, and other oddities, hanging from the beams.

There was an awkward silence as the mixed crew of adventurers gathered in Touchwood's kitchen. Touchwood, standing with his back to the wood-burning stove, looked about him expectantly, but nobody said a word. He bent down to the wood basket and placed a couple of turf blocks into the stove, then shut the door with a metallic clatter. This somehow broke the spell of silence in the room.

"Touchwood, old chap, I don't suppose you have any of that Redbreast left? The one you have secreted in your cabinet upstairs," asked Dafydd hopefully.

Touchwood smiled and chuckled to himself at the memory, "You remember that?" he shook his head in amusement, "That was over sixty years ago, that whiskey has long gone."

Touchwood, smiling and shaking his head at the audacity of the fellow, asked, "Anyone for tea?"

Looking around the room, it really was a very mixed bunch. Ruby and Victoria, his granddaughter, were, of course, human; Rumanadil was a shade and possibly a Dark Elf, but certainly an otherworld being; Morgana's shade, attracted by all the magical energy, had materialised in a corner of the room; Uncle Dafydd was, of course, a long-standing human friend and mentor, but just what he was right now, he just wasn't sure of.

Dafydd turned and looked uncertainly at the crowd of heads gathered at the doorway, jostling with each other to get a better look.

Touchwood took it all in and turned to Victoria. "Would you be a dear and make us all some tea? I don't think I have enough cups in here. Take Ruby with you to help. Oh, and shut the door behind you, would you?"

Victoria, sensing the uneasiness in the room, quickly understood his real meaning and nodded her assent. She took Ruby by the elbow into the hallway and closed the door behind her. Touchwood could hear the muffled barrage of questions shot at Ruby, which gradually faded down the corridor.

2

"Dafydd ap Gwilym, you dare to show your face before me! "Morgana stormed as she advanced on Dafydd.

Dafydd, surprised, turned to face the familiar voice from the corner, holding up both hands defensively. "Morgana? How nice to see you after all these years."

"You absolute idiot! What do you think you were doing, marching into the realm of the dark elves, stirring them up like a termite nest? Did you not know I was secretly in their realm on important business?" Morgana declared imperiously. She raised her arms and looked like she was about to turn him to stone with her magic.

"Morgana Dear! Now we mustn't be hasty," Dafydd said as he came to her familiarly. "You know how you become... 'ill-tempered'... when in the human realm." Tentatively, he placed a comforting arm around her shoulder.

"Ill-tempered? I will give you ill-tempered," she ranted churlishly. She made a sham attempt to shake off Dafydd's arm, but clearly was comforted by its presence. "I was particularly vulnerable at that point, you know. Freeing Pan from his imprisonment was no easy task, I can tell you. Laying spell upon spell can weaken one's aura significantly." She pouted like a child and coyly turned to him, appealing for sympathy.

"Yes, yes, you played a very important role in the grand plan, " Dafydd comforted her. "We are all very grateful for your contribution."

Touchwood looked on in astonishment, his mouth

open. He had never seen Morgana behaving in such a way. They were like an old married couple, but he could never imagine Morgana and Dafydd together!

"Anyway, it all turned out well in the end," Dafydd continued. "We all had a part to play, and now at least that scoundrel Indech is no more. Perhaps the dark elves will abort their plans now he has gone."

"Yes, Dafydd ap Gwilym," Morgana shrugging off his arm, suddenly became stiff and imposing again. "That's something else that's been bothering me. How did you, a mere human, kill an elf? We spiritual beings are supposed to be immortal…"

Touchwood and Rumanadil had been looking on with interest during this exchange, but now Touchwood caught Rumanadil's eye and an understanding passed between them. Keeping eye contact, Rumanadil took a pace forward. Touchwood nodded. So Rumanadil moved to intervene before the couple came to blows.

"Perhaps Dafydd, we should show Morgana our captured Void craft and…"

Morgana's angry face turned to see who it was that dared to interrupt her. But seeing Rumanadil for the first time, her face softened into a lecherous smile. "And who is this handsome warrior? Dafydd, you really are remiss. You haven't introduced us yet."

Turning her back on Dafydd, she nuzzled in close to Rumanadil, placing both hands on his arm. Speaking softly and close.

Dafydd seemed very relieved to be rid of Morgana, and came to stand beside Touchwood.

"Dafydd you old goat, I didn't know you knew Morgana," teased Touchwood.

"Oh, we go back a long way. We had a bit of a thing going for a while. But long-term relationships with elves rarely work out."

Touchwood nodded as if he understood, but asked, "So what is this silver ball thing that is parked in my garden? I assume you somehow travel in it."

"I'm surprised as you are, Touchwood, old chap. I had no idea the elves had such technology as this. It's quite worrying really and there is much more I must share with you. Which is why we came here. It's been quite a turbulent time for me. I was captured by the dark elves, you know. Are you sure you don't have any whiskey left?"

"Yes, so I heard. You were lucky to escape. Look, I will see what I have in my vice cupboard upstairs."

Touchwood climbed the ladder to his loft space above the wood stove. It was where he had his bed and some bedroom furniture.

Meanwhile, Dafydd eyed Morgana, who was busy flirting with Rumanadil, who seemed to quite enjoy the experience. Dafydd heard the chink of bottles upstairs and licked his lips. Like any prisoner suddenly released, he and Rumanadil were keen to experience the pleasures of freedom.

3

Touchwood returned from his bedroom space, clutching a bottle of some deep red liquor. Then went to a shelf to retrieve some glasses. Touchwood eyed Morgana and Rumanadil, who seemed to be involved in an intimate conversation, and decided it was probably not wise to interrupt. So, clutching two shot glasses, and the bottle returned to Dafydd, who was beside the stove.

"Don't have any potcheen at the moment, old friend, but here is an untouched bottle of sloe gin for us to sample."

Dafydd seemed to brighten considerably at the prospect and accepted his glass gratefully. As Touchwood poured the ruby red liqueur, an intense raspberry-like aroma lifted from the glass. It reminded Touchwood of his visits to the otherworld forest grove, where ripe plumbs fell from the trees. A tinge of regret gnawed at his soul, as he hadn't been there for such a long time, having had his hands full with the search for the missing Syrinx, and afterwards recuperating from it all.

He realised too that he missed his spirit guide, the Oak King, who he had foolishly begun to mistrust. And realised that, after all his adventures, what a staunch friend he had been, after all.

"Touchwood, old chap! I wouldn't mind sampling some of that now, if you don't mind."

Suddenly brought back to the present, Touchwood realised he had stopped mid-pour and hadn't filled Dafydd's glass yet.

"Sorry, old friend, the smell of this liqueur somehow reminded me of the otherworld."

"Yes, it smells particularly delicious," he remarked as he wafted a hand over his glass to bring the smell to his nose, then took a sip. "Ahh! And the taste… plumbs… with bittersweet flavours of almonds… liquorice. Yes, and the tartness of sloe berries with a lovely warm glow. Quite delightful. It's been a long time since I have had something quite so good."

Touchwood sat on a hardback chair by the wood-burning stove and Dafydd took another the other side. They ignored the other two, who seemed to be lost in a world of their own.

"So I'm interested in this silver ball. What exactly is it," asked Touchwood?

"Rumanadil called it a void craft. He told me it has the ability to travel through the void between dimensions. Consequently, it can move between the Otherworld and the world of physical beings. Rumanadil controls it with the power of thought. It's designed to respond to elf magic," Dafydd took another sip of the sloe gin while considering.

Then shaking his head, "I don't really understand how it works, which is bothering me. I don't like not knowing things. But apparently, it is a combination of high elf magic, and high-end human technology, that can manipulate a quantum of light, to create a portal in the fabric of the universe."

Touchwood took a sip from his glass, looked at Dafydd, and smiled. He hadn't changed a bit, he thought, still the same old Uncle Dafydd.

"But the really interesting thing about it is," Dafydd continued, "That it creates a quantum field about it, which can sustain a spirit body in this physical world indefinitely."

"Ah really? How interesting, because I know when Adge came here, as a shade, he didn't have enough magical energy to stay very long. And even Morgana, who had more magical energy than Adge, had to move up to the Dolmen to recharge."

Both men seemed to be enjoying conversing with each

other in this way. It had been too long.

"Ah, I see," remarked Dafydd. "So this is why even though you see Rumanadil and Morgana as appearing normal, it is really their spirit body you are seeing. The Void craft is maintaining their spirit field. In many ways, the Void craft is behaving like a portable sacred site or megalith."

"Very interesting," said Touchwood distractedly. "But there are so many things I have been wanting to talk to you about Dafydd, my poor head is bursting with it. But I am most concerned about my granddaughter Victoria."

"Is she the girl with the blond hair I first met in the garden?"

"Yes. She came to me to tell me about your arrival. You frightened her to death, poor thing."

"I do apologise for that Touchwood. In retrospect, I should have just walked down here in the daytime."

"Perhaps. But you see, ever since I 'mistakenly' transported her to the Otherworld; don't ask how it happened; she seems to have developed 'green fingers'. Every seed and plant she touches seems to grow much better than any of the others. Community members have commented to her that she must have inherited that from her grandfather, as I have similar power over plants.

"And another thing," continued Touchwood, "she seems to have developed all sorts of psychic gifts spontaneously. A spirit guide has not gifted them to her. And… and she just seems to 'know' things instinctively. Like the other day, some members of the community were attempting to lift a pallet of facing stones, using a pulley, up onto a second-story roof we are building on top of the barn. Victoria was just walking from the garden to the kitchen with some vegetables she had gathered when she remarked in passing, 'That rope is not strong enough to lift that weight. It's going to break!' Well, those people there had lifted that weight between them. They knew how heavy it was, and they had previously made the rope and used it to lift all sorts of things, so knew its lifting ability. So surely they were in a better position to judge the situation. But somehow Victoria just knew that the rope wouldn't hold. And she was right, of course. When the people started to lift the load halfway up, the rope broke and the stones came crashing down. Fortunately, nobody was hurt, because even though nobody acknowledged Victoria's warning, they all proceeded more cautiously and stood well away."

"Hum, I see. You say she is your granddaughter. I didn't think you had married again."

"Well, it's complicated. But I didn't even know I had a son, either, until his daughter turned up here as a very small child. Oh, how can I explain?"

"Perhaps at the beginning?" suggested Dafydd.

"I think it all started with the yew tree ritual, many years ago, when Hazel and I were still working magic together. She had been told by her spirit guide that we should perform a very special ritual on the upcoming blue moon. We needed to do it at an ancient yew grove near Navern in Wales. One where there was an ancient grandmother Yew, called the Bleeding Yew. The date for the ritual was set at a very rare astrological occurrence. You see, the upcoming blue moon also fell on Friday, the 13th of May. So it was going to be our Beltane ritual as well. Hazel and I decided as it was such a significant and rare astrological occurrence, we should also have a full coven of thirteen.

"Well, I can tell you it wasn't easy to arrange, but anyway, somehow, it all came together. But the point I'm trying to make is that Sherrie and I coupled up and performed the great rite within the Yew Grove.

"I see. I'm starting to get the picture," remarked Dafydd.

"As it transpired, for her own reasons, Sherrie hid her pregnancy from me, and I was left in the dark about the son she gave birth to. His name was Jade. Unfortunately, I never met him. It was during those chaotic times, when the waters rose and governments were imposing martial law, attempting to control the situation."

"Yes, I remember it well," chipped in Dafydd. "Climate change storms were ravaging the land, there was fighting between various factions, and the situation became appalling. My old cottage on Anglesea became submerged under water, and I had to evacuate to higher ground. They were very hard times."

"Fortunately, we were spared most of it," continued Touchwood. "Being self-sufficient on the west coast of Ireland, at the edge of the world. But to get back to my story, Jade married a girl called Poppy, and together they conceived Victoria. They both were eco-activists, and unfortunately during those troubled times, both of Victoria's parents were killed. As an orphan, she was evacuated to us here on this island, her only known family. So she grew up here. She doesn't remember any other life."

"So it seems then that Victoria," remarked Dafydd, "has inherited some of your 'fay blood' Touchwood. Do you know anything about Sherrie's family?"

"Unfortunately no. But knowing her, I would say she had some oriental blood. Even though she was brought up European, she had similar facial features."

"Hum, I see. Perhaps she had some fey blood too. You say that it wasn't Victoria that was conceived at the yew tree ritual, but her father."

"Yes, Jade was my son, conceived at that powerful yew tree ritual all those years ago. As I said, I didn't even know him. He was Victoria's father - and led a group of eco-activists on the Mendips, is all I know of him. Victoria arrived here as a small child, with a letter from Poppy explaining it all. I know nothing about Poppy either. But I guess it's possible that both Sherrie and Poppy had fay blood."

"It's possible. There were a lot of gifted children born in those last days before the waters rose. Some of the other Dyn Hysbys or Master Magicians I knew, said that there were a lot of 'advanced souls' incarnated to witness those last years of humankind's folly…"

4

At this point, Touchwood's kitchen door flew open and Ruth walked in bearing a tray full of cups and a large pot of tea. She was followed by Victoria, with another tray bearing griddle cakes and a sizeable chunk of cheese.

"Here we are, gentlemen. Thought you might be hungry. Sorry, we seem to have run out of bread, so I brought plenty of griddle cakes and cheese and…" she stopped mid-sentence looking around. "Where is everyone?"

Dafydd and Touchwood looked up, startled by the sudden intrusion. They both looked about them, surprised, only then noticing that Morgana and Rumanadil had disappeared.

"Err… perhaps they have gone out to the silver ball in the garden," Touchwood offered. "Anyway, I'm sure Dafydd is famished after his adventures. We will have to use my workbench and put the trays on there." The heavy workbench was one of the few things remaining after Morgana's tantrums.

Ruth and Victoria unburdened themselves of the trays. All the while Ruby was eying Dafydd suspiciously. Then she said, "I really must return to the kitchen to help Ivy prepare the bread for rising overnight, as we have run out."

She seemed to expect Victoria to come away with her too. But Victoria looked at her Grandpapa pleadingly. She clearly wanted to stay.

"Thank you so much, Ruby, for your trouble. Victoria this is Dafydd." He waited till Ruby had closed the door behind her, then. "He is a very old friend of mine, and has been my magical mentor for longer than I care to remember."

"Victoria, so please to meet you at last." Dafydd gently took her hand and shook it in a gentlemanly way. "Touchwood has told me all about you. But first, forgive me, I must apologise for startling you in the garden just now. Bit of a grand entrance really," he said bashfully. "The intention was to land the craft in the dark unnoticed, and for me to knock on Touchwood's door, as an ordinary visitor. But best-laid plans etc…"

"Is that silver ball one of those fairy light thingies… er, UFOs that Grandpapa told me about," Victoria enthused?

Dafydd was stumped for a moment. Not quite sure what she meant. But then replied, "Well, yes, I suppose you could say that. They have probably been developing them for some time but…"

"Oh, I soooo would love to see one close up. Perhaps I could go inside. That would be soooo exciting. Grandpapa, do you think we could? Please…"

Victoria was so lovely and cute when she occasionally begged him for things. He could never resist. Touchwood looked at Dafydd helplessly. He looked helplessly back.

"I suppose there could be no harm in it. I've been itching to show you inside, anyway. Besides, we need to rescue poor Rumanadil from Morgana; I don't trust that woman," pronounced Dafydd as he marched towards the kitchen door. "If she gets her hands on that void craft, it might be the last we see of it."

Chapter 14

The Mirror Pool

1

Since childhood, Star had had premonitions. They came completely at random, often at very inappropriate times, like in the middle of a family dinner. However, these powerful feelings or visions of events that something was going to happen in the future; often came true.

But as a child, they were only minor things, like the time she had 'seen' how her friend's lost kitten had fallen down a rabbit hole. Or perhaps a 'vision' of a rainstorm just before she went out, so she remembered to bring her cloak.

However, during her training as a priestess, they had called this gift far-sight or seership. And this seership had been developed and honed. She had been taught to harness this power, so the 'visions' only came when she wanted, like when she visited the mirror pool.

The mirror pool was a sacred space within the Temple of the moon's confines, and was a natural spring that flowed into a series of shallow ponds, surrounded by a thicket of hazel trees.

On this particular evening, something she couldn't name had drawn Star toward the sacred pool. Above the trees, the pure, slim crescent of the virgin moon, barely visible, shone like the silver torc about Star's neck. The water was clear, reflecting the moonlight of the new moon.

She dipped her hand into the cool water and drank. For she knew it was forbidden to place any man-made object into the pool. Even the small spring issuing from the rocks above was sacred and the water only used within the temples, being collected only by clam shells or bone drinking-horns.

The spring had been flowing since anyone could remember, and had a sulphurous smell and tasted like the waters of the hot baths in the Sun Temple. It was said by the high druids that these springs were heated by the volcanic rocks far below the island.

She set her small lamp on a stone beside the sacred pool, one she had lighted from the eternal flame that burnt in the temple perpetually. The four elements were now present: the water from the pool; the rocky earth on which she sat, the air and sky about her, of which the moon was a part.

In a meditative trance, she stared into the pool. At first, she saw only confused images. But then she saw a blazing comet drifting through the blackest night. In her young life, she had seen several comets and was in awe of all of them. But this... this one caused her to shudder. An icy shiver played down her back and seemed to enter the pit of her gut. Churning in her deepest bowels.

The name 'Wormwood' came to her and even though she shrank back from the pool, she could not help but see the comet explode into a hundred pieces, each one plummeting to the earth.

The vision changed. Now she could see a great wall of ice, such as had been reported seen in the lands across the Great Ocean, in the north of that land, where the great ice lay. The ice wall seemed to be hundreds of feet high, and as her spirit vision floated above it, she could see a vast lake of ice. A great plain of flat, frigid ice.

On it, she could see huge white bears prowling the acres of ice for prey. One such bear looked up at the sky. It watched as one of the splintered comets came crashing down upon the great ice wall that held back the waters of the gigantic, icy lake. The massive impact of the comet caused the ice wall to crumble and fall.

Star watched in fascinated horror as great icy mountainous chunks of ice fell onto the tundra below. These were quickly followed by a tremendous waterfall of icy water that had been under the great ice plain.

Tears formed in her eyes as she saw one of the great white bears fall into the turbulent waters, as the ice of the great plain collapsed and joined the raging torrent, now flowing through the gap in the ice wall made by the comet.

Massive chunks of ice sheet, bombarded the remaining ice wall, destroying that which dammed the ice lake. In horror, Star watched the catastrophe unfold as frigid water flowed over the tundra below, destroying all in its path. The cataclysm of ice blocks and rocks, continued to flow into the Great Ocean, and caused a tsunami of monstrous size to flow across the Ocean, till it reached the archipelago of Y's, causing disaster and carnage to all life on the islands.

In trauma and shock, Star backed away from the mirror pool and raced away to hide her head in her bed. But try as she might, she could not remove the image of that great disaster from her mind.

2

The following morning, after an anxious and sleepless night. Star made her way to the apothecary, and reported between a river of tears and sobs, what she had seen in the mirror pool for her mentor Selen.

Selen sat in a comfortable chair, tucked into a corner of the apothecary. Star was still sobbing, her head on Selens' knees; who was comforting her protégé. After some time, Star settled and seemed more in control of herself; it was then that Selem made a decision.

Star had never been to the cauldron room, no sixth-degree priestess was allowed there. She didn't even know where it was, but had only heard talk of it. But Selen retrieved her staff by the door and took her out of the apothecary.

It was a short walk, as Selem led her to a narrow area between the high surrounding garden wall and the main wall of the temple building. A thicket of hawthorn bushes had grown in the small space, blocking the way. But Selen deftly slid along the temple wall and disappeared into the thicket.

"Follow me," Selem whispered. Intrigued, Star followed her mentor, discovering there was a small clearing in the thicket.

Then Selen started to sing, or rather it was more of a chant or utterance, of an oddly inhuman syllable. She repeated this, till she caught a sort of double pitch, the voice ringing in both registers at once, harmonics of the same note, which resonated together, becoming louder, till it started to hurt Star's ears.

Then suddenly, with a stony scraping, an undetectable door in the solid stone wall started to open; revealing a gloomy void. Star's eyes became like saucers, as she looked bewildered from the hole in the wall, to her mentor and back. It made Star look at her mentor in a whole new light. But Selen surprised her again, as she drew a complicated gesture above the top of her staff. Instantly, the yellow crystal affixed to the top of her staff started to glow with a yellow light; Selen stepped forward into the gloom.

Bewildered, Star followed her into the small room now revealed. As Star's eyes were getting used to the gloom, Selen started to sing another chant, subtly different to the first. With a stony scraping, the stone door closed shut behind them. As the nimbus glow from Selen's staff increased, Star could see the small secret room was empty; except for some ancient tapestries hung on the wall.

Star looked about her in wonder, whispering, "Where are we Selen? I thought I knew every part of this temple."

"This is the cauldron room of Cyrridfen. There are many hidden spaces within the Temple of the Moon. As you progress in the grades, you may learn of some of them, but even I don't know of them all."

Star looked about her again in dismay. "But where is

the cauldron?"

"That's a very good question Star. But the answer is, I do not know." Selen nodded her wise head in confirmation. "There are too many secrets in the Temples these days. And I like it not. But I do know it is connected with what you saw in the mirror pool. Which is why I brought you here. In this room, no one else can hear us, for I must tell you that what you have seen is already known to many of the elders; but it is kept secret. Over the years, many have seen the 'Comet of Destruction' in visions and dreams or sendings. We know it is coming, but no one can tell when it will be. The 'Stars' tell us nothing."

Star looked at her mentor in horror, half disbelieving what she heard. She was hoping her mentor would tell her that her 'horrific vision' was just a random fear dream. Nothing to worry about. But this?

Selen continued, even though she saw the fear in the young girl's eyes, "Because of this, the Cauldron of Cyrridfen is gone, along with the other three magical treasures of Y's. All moved to safe locations, in high places on the mainland."

Star suddenly felt sick and woozy. Her knees trembled. Thinking she might faint, she sat down quickly on the stone floor, back against the wall, and started to do the breathing exercises that she had been taught.

Selen looked upon her young student, pity in her eyes. Then turned and squatted beside her, the wall supporting her back.

"You know Star, you have moved through the grades quickly, retaining everything I have taught you. I have said it before, but I know you to be one of the 'Old Souls'.

You have been born and reborn again and again. At your young age, you are far wiser than I ever was as a silly young priestess."

Despite her wooziness, this made Star smile. She could not have imagined that Selen would ever have been 'a silly young priestess.'

"Back in the old days," Selen continued, "We didn't bother so much with all this grading system. An adept took on an apprentice, and she learnt on the hoof. Wherever the Adept was needed for healing, the apprentice went with her, learning as she went. If I had my way..." but she left it unsaid. But instead said, "Look, I believe you are wise enough to know what I'm about to tell you." Selen moved her hand to rest tenderly on top of Star's.

"I know you have been taught Star, that in nature there are two forces at play in the universe. That which 'creates', and that which 'destroys'. The seasonal cycles of the year: spring and summer are creative; fecundity and fertility; everything grows.

"But it must be followed by autumn and winter, where things die back and rest; the Winter Queen reigns. It is the eternal cycle; it is the natural order of things."

Star nodded her acknowledgement.

"And so it is in the temples. You and I are healers. We restore a natural, healthy balance in a body that is plagued by destructive forces. We are one of the forces of light, of creativity."

Star nodded her head again in acknowledgement that she understood, but then said, "But what of the destructive forces in the temple? I see none of that."

"There are always a few magicians who cannot resist dabbling in the dark and forbidden arts of the past. We call them 'The Hidden Ones,' they wear the Black robes. And practice in dark shrines, out of sight, below ground, even below the temples of light."

At this, Selen heard Star take a quick intake of breath. But she continued kindly. "That's an inevitable part of the cycle child; you know we have Temple Laws. The law of balance is one of those. It is a way of limiting our power. We are committed to keeping the balance of power between creative and destructive forces. Ever are we seeking a balance between the two."

Star, her eyes wide, asked, "We are light healers, but what do the black robes do?"

"They are apostasy of the light. The black robes seek to divert power. To change nature's balance by bringing rain from reluctant clouds; create blinding mists; bring down fear to an opposing army, and they lose lightning on their enemies." Selen paused a moment, allowing Star to take it all in.

But then she shrugged her shoulders, "The black robes have their place when enemies seek to war with us. As does happen from time to time. It's when they start upsetting the balance that the problem occurs."

"What do you mean mistress?"

"The black robes now seek to upset the balance, in favour of the dark side. The temple elders seem blind to them. But I fear the black robes have got out of control, creating magics that have a very detrimental effect on the balance between creative and destructive forces. In these unprecedented times, where the balance has been pushed too far over to the destructive side, I feel I must break my usual taboos about sacred knowledge. And so I tell you all this."

Chapter 15

Void Talk

1

The rain had stopped as suddenly as it started. The clouds dispersed and the Goddess full moon could be seen again high in the sky, giving off her silvery light. Touchwood, Victoria and Dafydd stood in the garden, searching the shadows under the trees for the magnificent silver ball. Even though they knew it must be there, it was impossible to see it. However, Dafydd walked boldly into the shadows, almost bumping into the craft in his eagerness to be aboard again.

"Found it," he called back to the others. "Come over here and I will get you aboard."

With Touchwood placing his hand on Dafydd's shoulder and Victoria putting hers on Touchwood's, Dafydd summoned up the magical energy required to travel through the walls of the craft.

2

The void craft had no doors or windows. The only

way to enter it was to teleport, in the same way that Dafydd and Touchwood, had teleported through the matrix of interconnecting ley lines, when they were searching for the missing Syrinx. It required the discipline and specially trained mental powers of an experienced magician for someone to travel in this way.

They must know how to manipulate clouds of Orgone energy that gather along the earth's energy lines, with megalithic sites at the nodes. Just like the druids of old did thousands of years ago. And is similar to the way acupuncturists utilise the bodies meridians and use tiny needles to puncture the skin at places called 'acupoints'.

Magicians, likewise, for centuries, have also known about the tiny holes in the fabric of the universe, through which energy can flow both in and out. In simple terms, it's like the fabric of the universe has tiny faults in it, and there are lots of them all over the place. It's where the veil is thin.

But places that have megaliths, like standing stones or barrows and stone circles, have large concentrations of them. Some magicians like Dafydd still know how to work with them by creating large concentrations of Orgone energy. In this way, they can create a large enough portal to travel through.

And so it was with the Void craft using magic and technology that could create a quantum field about it. It behaved somewhat like a portable megalithic site.

3

Victoria stood, eyes as big as saucers inside the void craft. She had expected to see concave silver walls, and a cramped space. But it was nothing like that at all. She stood in a vast white space with corridors leading off in every direction. The walls were white; the floor was white, and the ceiling seemed to disappear into a white mist. This place was enormous.

Dafydd looked at Victoria's amazed face, expecting her reaction, and said, "Inside the void ship is like the otherworld, a timeless space. But unlike the otherworld, it does not have the spirit essence of the physical world. As Rumanadil explained it to me: instead it is timeless and spaceless. Everything you see has been magically glamoured by the dark elves and remains indefinitely supported by the craft's quantum field."

But Victoria wasn't listening at all. She had wandered off and was running her hands up and down a white wall to test its reality. But Touchwood too stared about him in wonder and whispered to himself, "It's bigger on the inside!"

Dafydd smiled at the response, "Yes, it seems to go on forever. You two had best follow me, or you might get lost in here."

Dafydd marched off down one of the corridors, with Touchwood following, holding Vitoria's hand very firmly.

Shortly they came to a series of open doors, inside the rooms looked to be crew quarters with four bunks to a room. But Dafydd continued along the corridor till he heard voices, and throaty laughter. It was Rumanadil and Morgana. The door of the room was left a jar. Dafydd and Touchwood listened for a moment. Then, as Victoria pushed through to listen as well, Dafydd became agitated, grabbing Victoria's hand, and quickly pulled her away saying. "I don't think they want to be disturbed right now -- let's find the kitchens."

Touchwood reacted similarly and took Victorias other hand, following Dafydd further along the corridor, till they came to a large room, filled with tables, benches and what looked to be a very modern kitchen; nothing like the one Victoria was used to. Dafydd immediately went over to a cupboard and brought out some army rations, placing them on the counter.

"Here, Touchwood, try some of these. They are not half bad."

Touchwood picked up the plastic sack with a straw attached and looked at it dubiously.

"Here," said Dafydd, "All's you need to do is twist the top like this. And then you can suck out the nutritious contents. Mmmm! I think this one is strawberry."

No one noticed that Victoria had wandered over to a what looked like a hatch in the wall, and was examining the console. Touchwood halfheartedly twisted the top of his army ration sack. But curiosity got the better of him and he tried sucking on the straw.

"It tastes strangely like lamb and mint! Most peculiar." Then, pulling a sour face, dropped it back on the counter and turned to Dafydd.

"Look, I know this void craft is all very fascinating, but my friend Adge has been spelled by Morgana into a tree. We need to devise a rescue plan."

"Morgana did this? How do you know?" replied Dafydd, suddenly looking very serious.

"She told me herself. Said it was an accident."

"Sound's typical of the woman. But I must tell you about what else we have discovered in the dark elf's realm…"

Just then an excited scream followed by, "That's amazing! I don't believe it."

All eyes turned to Victoria, who was busy spooning something into her mouth. Touchwood, a little concerned, went over to her and said, "What's that you're eating?" then dipped his finger into the bowl to sample it.

"That's chocolate ice cream," he declared. "Where on earth did you get that?"

"I know, isn't it heavenly," Victoria enthused between mouthfuls. "Yum! It's the one thing we can't make ourselves. Ruby tried to explain it to me. She said she still remembers it from when she was a child."

"But where did it come from," Insisted Touchwood?

"Well, while you two were talking about the food sacks, you were eating. It got me thinking about what food I would like most of all. I was standing by that little hatch thingie in the wall over there, when a bowl of ice cream suddenly appeared, behind the window like magic."

Touchwood's mouth, still agape, looked over at the hatch she had indicated. But Dafydd was already there with his back to them. There was a little stifled exclamation from him, then he slowly turned around with the biggest grin on his face. Lovingly, cradled in his hands, was a bottle of red wine.

"Do you know what this is?" he asked reverentially.

"Looks like a bottle of wine to me," remarked Victoria, still scoffing mouthfuls of ice cream.

"Correct. But not any bottle of wine. This is Chateau Lafite Rothschild vintage 1953," said Dafydd as he held up the bottle; looking at it adoringly.

"Yuk!" said Victoria. "It must be disgusting being that old. Me and Forge found a bottle of homemade wine in his dad's old barn. The label said it was ten years old. When we drank it, it tasted revolting."

Touchwood gave his granddaughter a hard stare for being so rude. Victoria lowered her eyes and blushed.

Touchwood returned his attention to Dafydd, "But surely it can't be the real thing. Where did you find it?"

"This little hatch here. Seems to be a food and drink synthesiser. I decided ice cream was a basic item, so I thought I would give 'the thing' a harder task."

"Looks genuine enough. But maybe we should try drinking it and find out," said Touchwood as he walked over to Dafydd and tried to take the bottle from his hands. But Dafydd wasn't having any of it and held onto it for dear life.

"No way," Dafydd shouted stubbornly. "This is probably the only one of its kind left in the world. It must be worth thousands!" He struggled with Touchwood to keep hold of it.

"Come-on Dafydd, we need to share. Let's set an example for the children," Touchwood said as he tried to pull the bottle from Dafydd's hands. But Dafydd furiously pulled back. Unfortunately Dafydd was a little unsteady on his feet and he fell backwards to the floor with Touchwood falling on top of him.

"Er …hum! I thought you said we needed to act quickly at all costs to save you humans." It was Rumanadil's loud voice. He stood in the kitchen doorway looking on, with Morgana at his side, her hair dishevelled but a contented and amused look on her face.

Dafydd and Touchwood lay in a heap on the floor, squabbling over the rare bottle of wine. While Victoria, with chocolate ice cream all round her mouth, looked on with a bemused expression.

Both Touchwood and Dafydd struggled to stand up. Looking very embarrassed, they hung their heads, saying nothing, looking for all the world like two naughty schoolboys stood outside the headmaster's study.

"It is, as I told you Rumanadil," remarked Morgana. "I do wonder, would the earth be a better place without humans?"

"Maby you are right Morgana. They squabble over possessions when their very existence is in jeopardy."

But it was Victoria who spoke out next. "You high elves have no room to talk. You only seem to care about hedonistic pleasures. You stood by and did nothing while the dark elves sought to upset the balance of the world. Now they are out of control, you come to hide with us."

Both Touchwood and Dafydd cringed at this outburst, expecting Morgana's wrath. But Morgana only looked at Victoria with a hint of amusement in her eye and an appreciative smile, like a proud mother.

"Yes, well... perhaps we are all at fault in some way," said Touchwood, trying to calm the situation. "There is little to be gained arguing about who's fault it is. Perhaps this would be a good time for all of us to sit and talk and try to work out our plan of action. We only have a limited window of opportunity."

Rumanadil, looking a little taken aback by Victorias out burst, replied, "That sounds like a very good idea

Touchwood. Let us move to the mess hall tables over there and each can tell what they know and then we can begin to work out what is to be done."

4

Inside the void ship, the weary travellers had each told their story. Dafydd and Rumanadil, for the main part, with Touchwood adding what little he knew. Morgana kept a regal silence, listening to all, while sipping Dafydd's prized wine, which she had opened with her magic. Victoria looked on silently too, soaking up everything that was said. Terrified by what she heard but secretly very excited to be a part of it.

Discussions had gone on for hours, although inside the void craft it was impossible to tell for how long. However, the discussions had been inconclusive. The only actual decision made was to call this odd group of friends 'the war council'. Even though nobody voiced it out aloud, most felt they were in an impossible situation. Nobody could think of an effective plan of action.

Touchwood had eventually nodded off in his chair. Victoria too, had sleepily laid her head on the table, using her arms as a pillow.

At some point, Rumanadil had looked at Morgana with a twinkle in his eye, and Morgana had nodded assent. So they had silently sloped off, back to their chosen room, leaving Dafydd to finish the remains of his prized wine. But shortly after, he too had nodded off.

5

Outside the void craft, the first light of dawn crept up

the eastern horizon. The full moon, having long before, slipped below the western edge of the horizon. The neat vegetable gardens of Rath Grain glowed dully in the twilight. Today the dawn chorus seemed subdued. The birds somehow seemed to be aware of the impending situation.

In the deep shadows under the trees, the void craft reflecting the surrounding environment could not be seen, but two glowing nimbus clouds appeared beside it, which slowly lowered towards the earth. When they touched, a momentary flash of light radiated in all directions — then was gone. Two figures silently walked to the end of the community garden.

Dafydd and Rumanadil stood looking through the willow trees at the mists that surrounded the island.

"Is it always like this, shrouded in mists? Rumanadil asked.

When the two had escaped from the dark elves' prison with the help of Goibniu, the smith. Under the cloak of invisibility, they had made their way to the void craft that Rumanadil had seen while spying. Once inside the craft, they had made haste to leave as soon as possible. They were keen to leave the Otherworld and the realm of the dark elves behind.

Rumanadil found he could control the mysterious vehicle with his powerful Elven mind, and had piloted the craft to the physical realm. As Dafydd had been spirit walking in the otherworld, when he had been captured, the first thing he needed to do, was to return to his physical body in Anglesea and reunite with it.

He had been away from it too long and it had suffered as a result. He was so stiff he could barely walk.

Rumanadil had to carry him. However, once inside the void craft again, he found the healing process began rapidly.

But now that the Dark elves knew of him, he felt it was too risky to return to his cottage on Anglesea, as they could too easily link him to it. Instead Dafydd had suggested they head for the top of the mountain of Sliabh an Iarainn, as it was a place he knew to be deserted. He had projected the image of it to Rumanadil's mind.

Once there, and feeling safe, Dafydd's body continued to recover. At their leisure, they had explored the ship, and had found kitchens and food stores, enough to feed an army. They had also found many store cupboards filled with fresh clothes in dark elf styles. Close by, they found the shower rooms, which they quickly availed off, discarding their ruined clothes and washing off the filth of their prison cell.

The clothes were all dark Elven warrior style. But Dafydd had chosen what seemed to be an officer's clothing, as it didn't have the leather armour and combat belts that the warriors had. But had a hooded cloak of fine cashmere that seemed to change colour as it moved. And a tunic of crimson with gold trimmings.

However, Rumanadil chose the warrior style. His tunic was a dark midnight blue with a lustre like a stormy sky. And leather belts across his chest with intricate knot-work tooled into it. About his shoulders he wore a collar of thick, grey wolf fur.

Now feeling clean and refreshed, they explored further and had found many rooms that looked to be crew quarters with four bunks to a room. Dafydd quickly decided they should get some sleep in comfort while they could. As, while on the run, one never knew for sure what the next day might bring.

Inside the void ship, like the Otherworld, was a timeless space. They could not tell how long they had slept. But they could feel that the sly spells of the dark elves still lay over them, for when they did awaken they were famished - they hadn't eaten anything while in prison. Consequently, they raided the kitchen and food stores, gratefully consuming several helpings of surprisingly tasty army rations.

While eating, Dafydd's sharp mind slowly returning after a peaceful sleep, wondered why if this craft was made by the dark elves, who were Otherworld creatures, why they needed any food supplies at all. And remarked as such to Rumanadil. He answered that perhaps it wasn't for the dark elves at all, but for the elf-human hybrids he had seen, who, if they were bred to live in the human realm, needed to eat like humans.

Now as Dafydd and Rumanadil stood at the end of the community garden looking down at the mists below, Dafydd answered, "Yes there always seems to be mists about Sliabh an Iarainn. Touchwood calls this the magical mountain. Perhaps he is right, and it is becoming halfway to the land of fairy."

"Sliabh an Iarainn you say?" Rumanadil queried, then his eyes seemed to stare into the middle distance and quoted with a storyteller's cadence:

"And the magical race of the Tuatha De Danann came sailing the winds over the purple mountains of Connemara and beyond. Shrouded in magic mists, was a great fleet, born on the strong winds. Their great sails fully stretched, bearing a raven crest. At last they landed on the mountain of Sliabh an Iarainn and from there, spread to the rest of Ireland."

Dafydd turned and looked at him, wonder in his eye, "You know this place then?"

"Only from the old ballads sung to us by our bards. This one is very old and tells of a time before we ever transcended to Tír na nÓg. According to the tale, before even we lived in Ireland, our ancestors fled here from a great destruction of our homelands. The tales tell of a great civilisation which blossomed on many islands in the great ocean to the west."

"Atlantis?" Dafydd whispered. "You have ballads of it, even in the otherworld.

"Atlantis? I know not that name. Our bards sing of the 'land of the wise,' or the bards sing of our ancestors as the 'wise ones'."

"We humans have many myths about lost lands to the west," said Dafydd. "Antilla, Hy-Brasil, Lyonesse and Mu, to name a few. However, the Irish have legends about the 'land of the ever young' or 'the land of the wise'.

"But to get back to our present situation. I thought all would be well once I killed king Indech. But you have seen that there is much more to concern we humans. After our discussions last evening, I was thinking perhaps we could call upon the high elves to help us. Surely, as you know the high Queen, you could enlist her to help us?"

"I would dearly like to, friend, if I could. But the Queen has made it clear to me that she has no will to cause a war in Tír na nÓg between Elven kind. Which is why she could offer us no help to escape. My espionage was a covert mission denied by the Queen."

"This gives me little hope, Rumanadil. And there are few humans left on earth who even know of the danger. What do you think about Morgana? Do you think she will help us?"

"With sufficient motivation," considered Rumanadil. "And if she can find benefits to herself, she could be persuaded. She seems quite taken with Victoria. Perhaps there is some way there."

"Yes. Touchwood has mentioned his concerns about his granddaughter to me," remarked Dafydd. "But I had not met her before. However, there is something about her that I can't quite put my finger on."

"She is tall and very beautiful," said Rumanadil. "With hair the colour of corn before the harvest, and green eyes that take on all the shades of the sea. She, is a dreamer. I know it to be true. Something that may prove very useful in the times to come."

"She certainly has that otherworldly look, admitted Dafydd. "I believe she knows more about all this than Touchwood wants to believe. And as regards Touchwood himself, I have been mentoring him in magic for many years now. I have taught him to create portals large enough to physically crawl through and to 'teleport' from one megalith to another. He has also been receiving messages from the otherworld since before I knew him. I believe him to be of a Fay bloodline.

"We should all be eternally grateful to him as it was him and his druid brother Adge who found the missing Syrinx - Pans' magical pipes. And it was him and Victoria who returned them to Pan. That reminds me, we really should find a way to rescue Adge the druid. He has proved to be a budding alchemist."

"I can only agree with you Dafydd," confirmed Rumanadil. "There is indeed much to be done. Not least, is that we need to deal with the Dark Elf councillors before they recover and elect a new king and continue with their evil plans. But for the life of me, I cannot see how we can achieve that."

Dafydd, staring off into the boiling mists below, looked very grim as he slowly shook his head and admitted, "No, neither can I."

Chapter 16

The Oak King

Speaks

1

Touchwood had awoken with a jolt. Opening his eyes, he realised he was still in the mess hall of the void craft. Victoria was still asleep, head resting on her arms on the other side of the mess hall table. But no one else was there.

Cursing the uncomfortable nature of the chair he was in, he stood up, stretching his aching back. He was gasping for a cup of tea.

Looking about him, he could see no stove or kettle to make one with. Muttering to himself about the stark nature of the void craft, he painfully walked into the kitchen to double check. Then he remembered the food synthesiser hatch, and was tempted for a moment to ask it for a cup of tea. But decided he didn't trust the thing, and would rather do without. Walking away from it in disgust.

Feeling quite grumpy now, he remembered the disheartening discussions they had had before he fell asleep. This did nothing to improve his mood, and he began to despair that nobody could think of a way to defeat the dark elves. He decided to go and find one of the dormitory rooms, so he could lie on a bed to rest his back. That, at least, was a positive move.

Sitting on the edge of a bunk bed, it came to him that he should contact the Oak King. His spirit guide had always given him sound advice in the past and realised yet again that he had been a fool to suspect the Oak King of consorting with the dark elves.

Thinking back to his encounters with the Oak King, apart from withholding information, there had never been any cause to doubt his integrity or advice. The thought brought him new hope. So, with a new resolve, he lay down on the thin mattress and prepared himself in the usual way to enter the otherworld.

Perhaps it was because of the quantum field about the void craft, but he found it much easier than usuall to get there; it almost seemed effortless.

2

…Almost immediately, Touchwood manifested directly into the familiar forest grove. He was sitting on a log with a small campfire flickering before him. Dreamily, he looked about him at the iridescent colours, and the fecundity of the natural world about him. Above him was the shimmering blue of the sunless sky. Under his bare feet was a soft and spongy mossy floor in variegated greens. He looked about his feet in wonder. There, a fairy-ring of champignon mushrooms, nearby a harvest of fly agaric, with its fairy-tale red hood, and white spots. In the trees, a crop of bright red rose-hips and elderberries hung in sumptuous black bunches.

The air, too, seemed filled with an enchanting bird song. It was truly surreal. But Touchwood had long ago come to realise that this 'Other-world' was archetypical for everything in the physical world. Each tree here was the 'spirit essence', the Quintessence for its shadow, in his own world.

Still lost in the magical world that surrounded him, he suddenly noticed that the Oak King had appeared a little distance from him at the edge of the grove. The thick lips of his enormous mouth gave a wide smile that matched the humorous glint of his deep brown eyes.

"Hail and welcome, brother Touchwood. It has been a long time," he greeted.

"Good morrow Sire," Touchwood replied, automatically deferring to the traditional greeting he had been taught to say when addressing the Oak King. "I apologise for my long absence. But much has happened since we last met."

"Time has no meaning to me here in the otherworld. But it is good to see you again, Touchwood. Perhaps you may not realise, but I have been taking an interest in all you have been involved with. However, I admit the Dark elves had taken we old Gods by surprise. We hadn't realised just how powerful the dark elves have become. I myself am ashamed that we let this happen, right under our noses."

I looked over at the Oak King. He truly was a magnificent creature. A tall giant of a man, his body was lean and hard, his powerful thighs rippled with strength. The short tunic he wore was all different shades of green. His weathered skin was toned with the colours of the earth. But his noble head, crowned with a circlet of oak leaves, was bowed in sorrow. Touchwood almost felt sorry for him.

"Oak King, I come to you humbly, and ask for your guidance. What can be done to thwart the wicked plans of the dark elves?"

The Oak King lifted his magnificent head, so that Touchwood could see that there was a look of great sadness in his eyes before he answered, "Touchwood, I have mentioned this to you before, but we have had to intervene occasionally before when certain civilisations have become too troublesome. The Atlanteans got out of control, creating magic that had a very detrimental effect on the balance between creative and destructive forces.

"Several other great civilisations have also necessitated our intervention, such as the Ancient Sumerians, the Indus civilization, the ancient Greeks, and more recently, the Roman Empire."

"Yes, I remember you telling me. So could you stop the dark elfs, or 'intervene' I mean."

"But those civilisations I mentioned were all on the physical plane."

The Oak King paused a moment before continuing with more gravity. "There are ancient laws that were laid down eons ago. They prevent one God from interfering with another. Even though some in the past have gone against this ruling with disastrous results. A celestial war is not pretty and often ends up destroying all life on the physical plane. It has happened in the past eons ago, which is why we have these laws. All the old Gods now abide by them rigidly. None of us wanted a return to those terrible times, where we almost lost humanity, in our wrath, to battle with each other.

"So you must see my problem," Oak continued. "It is these new-comers to the otherworld, the hyper-human race that transcended to live here amongst the old Gods. Those which we call Elven kind. Because of these laws, we cannot move against them. Even though they are only Demi-Gods, we are bound by those ancient laws, because now they are part of the otherworld, too."

Touchwood looked at the Oak King in utter dismay.

"But we may help you in other ways," consoled the Oak king. "I can remind you that as humans, you are allowed to move against them."

"But how can we? The dark elves are so powerful," said Touchwood in despair.

"Perhaps I should remind you that Brother Dafydd, worked it so he could kill Indech, their leader," replied Oak, with a glint in his eye.

A sudden ray of hope shone in Touchwood's mind. "Of course! He used the Spear of Assail, one of the magical treasures of the Tuatha de Danna."

"He did. And this is why those magical tools were created in the first place. They were gifts from the otherworld to human kind. Do you really think there have not been problems similar to this before? When the Tuatha tribe still lived in Ireland, the Fomorians were Demi Gods who worked their dark magic against the Tuatha race."

"The Fomorians," Touchwood queried? "Dafydd told me that king Indech, the Lord of chaos was a Fomorian, not a Dark elf. I wasn't sure what he meant by that."

"The Fomorians were a very ancient race who inhabited the northern parts of Europe before the great ice came. In those days, life on the surface was very treacherous. It was a period when storms of comets plagued the earth, wreaking havoc and causing great disruption. The Fomorians evolved to live underground, creating a labyrinth of tunnels and caves. You should know that they had a deep understanding of the magical arts and could shapeshift into any form they needed. Some of their tunnels even emerged under the sea, where they took the form of fish-men. I believe that you humans have many legends about these folk.

"But in any case, the important thing to know about them is that in their dark caves, they turned to the dark side, creating dark magics. And worst of all, some of them learnt to transcend to the otherworld and dwelt there for many years as dark Demi Gods.

"But it was during this time that another noble race came to live upon the earth plain. They too were highly evolved - a hyper human race. They were called the nation of Y's, or as you humans now call them, Atlantean.

"But they too had a dark contingent. Though small in numbers, they worked with the wild, destructive powers of nature; the powers of chaos, darkness, death, blight and drought. They built devices that could temporarily enable them to visit the otherworld. It was here that they came upon the Fomorians. Together they worked on dark magics that had a very detrimental effect on the otherworld, wrecking havoc with the very essence of nature itself.

"It was because of this that we old Gods intervened and used the cosmic powers of nature to destroy their homeland. It was this that caused the great Ice to recede in the physical world, the sea levels rose and the lands of

Ireland became habitable again. I am sure you know the story from there."

"Yes," said Touchwood. "I am familiar with the ancient hero tales of Ireland. But you were telling me about the four magical tools of the Tuatha."

"Ah yes! After we had destroyed the homelands of Y's and the dark contingents along with it. We still had the problem of the Fomorians, the dark Demi Gods residing in the otherworld; we needed to cast them out. But we old Gods, as you know, could not move against them. But we enlisted the help of those few wise wizards that had escaped the drowning of Atlantis.

These few wise ones, resided in Ireland, and were then known as the Tuatha tribe. But hundreds of years had passed in the physical realm, so they had well established themselves in their new homeland. However, as I was saying, the Fomorians were harassing the Tuatha tribe and worked their dark magic against them. So as you might imagine, the Tuatha were more than willing to accept help to defeat the Fomorians.

"It was a long and convoluted series of battles and events, but the main thing you need to know is that we helped their alchemist-smith Goibniu, to produce those four magical tools. An Omphalos stone that facilitated direct communication with the old Gods, so as they could not be misled by other entities from the otherworld. The Tuatha tribe called this stone the Lia Fail.

"The Claíomh Solais, a sword with magical properties that makes the keeper insuperable and impossible to defeat. This was given to their king, Núada. Also, Goibniu made the Coire Ansic, a magical cauldron that had many properties. Among them was the ability to feed an army from the one cauldron.

"But perhaps the one thing that Goibniu made that caused the most controversy among the old Gods was the Gae Assail. A Spear, whose magical properties were that 'none could stand against it.' This included mythical creatures and other spirit beings.

"I can tell you Touchwood, that this spear was the one magical gift that was opposed by the most in the otherworld. But it was only allowed to exist at all, if a closely guarded magical incantation, which was entrusted only to its maker Goibniu, the metalsmith of the Tuatha de Danann. So this severely restricted its use."

"That was the spear that Dafydd used to kill king Indech," replied Touchwood. "But he told me that the dark elves now have it securely locked away."

"Indeed. And it is this that bothers us old Gods the most. The Dark elves had been looking for it for long ages. If they found it, they had intended to destroy the Great God Pan. Now they have it. They could destroy any of the old Gods, including me!

"This is the main, and only, reason that we have agreed to 'Gift' you with special powers in a bid to help you to destroy the dark elf leaders for the good of all."

"Help me destroy the dark elves?" Touchwood cried incredulously. "I have not the power to do that."

"No. Not yet. But the power we 'gift' you is not given lightly to any mortal. The last time this was done was for Goibniu, the smith of the Danann clan. They were in dire need too. The power we gift you is the magical power to 'charge' any weapon so that 'none can stand against it.' This includes Gods, mythical creatures and other spirit beings."

Touchwood was silent for some time. Shocked into silence by the magnitude of what the Oak King had said to him. The Oak King glanced at his face. He had seen that look before in a man. But only once, and that was in the face of Goibniu the smith, just after Oak had said the very same words to him.

Eventually Touchwood managed to raise his eyes to meet those of the Oak King and whispered, "You would do this for me?"

"There have been very few times throughout the history of mankind, when the need for such power as this, has come about. And at those times, very few humans that we could trust with that power. I believe, you Touchwood, are one of them."

Touchwood felt humbled beyond words. But before he could contemplate the implications too much. The Oak King spoke again.

"But even this great power will not be enough. I need to ask you to revisit the Crystal Cave again. From there, retrieve Núada's Sword of Light, who Merlin renamed as Excalibur; so too the Knife of Llawfrodedd; as well as the Stone and Ring of Eluned and lastly the cauldron of the Dagda."

"The cauldron of the Dagda. Why would we need that? The legends say it could feed an army. We are hardly that."

"Over time, human legends have become garbled. The mysterious cauldron of the Dagda has many powers and many names. Cerridwen claimed it as her own, as did the Dagda. In later years, it was named after Bran the

Blessed. The Atlanteans named it the cauldron of Cyrridfen. And they knew its full power and used it for regeneration and rebirth. For them, it was a magical cauldron able to resurrect the dead."

Touchwood's mouth dropped open at this, "This is great power indeed, Oak king."

"It is, and I believe before the end, you will need it. So do as I say and retrieve these wonders from the cave, but be sure to take only those I have indicated. Then you are to charge the weapons with the power I am about to give you. The spear of destiny is lost to us, so I charge you to make another. But here is something that you must know. You must not make weapons of iron if you want the Elven folk to help you. Of course, they are not afraid of iron, as some of your mythology tales report," he chuckled. "But when they are around it, the iron interferes with their magical powers and makes them weak. It prevents their magic from working, so they tend to avoid it. They can also detect it from a fair distance, so if you are engaged in covert missions in the dark elf realm, iron can give your presence away. This is why the spear of destiny was made of Yew. And the other weapons in the treasures made of bronze."

"This is good advice Oak, I shall well remember it. We will need to check our clothes as well."

"So when you make a new spearhead, or any other weapons you use against the dark elves, be sure to charge them with the power that 'none may stand against it.' - Now it is time," the Oak King declared.

As before, when the Oak King had gifted Touchwood the power to shapeshift into animals, the Oak King moved behind him and placed one large hand on his head. It felt heavy, but with it came a feeling of euphoria, somewhat like the energy healing Victoria had given him, but considerably more powerful. The feeling flowed through him, seeming to invigorate and 'charge' every cell in his body.

Somehow, he felt new and more alive than he had ever felt before. And with it came understanding. Touchwood suddenly knew, strings of energy connected everything and that he was energy, or rather, his body was energy. Who he was, his 'consciousness' was something else he had no words to explain. But gradually he became aware that he could move that 'consciousness' to whatever he focused on.

The Oak King now spoke out loudly, declaring, "I, Oak King, gift you with the power to 'magically charge' any object with the supernatural power of your intent."

Suddenly, Touchwood's mind spun wildly, as if caught up in a whirlwind. Faster and faster it spun, yet at the same time he seemed to be getting smaller and smaller, till he began to see floating about him molecules and atoms and probabilistic clouds of electrons, that where vibrating so fast as to appear to be anywhere and everywhere at the same time.

Yet he became smaller still, inextricably drawn to the swirling vortex inside the nucleus. Now he was falling. Falling through blackness that seemed to go on forever...

3

Suddenly, Touchwood awoke with a jolt. He found

himself sweating profusely and was lying on a bunk, inside a dormitory room, inside the void craft.

Chapter 17

War Council

1

To a background of chinking cutlery and the murmur of contented voices, the warm, aromatic smells of fried bacon and freshly ground coffee wafted through the air. Along with the comforting smells of hoppy ale, pancakes, and maple syrup.

It had taken some considerable work, but Touchwood had eventually managed to gather all the members of the war council to meet again over breakfast, in the Void ship's mess hall. Everyone had chosen their favourite foods for breakfast, magically produced by the food synthesiser hatch. It seemed everyone felt the need to comfort and pamper themselves, perhaps because of their situation, or perhaps it was the white, soulless environment of the Void craft.

Towards the end of breakfast when everyone, even Morgana, seemed contented. Touchwood stood up and informed the group about the meeting he had had with the Oak King, and all that he had advised. This seemed to raise everyone's spirits even further. People sensed a change in energy; 'something' was happening.

Plans were quickly developed, and sub groups formed. But from the start, they realised that they needed more members of the war council if they ever hoped to succeed. With this in mind, they tasked Morgana with freeing Adge from entombment in the tree. Much to his chagrin, they assigned Dafydd to aid her with his magic.

Victoria reminded everyone that Brad from the Rath Grain community had army experience, and could be an invaluable member of the group. She volunteered to approach him and bring him up to date with all the developments in the otherworld; Touchwood didn't envy her that job.

But Touchwood had also suggested to Victoria that once she had inducted Brad into the war council, that the two of them go across the island and ask Forge, the blacksmith's son, to make a bronze spear head for her. But not to tell him why she wanted it. He said to just make up some story, that you want to use it for hunting deer.

However, Touchwood quickly realised that they all needed effective weapons to achieve any of their plans. So Touchwood told the group that he would immediately return to the Crystal Cave and retrieve the magical tools that the Oak King had suggested. Morgana had volunteered to go with Touchwood as she wanted to say her last fair wells to Merlin. Rumanadil meanwhile had volunteered to search the void craft to see what it held, and if there was anything useful that they could use for their plans.

2

There was darkness all about them. Then, in the slowly growing nimbus glow forming between Morgana's hands, Touchwood could see the wondrous cave. Morgana's face, lit by the glow, looked about her in wonder. As she looked, she continued twisting her hands in a slow swirling motion, somewhat like Tai Chi, about the ball of light forming there.

This nimbus glow still intrigued Touchwood. He remembered the first time Dafydd had taught it to him. Dafydd had said he had perfected it while he was trying to build up enough Orgone energy to open a portal big enough to teleport. He had told him that once you build up enough energy with your hands, the concentrated Orgone produces a glow. He had gone on to tell him that we often see these glows at sacred sites at certain times when the energy is strong; people often mistake it for UFOs. However, this ability seemed to come to Morgana instinctively.

As Touchwood looked about him in wonder, he could see the walls and ceiling were covered in purple crystals that had grown from the very walls of the cave. The floor too was of the same crystal, making it difficult footing.

The cave, or rather a small cavern, was some eighteen feet long by a little less across and of a similar height. There was no entrance passage to this cavern, the purple crystals surrounded at every turn. The only way into this secret chamber was by teleporting from Knowth's main corbeled chamber.

They were in the Crystal Cave, talked about in all the Arthurian legends. In reality, it was a huge geode within a massive bolder that the megalith builders had placed right in the centre of the Knowth mound, exactly between the ends of the two opposing passageways.

As in his previous visit, Touchwood's eyes became adjusted to the dim light. Now he could see the treasures within. At one end of the cavern, an enormous cauldron sat, made of burnished bronze and etched with intricate designs on its sides. Interweaving knots and animals, crescent moons, and zigzags; with inlaid pearls around its rim. Touchwood knew this to be the cauldron of the Dagda, one of the four treasures of the Tuatha de Danann. The Lia Fail- the stone of destiny and the Spear of Lugh were, of course, missing.

But at the darkened end of the cave, could be seen the ancient, mummified remains of a tall man. He was wearing around his neck a golden crescent shaped lunula. Clutched across his chest in his bony arms was a magnificent sword, the legendary Excalibur, Núada's Sword of Light. This Touchwood knew now were the remains of the hyper human wizard Merlin.

And now he could see that Morgana was staring in that direction too. Her eyes glistened with tears, with an expression of such lonely sadness; it was hard to behold. Clearly, she still loved that hyper human being, who had been her husband in ages past; who had sacrificed his own life for her, so that she could transcend to the otherworld.

Merlin, who had been left alone on the earth plain by all others of the Tuatha tribe. Then, disillusioned by the shortcomings of the native humans, he had at last come to the Crystal Cave to die.

Leaving her to her grief, Touchwood, lowering his eyes, turned, and looked about for the treasures they had come to collect. There, he could see, placed on top of a willow work hamper was the Knife of Llawfrodedd the Horseman, one of the thirteen Treasures of Britain. And so too was the stone and ring of Eluned; the ring would make its wearer invisible when it was twisted round the finger, hiding the stone inside the wearer's fist.

He had already spotted at one end of the cavern the mysterious cauldron of the Dagda that had many powers but most notably the power of regeneration and rebirth, a magical cauldron able to resurrect the dead.

Touchwood's eyes once again turned to the mummified remains of Merlin. Morgana was now kneeling beside him, an arm outstretched, resting on Merlin's poor skull. Morgana, head bowed, was now openly weeping before her dead husband.

Touchwood had never seen Morgana looking so vulnerable and human before. She had always been so imperious, so in charge, so… frankly, bossy.

He realised now that it had all been a reaction to the deep pain of grief inside her. Reaction too, perhaps that they had never had children together. Morgana had informed him that after the destruction of the nation of Y's, the few survivors, now displaced from their homeland, for some unknown reason, experienced very few successful pregnancies and very few reached adulthood.

Perhaps, too, this was why she had become so attached to Victoria, wishing her to be the daughter she had never had. Touchwood had noticed her mood had certainly improved of late.

But now, seeing her genuine grief, Touchwood felt moved to comfort her. Quietly walking over to her, he bent down and placed a comforting arm about her shoulder. Her reaction surprised him, for she nuzzled her head into his chest and allowed his arms to embrace her. There, safe in his arms, she sobbed and wept like a child.

3

Selen had committed an illegal act by confiding with Star about the missing cauldron of Cyrridfen. This was one of the temple secrets, and Star knew it should not have been confided to a mere 6th degree priestess. Talking to her about the presence of the 'Hidden Ones' was an even worse offence, she knew. It brought a shiver down her spine just thinking about it. Star knew she had been naïve, thinking that everything about the temples was sun and roses. But she felt unworthy of holding this knowledge, and was concerned too that she might be found out, or unwittingly reveal that she knew.

Next time she met Selen in the apothecary it became apparent that she too was worried about the consequences of this illegal revelation. And Star began to worry about Selen. If the other adepts found out, they may, regardless of her temple standing, demote her or exile her to some Atlantean outpost on the mainland.

Because of this, Selen revealed to Star that she was going to announce to the elder council that she wanted Star to be her apprentice. It was a forgone conclusion, anyway. Selen had known this was Star's true path a long time ago.

As apprentice to a temple adept, Star would be regarded as equivalent to a seventh degree priestess. Consequently, she would be eligible to be initiated into certain temple secrets, which included the cauldron of Cyrridfen.

4

It was some weeks later, after Star had officially become Selens apprentice, that Selen had taken Star outside the walls of the Temple precincts to the city hospital, where, apart from her many other duties, she was consultant healer. That day Selen was scheduled to attend a patient at the Murias sleep temple, which was a wing off the main hospital.

The Sleep temples of Y's were also known as dream temples, and these temples served as sanctuaries for healing various ailments, both physical and psychological.

In these temples, priests and priestesses would guide patients into a state of deep relaxation and suggestibility, often using rhythmic chanting, soothing music, and repetitive rituals. This process aimed to induce a trance-like state, which is a key component in accessing the subconscious mind. The priests and priestesses of the temples had a firm belief in the healing power of dreams and divine intervention.

Upon waking, patients would recount their dreams to temple priests or priestesses, who were skilled in dream analysis. The interpretations would guide the prescribed treatments, which could include herbal remedies, dietary changes, or specific rituals.

Occasionally patients were admitted with deep-rooted psychological or mental health problems. So it was necessary during induced dream sleep, to take the patient on a shamanic journey to the otherworld, and find the parts of the soul that had been traumatised, and left the everyday mind, perhaps hiding away, in some deep-rooted or inaccessible part of the spirit-world. Many destructive habits could be cured in this way as well.

However, on this particular occasion, the patient needed surgery, as she had broken her thigh bone on a building site. It was necessary for Selen to induce a very deep anaesthetic sleep. Therefore, beforehand, the patient underwent purification rituals, including cleansing baths, prayers, and offerings to the Goddess of healing. The patient was then led to a special chamber, designed to induce sleep through hypnotic chants, auto suggestion and sedative herbs.

While the patient was in this very deep dream state, Selen, assisted by Star, could perform the necessary surgery to repair the damaged bone. The patient could not feel a thing and slept on, oblivious.

Star was particularly intrigued by the power of the Sleep Temples, and asked Selen if she could be instructed in the methods used. She could see the incredible versatility of such work. Selen said she would be delighted to teach Star the secrets of the sleep temples. But reminded her, however, that she still had to continue with her commitment to teaching neophytes in the halls of learning, and that she had her regular class on the morrow.

5

"Today, neophytes, we are going to talk about Earth Energy and liminal space. Does anyone know what liminal space is?" Star looked about the room, but not one hand went up.

"Oh… OK. Right, let's try it this way. You are all probably aware that throughout our islands there are certain places that are considered holy."

"Like the Temple's mistress," replied Lana eagerly.

"Yes, that's true. More than you think. But we will come to that later. I was thinking more on the lines of places like waterfalls, holy wells, underground chambers, and even the shoreline. Places where the elements meet. Have you not noticed that there is something about those places that feel special? They have a subtle mystery attached to them. This is because they are a 'thin place,' they are 'betwixt and between.'"

"Yes, miss," chipped in Leo, "I have been to some of those places and it sometimes feels spooky and weird. But what is 'a thin place?'"

"Oh!" Star exclaimed in frustration. Her eyes looked up to the sky, as if seeking inspiration, then puffed out her cheeks and took a big breath to calm herself. This was harder than she thought it was going to be. She tried another tack.

"Ok. Between our world and the spirit world, there is something known as 'the Veil.' It is a boundary between the worlds. But in certain places that 'Veil' is thin. This is a liminal space. It literally means a 'threshold' between one place and another. A place where the veil between this world and the ethereal world is thin.

"A 'thin place' is where one can perceive both worlds, where the two worlds become one. Liminal space denotes a time and space between the physical world, where you and I live, and the spirit world. Does everyone understand what I mean now?"

A dozen hands went up. "Yes, Zane, you have a question."

"How do we know when we are in a thin place, mistress?"

"Thin places aren't perceived with the five senses. Experiencing them goes beyond those limits. Some people notice the thinness. Some do not. This is why we in the Temples train ourselves to perceive these things, so we can work with them. But describing the meaning of a 'thin place' to a newcomer or someone not trained in the Temples is like describing 'love'... 'or fear'... the feeling of holding your newborn child... the presence of the Gods."

Star looked about the room. Every youthful face was growing with interest and fascination. She knew she was getting through to them. So continued.

"With the training you will receive here in the temples, to heighten your perceptions and hone your natural abilities. Thin places will captivate your imagination... yet somehow diminish our existence. We start to realise we are very small, yet we gain a connection and become part of something larger than we can perceive.

"By third grade, you will find a thin place pulsates with an energy that connects with our own energy; we feel it, but we may not see it. A thin place becomes a place where connection to the Otherworld, seems effortless, and ephemeral signs of its existence, are almost palpable.

"There are places in the world where the veil is perpetually thin, making it easier to connect with spirit. Areas where the veil is lifted or even non-existent are known as vortices. Our ancestors have been marking such sacred sites for thousands of years. Sometimes they are marked by a single stone called a menhir. Or sometimes by a circle of stones. But the marking stones can't just be any old stone. These stones must be a special sort of stone, one that contains crystals."

"What sort of crystals are they mistress?" called Reed.

"The main crystals that we look for in a stone are feldspar, quartz, and mica. You will learn what each of those crystals is used for in more advanced classes. But for the moment, we are just giving you a general overview.

"Now at these thin places, a special type of energy gathers which emanates from the earth. We call these dragon energies or sometime serpent energies depending on how strong they are. All you need to know for the moment is that the crystals in the stones gather and stores the serpent energies.

"There are clever priests called Dragonmancers or Geomancers who specifically work with these energies. They constructed stone circles, standing stones and other megalithic structures, to either amplify or redirect that force. They know how to project these gathered energies from one stone circle to another, and these straight paths of energy are called dragon paths. Their aim is to create a network of dragon paths because these energies have beneficial powers to living things. They feed people with life energy through the human chakras. Also, they sustained plants and animals, and even soil would feel dead without them. This increases the fertility of the land, animals and the humans living on it.

"Now class," Star rounded up. "It is almost time for

the break, so I suggest you quietly meditate on all we have learnt till then."

Chapter 18

Finnbar the Smith

1

To most people within the small archipelago of islands that Sliabh an Iarainn belonged to, life struggled on the best it could. Aware that no main stream civilisation was there to back them up. But oblivious to the inter-dimensional drama unfolding. Oblivious to the impending invasion of elf-human hybrids spawned by the dark elves.

There was a strong tradition of trading and bartering occurring between community villagers on the island all year round and often between the local islands of Shee-Beg, Shee-more and the Kilronan mountains to the west. Some groups specialised in fishing, either going out in boats with lines or laying salmon nets. Others reared sheep to make wool items to trade. Some, like the Rath Grain community, specialised in market gardens. They also traded meat when they had some to spare. Touchwood often used the services of an old farmer in a nearby village to kill and butcher his domestic animals; for no one in his community village could face that task.

Some villagers made home-brewed cider and wine, which was always a popular trade. There was even a group on the other side of the mountain island who made Irish moonshine, which locally was called Potcheen. On that far side of the island, also lived a family of blacksmiths which had renamed themselves Armstrong. Victoria was friends with their son Forge who was often asked to do blacksmithing work for Rath Grain.

Further afield, there was a boat builder on Sidhe-Mor that made long boats with four sets of oars. With it, they could go beyond the shallow sea, much further out, and catch deepwater fish.

However, with the change to milder weather from winter to spring, occasionally Sliabh an Iarainn had visits from more adventurous traders. Some came from the islands of the Wicklow mountains in the southeast and sometimes even further afield from the Purple Mountains in Killarney, way down in the southwest.

Finnbar was one of those who arrived with a group of traders in long boats with sails and ten sets of oars. They travelled from island to island, trading on their way. These traders were always welcome, not only for their wares but also for the news from faraway islands that they brought with them.

Finnbar, a travelling smith, arrived that morning at the Armstrong holding, bearing bricks of salt and delicious Dulse seaweed from the Conamara Island group. He brought copper and tin ingots from the Purple Mountains and he also had with him a variety of decorative brooches, combs, dress pins, armbands and bracelets - all in gold, silver, copper and bronze.

News of the trader's arrival had travelled quickly. That day, they had visitors from all across the island. So it was no surprise when Victoria and Brad turned up at the Armstrong's smithy looking for young Forge. Many of the islanders had brought goods to trade, and the holding had quickly transformed into a marketplace.

Surprised but delighted by the pop-up market, Brad and Victoria wandered through the crowds of traders, delighted with the lively atmosphere and all the wonderful smells and colours. Traders had laid out their wares on animal skins or colourful woven blankets, and engaged in lively haggling and bartering all through the day.

Victoria lingered for some time viewing all the colourful jewellery, quite forgetting her allotted task. Brad, however, with his disciplined military background, quickly sought out Forge to assign him the task of making the bronze spearhead.

Forge had accepted the commission, but only because that very day Finnbar, the travelling smith, had brought with him some copper and tin ingots needed to make the bronze. He promised to work on the spear making as soon as the trading fair was over. Brad, however, tried to stress the urgency of their project, and urge Forge to begin the next morning. But couldn't say too much unless it caused suspicion.

However, Brad and Victoria, being the young people that they were, had wanted to stay overnight and enjoy being part of the festivities. That evening, as it was fine weather, everyone congregated around a campfire in one of the wintering fields. They arranged a selection of animal skins and logs around the fire for sitting on. Finnbar was given the place of honour, upwind of the smoke, but fortunately, the fine weather continued, making it a very still night.

Finnbar was known to be a wonderful storyteller and had a good stock of stories, many being new to the islanders. However, it was still early evening, so he was telling stories to the young children that had gathered round him. They had come from the various villages about the mountain. Finnbar, a great stocky man, was sitting on a log with children all about his knees, listening in sleepy fascination.

"Listen, come gather round and I will tell you a story," began Finnbar, waving his muscular arms and encouraging any children that were still in the outside ring to come closer. His voice exhibiting a well-practiced storyteller's cadence.

"Perhaps you may wish to hear a story about the creation of the world…" he asked then waited, like the bard he was, till everyone had settled and was quiet before he continued?

"In the beginning. In a world that was not our world, for it was a place without time or substance; there lived a Dragon. She was black as coal, yet everywhere she went, there was snow and ice. It was like this from the very beginning of time, for countless Aeons.

"However, by some mystery, it came to pass that the black Dragon gave birth to two other dragons. A red dragon and a white Dragon. The little dragons were very happy and played with each other for centuries; for these creatures are very long-lived.

"But eventually they grew up, and as is the nature of beasts, they mated...." At this, several little girls called out "Euew..." in disgust. While several little boys laughed at this.

Undeterred, Finnbar continued, "Now a strange thing happened, for wherever they mated, the physical world came into being; around the place where they joined. And this is how our world started. And the more they mated, the more the physical world grew and grew."

Now it had become a 'thing' with the children. Every time the word 'mated' was mentioned, several little girls called out "Euew..." and several little boys laughed at them. Finnbar was well used to this reaction from children and paused each time to allow the audience participation.

"Now the black Dragon, being ancient and wise, knew that there could never be limitless growth in any world. So, at regular periods, she came into the physical world to destroy some of what the red and white dragons had created.

"She also decreed that the red dragon should live on the Earth and rule the time of growth. And that the white dragon should live in the sky and rule over the time of abundance. And so it has been ever since. So you see, my friends, the need for all these aspects in our beautiful world. But as we are also part of this world, we must abide by those rules. For as it is in the world about us, so it must be within each of us."

Whether the children truly understood all they heard is a guess, no one can make. But you can be sure that each child went to bed that night, dreaming of dragons.

Most of the visitors from the island had intended to stay the night, so earlier had made makeshift shelters using skins and tree branches. Now the very small children, already asleep, were taken to their temporary shelters, others a little older, protesting and wanting to stay, were wrapped and laid down nearby so they could listen, but their parents knew they would eventually fall asleep.

This shuffling and rearranging of seating lasted a while, so the storytelling held a temporary lull. Finnbar took a long draught from his ale mug, then placed a piece of salty driftwood across the fire, sending up a flurry of blue and green sparks. As it caught, Victoria thought the flames produced were the prettiest blue she had ever seen. But the smell of it was evocative of the sharp tang of the briny sea.

Seeing everyone else was busy for the moment, Finnbar looked over at Victoria still staring into the flames and said, "You have the look of one who has travelled to otherworlds young lady."

Quickly brought back to the present moment, she cast her green eyes at the travelling smith across the fire. His steely grey eyes held her gaze with an intensity she had seldom seen. Victoria could feel her face flushing and lowered her eyes, taken aback by this random comment. She didn't quite know what to say, but eventually answered, "How can you tell?"

"You have the look of an elf about you."

"Do you know about them too," she asked, puzzled?

"A Smith's craft involves alchemy that attracts visitors from the otherworld. So yes, I know of them."

"Perhaps you should talk with my grandfather. He

has known them for a long time. And now there is dire peril coming from that place."

Finnbar looked about him, checking if anyone else was listening. "I am aware of this 'dire peril' you speak of, but did not know that any other humans knew of it."

"We have several at my village who work to prevent it. When you are finished here, I will take you to them."

People had started returning to the fireside now, the shuffling and rearranging completed. Finnbar, unwilling to say any more, caught Victoria's eye and nodded.

Early next morning more visitors arrived looking to trade goods. Finnbar and Forge were kept busy trading. Therfore Brad and Victoria thought it best to make their way back to Rath Grain, leaving with promises from Forge that he would get to work on the spear the following day. Finnbar too had promised to visit Rath Grain, once he had done all his trading.

2

Touchwood and Morgana had returned from their visit to the Crystal Cave. With Morgana's magical help, they had materialised directly back into the Void craft and brought the treasures they needed back with them.

The enormous cauldron, sword, knife, and ring were sat in a pile on the void craft's mess hall floor. Touchwood and Morgana were now sat sipping coffee, which Dafydd had prepared for them. All of them were now looking at the gathered treasures with a mixture of awe and inspiration.

After some minutes, Dafydd spoke out, "Victoria and Brad have gone seeking Forge, the blacksmith. And Rumanadil is searching the void craft for anything that he thinks may be useful in this coming war. I was thinking, while you were away, that once we have some weapons, we could chance the rescue of your druid brother, Adge. Rumanadil suggested he could pilot the void craft, under Morgana's direction, to where he is in the otherworld," as he said this, he eyed Morgana, who imperiously nodded her consent.

"With a suitable weapon," Dafydd continued, "he could stand on guard while Morgana and I, release him. What think you?"

"Sounds good to me," replied Touchwood, lowering the coffee cup from his lips. Then, eying Morgana, knowingly continued. "But first I will need to test my new power and charge the weapons."

"Rumanadil seems to have taken to a crossbow he found in the armoury," said Dafydd. "And I think he should have the sword of Nuada too, as he is probably the only one who knows how to use it."

"We definitely need to be carrying the sword of Nuada," stated Morgana. "Utilising its original power, the one that makes the keeper insuperable; impossible to defeat. We will need all the help we can get."

Touchwood nodded his head in agreement. Thinking to himself that there wasn't a moment to lose, he stood up and took up the sacred sword, laying it across his hands. Then, summoning up the power that the Oak King had given him, he focused all that power on the sword laying on his hands.

As Dafydd watched, Touchwood began to glow all about his body, till it seemed like there was an Aureole, a radiant egg shaped field, all about him. Then he spoke the words in a voice that was not Touchwood's own:

"I, Touchwood, charge this weapon with the power ordained in me, so that 'none can stand against it.' This includes Gods, mythical creatures and all other spirit beings."

As he spoke, rays of flaming golden light flowed out of his hands and into the sword, till it too glowed with the golden light. Dafydd stood amazed, never having seen anything like it before. Meanwhile, Rumanadil bearing a crossbow across his shoulders had returned and now stood in the doorway staring in awe at the spectacle.

Gradually the golden light faded, but Touchwood, still glowing with an Aureole, handed the sword to Dafydd, who almost reluctantly held out his hands to receive it.

Then Touchwood turned again to Rumanadil and said, "I will need to charge your crossbow so that any bolts fired with it may have the same power as the sword."

Rumanadil, still taken aback by the unexpected spectacle, stepped forward and gingerly laid his crossbow across Touchwood's glowing hands. Again the strange voice spoke the words:

"I, Touchwood, charge this weapon with the power ordained in me, so that 'none can stand against it.' This includes Gods, mythical creatures and all other spirit beings."

Again, the rays of flaming golden light flowed out of his hands and into the weapon laid across them.

Gradually the golden light faded along with the glowing Aureole that surrounded Touchwood, who now returned the charged crossbow to Rumanadil.

Touchwood, the miraculous power having left him, staggered to his chair, and flopping down, pressed his hands to his head. Dafydd, concerned for his friend, placed the sword on a nearby table and bent over him, saying, "Old chap, I have never seen anything like it. Is this the power that the Oak King instilled in you?"

Touchwood didn't answer. He felt sick and his head was spinning too much. Dafydd looked about him for something to aid him and said, "Look, old friend, I think you need something a little stronger than coffee. I'll see what I can russel up from that food synthesiser over there."

Rumanadil, still looking at Touchwood in awe, went over to the table and picked up the sacred sword. Slowly removing it from its scabbard, he swung it about testing its weight and balance. He seemed well pleased with the result.

Dafydd returned with a bottle of 18-Year-Old Glenfiddich, and two small glasses, "Here old friend, this should perk you up."

He poured two glasses of the whiskey with a slightly shaking hand, placing one on the table besides Touchwood. Then, pausing only a moment to sniff the pungent liquor, downed it in one. Touchwood, still too overcome to try his own, only sat there, hands still holding his head; perhaps a little worried that it might fall off.

Rumanadil, still swinging and thrusting the great sword, seeming well satisfied with it, eventually stopped and brought the sword up to his eyes to scrutinise it more closely. After a moment or two, he exclaimed, "Dafydd, I have never used a sword so perfectly balanced. It feels like someone made it especially for me."

Dafydd, while pouring another shot from the bottle, replied, "Perhaps that is a result of the magic with which it was charged. You have Touchwood to thank for that."

Nodding in agreement, Rumanadil stepped over to Touchwood and bent down on one knee before him. "Sir, I thank you for this wonderful sword. With it, I feel ready to rescue your druid brother. It is the least I can do for you."

Touchwood, slowly recovering now, looked up into Rumanadil's eyes, and smiling, replied, "I would be very grateful if you did, friend."

Then reaching for his glass of whiskey downed it in one, "Now I think I am ready for my own bed, above my own stove, in my own cottage."

With that, he walked, a little unsteadily, towards the mess hall door.

Chapter 19

Luminara

1

On returning to Rath Grain, Rumanadil had parked the void craft under the shelter of the trees in the community garden again. Freeing Adge from imprisonment in the Oak tree had been surprisingly uneventful. They had not encountered any dark elves or even grey guards, in that fetid marshland of Tech Duinn; a treacherous and oppressive corner of the dark elves' realm.

As Morgana's spell had put him there in the first place, it had been a fairly straightforward spell removal, but she still had to replace him with a handy boulder. Morgana, of course, had made much of it, seeking comfort this time from Rumanadil.

The only issue had been immediately after Adge had been released. Poor Adge had been so pleased to be free. On seeing Morgana again, he threw his arms about her in a great bear hug, then burying his shaved head in her ample bosom had wept copiously.

Morgana had found this performance very distasteful

and threw him off her. Rumanadil, protective of Morgana, approached, bearing his sword. Confused, Adge mistook him for a dark elf warrior and attempted to fight him off with a fallen oak branch. It wasn't until Dafydd had stepped in to try to calm the situation, and reassure Adge that Rumanadil was their bodyguard, and on their side that things calmed down.

Dafydd went on to introduce Adge to the void craft. And transporting him inside had kept Adge's confused and addled mind busy for the remainder of the voyage.

2

In his own room and in his own bed, Touchwood had slept like he had never slept before. He had come to dislike the sanitised, white, soulless environment of the void craft. With its utility, army bunks and hard benches.

But as he drifted off to sleep, his mind wandered randomly over the activities of the last few days. He realised that he had no idea how much time had passed, in the outside world, while he had been inside the Void craft. Did time pass differently, like it did in the Otherworld? The environment inside seemed timeless and otherworldly. But he had to admit that the concept of the void craft was ingenious. Its ability to travel between dimensions, and otherworlds, all the while maintaining an otherworld environment for those inside, was like the bubble of air maintained inside a submersible, exploring the ocean depths.

He began to wonder if there were other worlds besides the one he visited, when talking to the Oak King. He had come to understand that the 'Otherworld' was archetypical for his own world, the one he was in now.

Each tree in the otherworld was the 'spirit essence', the Quintessence for its shadow, in his own world. And that when he 'projected' to the Otherworld, it was his spirit body that existed there, and that he was, as shamans called it, 'spirit walking' while there. So he began to wonder what was happening when his physical body was in the void craft, talking to a spirit being like Morgana? And what would he be, if he did travel in the void craft, to those possible other worlds? It all began to seem very complicated...

"Grandpapa... Grandpapa, wake up," exclaimed Victoria as she gently shook his shoulder. "Finnbar is here to see you."

"Wha..." Touchwood groggily opened his eyes to find Victoria's concerned face looking down at him.

"You have been asleep for twenty-four hours! I was beginning to be concerned. Are you alright?"

Touchwood sat up in bed, the sleepy grogginess fading fast. He did a quick health scan of his body.

"Yes," he said. "I feel fine. In fact, I feel wonderful." Touchwood could hardly believe it. He felt better than he had felt in years.

"We came back yesterday to find you asleep. Me and Brad, that is. We have given Forge the details of the spear-head you gave us. He promised to work on it as soon as the traders have left. Oh, speaking of traders, Finnbar the smith has come to see you. He is down in the kitchen now with Brad. But there is something else."

She paused a moment, not sure how to say it. "He knows about the dark elves Grandpapa, says he wants to help. I said you would explain everything to him. The void craft is back in the garden now, so I'm going to find

Morgana to see what else I can do to help."

Without another word, Victoria clambered down the steps of the bed platform and slammed the door behind her.

After this outburst, Touchwood's head was spinning again. 'Teenagers,' he thought, 'they seem to operate at a thousand miles an hour'. Chuckling to himself, he got dressed and went down to the community kitchen to see Finnbar.

3

As soon as Rumanadil had finished piloting the void craft back to Rath Grain. Morgana at his side, had made it quite clear, that she required his attentions back in their chosen room, in the crew's quarters.

Meanwhile, Dafydd had continued his tour of the void craft, all the while bringing Adge up to speed with all that had happened while he had been imprisoned. He had told him about the war council and the retrieval of the treasures from the Crystal Cave. However, Dafydd had found it very hard going, for Adge kept being distracted by things he saw about him. Adge couldn't seem to focus on anything for very long. Dafydd realised therefor that being trapped and immobilised by an ancient tree in a timeless, gloomy and oppressive marshland had unfortunately addled Adge's mind.

After a while Dafydd had wearied of touring the void craft with Adge. He felt he was wasting his time talking with him. The man needed time to adjust to being mobile again; that he could understand. But perhaps harder to understand was that Adge was now a spirit being. Dafydd had never actually met Adge before, in physical form or in spirit body. He had only ever spoken to him over the phone. Dafydd had, however, been impressed with his abilities and had expressed that he thought the man was a budding alchemist. However, seeing him like this made him regret that he had not made the effort to know him while he was in his prime. He could not imagine what it would be like for a spirit being, who normally had all-sorts of miraculous abilities, while in the otherworld, to be restricted and entombed, yet still sentient. It would surely drive you mad. Dafydd sincerely hoped that the man would recover, given time. And thought that perhaps he could better serve Adge if he found him a room to sleep it off. Finding one of the crew's bunk rooms, he showed him the bunk bed and left Adge to sleep.

4

Victoria had found the void craft hidden under the trees in the community garden. She had seen what Dafydd did to gain access to the craft. So she thought she would try to 'will' herself aboard. She thought very hard about being inside and strongly visualised the mess hall inside the craft.

Suddenly she was there inside the void craft again. There was the kitchen, the mess hall tables, and the benches. And the food synthesiser hatch. But nobody seemed to be there. She called out, "Morgana!"

No answer.

"Dafydd!"

No answer.

So she walked around the Mess hall. There seemed to be several hallways leading off in different directions.

But she remembered Dafydd's warning about getting lost on the void craft and decided she didn't want to risk that. She looked again at the food synthesiser hatch, the one that had produced the delicious chocolate ice cream. Without a second thought she went over to the hatch, thinking about the ice cream with its delicious creamy coldness. And there it was, in the hatch like magic.

After two more helpings, she began to feel she had had enough. Her tummy was bloated and now feeling slightly sick. She felt like a little nap would do her good. She might as well while she waited for the others. Resting on her arms on the mess hall table, she bent her head down on them and immediately drifted off.

After a period of deep REM sleep, she entered that semi-waking state, somewhere between sleep and awake. Hypnotherapists call this the twilight state. Brain wave measurements during this state oscillate at about 3 to 8 Hertz, and we call them Theta waves. It is a semi-dream state, dominant in deep meditation or deep hypnosis, where subjects get vivid imagery and strong intuition. And where they often receive uncanny information beyond our normal awareness.

Of course, Victoria didn't know any of this. She just found it remarkably easy to drift off into the otherworld, where she wandered through a forest of noble trees that stood so silent and still.

The trees were immense. Dark and overpowering, they shouldered over the track, towering like castles. As she continued walking, she had a wonderful sense of euphoria. The lucid colours of nature delighted her, feeding her soul.

Further on, she came to an area of great gnarled

oaks and yews that looked to be hundreds of years old. On her island home, she had never seen trees like these. After a while of walking, a clearing appeared before her and a circle of hazel trees. As she walked into the clearing, gradually she began to see the wonderful shimmering crystal-clear pool she had seen the last time she visited, and sure enough, nine hazel trees bearing fruit surrounded it. Bright birds were in the branches singing happily as they might during the dawn chorus. Victoria stood transfixed by the beauty of the place.

But then suddenly, it seemed to Victoria that everything grew still, and all around her, things seemed to distort and shift like it was very far away. Everything seemed all at once distant and small, yet somehow looming over her.

Then, a glowing nimbus of light suddenly appeared before her, the intensity almost blinded her, and she instinctively stepped back, raiseing her hands to her eyes to protect them. An icy shiver ran down her back.

Then the intensity of the glow slowly diminished, and she began to discern a shape within the glow. The shape seemed to be human, but there were streamers of multicoloured light emanating from it in all directions. This too slowly diminished as she squinted through the slits of her eyes, till she could just discern a womanly shape. A fiery flame emanating from the shoulders of the figure, looked somewhat like wings.

"Do not be afraid Victoria. I have not come to harm you." The glowing light being seemed to say; although she could see no lips moving.

Victoria was terrified, for she had never seen anything like it before. The terrifying power of the being was tangible, like staring into the bubbling magma chamber of a volcano. But Victoria held her ground, straightening her back, standing firm and centred, and asked.

"Are you the Goddess, come to me?"

"I am not the Goddess Victoria. My kind could be called Her emissary's if you like."

"What is your name," asked Victoria?

The luminous being drew near to her. "You may call me Luminara, if it pleases you."

But then Victoria noticed that there seemed to be a strange smell that came with this glowing being. Not unpleasant, but a curious fragrance like some unfamiliar herb cast onto a fire.

Victoria lifted her hand to touch the glowing light being. But immediately the being drew back saying, "You cannot touch me, and live Victoria. Be careful."

Victoria immediately lowered her hand but smiled at the being and asked, "What is it you require of me, Luminara?"

"Rest assured, we are aware of the plight of humanity Victoria, and how it terrifies you. We have come to make you strong, for you have been chosen. Chosen to help restore the balance."

With these words the light being lifted both her hands towards Victoria. Suddenly a terrific wind blew up, the ground began to shake like an earthquake. A fiery flame emanating from the hands of the light being, flowed towards Victoria, engulfing her entire body. Everything about her seemed to distort and shift and swirl about like an enormous whirlpool. The fiery flame emanating from the hands of the light being, swept up Victoria like a paper boat, swirling he round and round, and down and down, deep into the maelstrom.

Victoria awoke with a scream on her lips, violently jumping bolt upright. To find herself alone in the mess hall. The table covered in water. All her clothes and hair were soaking wet.

Chapter 20

The Forge

1

"Finnbar old friend, it is so good to see you again. It has been too long since you saw fit to visit this old man," said Touchwood, as he strode over to Finnbar, extending his hand.

Finnbar was sitting at a table in the community refractory. Brad had found him some leftover goat stew from the previous evening. And a hunk of barley bread to mop up the sauce. But immediately Finnbar stood up when he heard Touchwood's voice and the two clenched arms in a warrior's greeting.

"Ye Gods, you seem to look younger and fitter than the last time I saw you old friend. Please tell me your secret," Finnbar chuckled as they both fixed each other with their eyes. Then embraced in a great man hug.

"I have to admit, I feel better today than I have in a long while," replied Touchwood. "But this is what we need to talk about."

Touchwood looked about him cautiously. Besides

Brad, there were several other community members ostensibly going about their work, but clearly eavesdropping their conversation.

"Err… I have something to show you in the workshop friend, that may interest you," continued Touchwood as he placed a friendly arm about Finnbar's massive shoulders and led him out of the refectory.

Once in the workshop and alone, Finnbar spoke out, "You old goat Touchwood. I've known you all these years and not once did you mention the elves and the mischief they are getting up to. You have Victoria to thank for enlightening me. I had been thinking I was the only one; or perhaps going mad."

"You are not mad, my friend. There are several here who know of this. But what has Victoria said to you, and how much do you know?"

The conversation continued, Finnbar relating what little he knew and Touchwood bringing him up to date with all that had happened in the otherworld in recent years. Poor Finnbar was white as a sheet towards the end, for he had not known how bad things had become.

Eventually Touchwood said that he needed to visit Forge, the blacksmith's son, to retrieve the bronze spearhead. Finnbar had volunteered to stay and help as much as he was able. So Touchwood asked him if he wouldn't mind making a spear shaft for the bronze head. As it transpired, Finnbar had had experience making spears before, as previously several people on the islands he had visited had requested spears for hunting. So Touchwood showed him the wood pile and gave him free rein to all the tools in the workshop.

2

Touchwood eased his hand around the edge of the cowhide that covered the doorway. A blast of heat hit him in the face. Inside, the brightness of the fire hurt his eyes, but he could see the silhouette of a stout youth bent over the forge.

"Shut the flap quickly and stand over there," the voice, harsh with impatience directed.

Touchwood did as he was bid. As his eyes adjusted to the flames, he could see the young smith knew his trade and how to build a smelting fire, stoking it small and hot and banking the edges so that the heat turned in on itself. The charcoal at the core glowed white, with small puffs of smoke and the white ash falling away. Now he could see the mould that stood in the heart of the fire, and the halo of blond hair as Forge reached up to pump the bellows.

Forge turned to him now and smiled, "It's almost ready to pour, your timing is perfect," his voice dry as the wind blowing through bulrushes. His leather apron of boiled ox hide was scorched with a myriad of burn marks. The bellows sighed again as he pumped, the fire crackled and roared, the mould glowing white hot at its core.

Now the young smith's muscular arm reached for a set of large tongs, and edged them into the fire, searching for the crucible of molten metal. Finding it, his hand slowly withdrew the crucible to the edge of the fire. He held his breath as he watched the surface of the liquid bronze. Satisfied, he then cast a sprinkling of flux crystals over it. Now slowly withdrawing the mould, both were now ready for the pour.

The smith bent his head and drew in a long breath, held it and with a steady hand, poured the thin stream of molten bronze into the cavity made in the mould. Mesmerised, Touchwood could hear the hiss and sigh of the air from the side vents, and little puffs of smoke could be seen emerging from the four vents.

The pour was good. Crucible, left to one side. The young smith now tapped the mould several times, knocking out any air bubbles. Finally he breathed out a long breath, the worst over.

With the long tongs, he placed the mould on his anvil.

"Now we have to wait for the mould to cool," said Forge as he turned towards Touchwood, removing his gloves and held out his calloused hands for him to shake. His muscled grip almost crushed Touchwood's bones, but he tried to give as good as he got.

"So, what's this all about Touchwood? Nobody uses bronze tools anymore."

Touchwood had hoped that Victoria had explained to him some ruse about the bronze spearhead. Now he had to think fast, "Ah… it is for Victoria… er, she is learning to hunt. And er… says that an iron spear is too heavy for her and needs one of bronze."

The young smith gave him a long stare. Touchwood felt embarrassed by the lie and could see disbelief in Forge's young eyes. But he said nothing, except to shrug and remark that perhaps she would be better off with wood.

All during their conversation he had been watching the surface of the metal in the mould, waiting for the scum on the surface to harden. Now it seemed ready for he stopped talking, reached for his hammer, and let it fall, splitting the mould in two, giving birth to the shining metal spearhead.

The smith took up his shorter tongs and dipped the hot spearhead in the quenching bucket, producing a peculiar high-pitched hiss while steam belched from the bucket. After a moment or two, he withdrew the tongues and placed the still-hot metal on the workbench. The workbench was already littered with a thousand blackened scorch marks.

"Can I touch it?" Touchwood asked?"

"If you want to burn your fingers?" Forge remarked with a smile. "Patience, is one of a blacksmith's hardest learned skills."

3

Touchwood, having walked across the island from the Armstrong's holding, decided it was best to go directly to the workshop. Having obtained the newly cast bronze spear head he wanted to see how Finnbar was doing with the spear shaft.

As he opened the workshop door, the pungent smell of beeswax and turpentine assaulted his nostrils. Oh, how that familiar smell, brought back the memories of years spent in this very workshop, making magical tools to sell at the markets. Brother Adge at his side, spouting some rubbish about how he had once been a roadie for Hawkwind, at the Stonehenge festival, back in 1983.

But now, there was Finnbar bent over the workbench, polishing rag in his hand.

"Finnbar! How goes it.?" called Touchwood as he entered the workshop.

"Perfect timing friend. Just applying the final polish. I

decided to go with a yew wood shaft. Not traditional I know but Yew trees have links to the death Goddess, and yew as a weapon is also said to bring swift, fast death. Yew wood, they say, has the ability to destroy established order. Which is what we need right now, is it not?"

Touchwood raised an eyebrow, impressed with Finnbar's knowledge of such things. "You sound like a druid old friend. I had no idea you had leaning's that way."

"Ah, Touchwood, you are not the only one with secrets. I have found that even today, it is best to keep those things close to your chest."

Touchwood nodded sagely as he bent to inspect the spear shaft. Finnbar had done a wonderful job of craftsmanship. Carved runes along the shaft acted as a grip for the hand and the beautiful colours of red and yellow and black stood out with the beeswax polish he had applied.

"You have excelled yourself Finnbar. It is truly a wonderful piece of craftsmanship. But now for the moment of truth. We need to marry the shaft with the head."

Touchwood reached inside his cloak and produced the bronze spearhead. He laid it across his hand, shining like burnished gold. The craftsmanship was superb, and Finnbar said as much, as he reached to lift it from Touchwood's outstretched hand. Lifting it close to his eye, he examined the flowing leaf shape of the blade, that complimented the shape of the gradual transition, from socket to blade. The design was very simple, with no embellishment to distract from the beautiful shapes created by the curvature of the blade and the shape of the transition.

Finnbar wasted no time. Laying the spear head and shaft on the bench together, he then made a detailed drawing on a flat piece of wood with a pencil, measuring carefully the inside and outside measurements of the socket. Then went to work with his whittling knife, cutting the shaft in a perfect taper to fit the spear socket perfectly. When he had finished, he pushed the whittled shaft end into the spear socket. The fit was tight, as it should be. But then Finnbar held the spear vertically with the head uppermost; it was half a head taller than he was. Then he lifted it a foot or so, and dropped the end onto the stone floor, several times. Now he tried to pull the spearhead from the shaft. It was solidly in place, with no adhesive necessary. However, not content with that, he took it over to the drill stand and asked Touchwood to crank the handle, which, through a series of gears, turned the drill chuck. Using a small drill-bit, he drilled a tiny hole right through the bronze socket, through the wood and out the other side. Then, placing a nail he had sourced earlier, punched it through socket and wood, cut the protruding nail off close and taking a ball-peen hammer, he deformed the rivet tail.

"That spear head will never pull off now," he declared with a chuckle, as he passed the finished spear for Touchwood to inspect.

4

Touchwood had transported Finnbar into the void craft. They were now walking through its corridors towards the mess room. He had promised Finnbar a cup of real coffee, as a reward for his hard graft in the workshop. However, Finnbar was still in shock at discovering the existence of such an outlandish device, that seemed to be a silver ball on the outside, but was vast inside. As he and Touchwood walked along a corridor, he was looking about in wonder.

Suddenly, they were in the mess hall. But Touchwood could not believe his eyes, for there, was his druid brother Adge. He was sitting at a table, munching away at a sizeable chunk of blue veined cheese.

Touchwood stopped so suddenly, that Finnbar almost bumped into him. "Adge?" he whispered. "Is that really you, old druid friend?"

But Adge didn't respond. He was so engrossed in a world of his own; munching the cheese was his whole being. Touchwood strode up to him, and placing a friendly hand on his shoulder, calling, "Adge, it's me, Touchwood. So good to see you. It is you, Adge, isn't it?"

The poor creature looked up from its meal, clutching his prize close to his chest. Then slowly, very slowly, recognition dawned in his eyes.

"Touchwood?" Adge managed in a rasping voice.

"Yes friend, it is me. We have been so worried about you. Morgana told me about how she had accidentally imprisoned you in a tree. But the dark elves were running crazy, after Dafydd killed their king. It became too dangerous to attempt a rescue, till we had suitable weapons and…"

But it became obvious that Adge was no longer listening. His attention had wandered back to the hunk of cheese clutched in his hands. Like some feral creature, he began to nibble away at a corner of it. But Touchwood noticed that his hands were trembling, and he was sweating profusely.

Puzzled by his strange behaviour and feeling hurt now, Touchwood tried again.

"Adge, it's me. Don't you recognise me, old friend...?"

But Finnbar came behind Touchwood and quickly grabbed his arm before he could start shaking the poor creature's shoulder.

"I think it might be best to leave him for a while," advised Finnbar. " I'm sure he is suffering from PTSD. I have seen it too many times these last years. Your friend might become violent if he feels threatened. That sort of trauma stress is a terrible thing."

Touchwood let his hand fall to his side. Looking at Adge a moment, and then again at Finnbar, then nodded.

"You might be right Finnbar, my druid brother is definitely not himself. Perhaps we should show him to a room where he can rest and maybe recover."

Finnbar nodded. So the two of them, one to each arm, very gently led the poor creature, still clutching his chunk of blue veined cheese, to one of the single rooms.

When Touchwood and Finnbar got back to the mess hall, Dafydd was there.

"Ah, Touchwood. We rescued your friend Adge. But he does not seem at all well. I put him to bed. But later found him wandering the corridors. I was afraid he would get lost in here forever. So I dropped him off in the mess hall, and showed him the food synthesiser, taught him how to use it, and left."

"Yes, I found him here with some blue veined cheese. He is back in bed again now." Touchwood then introduced him to Finnbar the smith, and informed Dafydd that he was willing to be part of the war council. Finnbar showed the finished spear to Dafydd, who greatly admired it, saying that the craftsmanship was every bit as good as the original Spear of Assail.

Then Dafydd pricked up his ears, for he heard footsteps in a corridor and said, "Oh, by the way Touchwood, I've been meaning to tell you. I think there is something that you need to see."

Touchwood turned to Dafydd with a questioning look. "What do you mean?"

But just then there was a loud blood curdling battle cry from across the room. All eyes quickly turned to see three figures stood just beyond the doorway. Touchwood immediately recognised Rumanadil, who was still dressed as a dark elf warrior, but his face was now painted with war paint, and he carried a mean-looking crossbow. He stood on the right.

On the other-side was another male warrior, dressed somewhat like Rumanadil. But after a moment or two, Touchwood realised this must be Brad. He carried a curved Arabian type sword. Both male warriors looked very intimidating, but no less was the female warrior who stood between them. But who was she?

Her blond hair, braided in a warrior's plait, ran halfway down her back. She had blackened her eyes with a wide band of paint, and painted two red finger width bands from her bottom lip down her chin. Blue woad spiralling patterns, adorned the rest of her face.

Her half naked body, was adorned only by a wide plaited leather band, about her chest, and large areas of her lithe body, were painted with woad spirals and streaks. She sported soft leather leggings, supported by a wide plaited leather belt, from which hung several leather pouches. Slung across her shoulder was a quiver full of deadly arrows, and in her hands, she clutched an ancient yew bow, yellow and black.

But her face! Her face looked so fierce. And those eyes! Those eyes, green as grass.

"Victoria!" exclaimed Touchwood, half disbelieving.

From her mouth came another blood-curdling scream, so loud he could feel its vibration in his chest. She crouched down on one knee and quickly drew her bow, an arrow notched ready to fire, pointing directly at him.

Touchwood backed away in horror. But the challenge was obvious. Victoria was leaving no room for argument from her grandfather.

"Look's like our SWAT team is ready to go," declared Dafydd with an amused grin.

Chapter 21

Weapons

1

Three mugs of strong coffee sat steaming on the mess hall table, deep within the Void craft. Touchwood, still recovering from the shock of seeing his granddaughter transformed into some sort of shield maiden, was sitting in a heap on the uncomfortable chair, and had not touched his coffee yet.

Dafydd stood talking to Finnbar, getting to know him in his own ineffable way. Finnbar, eager to sample the promised 'real coffee', reached for his mug and tentatively sipped. Raising his eyebrows in surprise, he declared it was the best he had tasted for many a year.

Victoria, Brad and Rumanadil had gone back down the corridor to look for Morgana.

"So, all in all, it looks like we are almost ready to raid the Dark elves, Touchwood. Don't you agree?" remarked Dafydd as he strode over to Touchwood.

Touchwood distractedly looked up at Dafydd. "What was that?"

"Drink your coffee man. We need to be on high alert, now that we are almost ready to make our raid on those dark elf councillors. We need to make plans and quickly, before they have got themselves organised again."

Touchwood reached for his coffee and took a deep gulp of it., "What on earth has happened to Victoria? I thought she was going to kill me."

Dafydd smiled and asked, "Did you notice how she had changed?"

"She has changed beyond all recognition Dafydd."

"No. I mean yes. But, did you notice her ears?"

Touchwood looked at him blankly.

"They have grown pointed like an elf's," said Dafydd.

"I thought she was indeed an elf warrior," said Finnbar, nodding in confirmation. Then sudden realisation hit him. "Was that little Victoria, your granddaughter Touchwood? Last time I saw her, she was only as tall as my chest."

Touchwood looked about him, bewildered. "Now you come to mention it, I did notice something. But her clothes and weapons and ferocious actions were so distracting, it didn't register till now. What has become of her Dafydd?"

"I had a chance to talk with her earlier, while you were away. Apparently, she has been experiencing some sort of temporal entanglement, with a priestess from the lost nation of Y's, that was destroyed some twelve thousand years ago. Through this entanglement, she has gained much secret knowledge - herb lore that only the mystery schools knew. She also has developed certain magical powers. She said she has also visited the otherworld, and encountered a light being who, in

Victoria's words, 'made her strong.'"

During all this, Touchwood, still holding the coffee mug halfway to his lips, stared at Dafydd in shock and disbelief.

"I think you need to face up to it old chap," continued Dafydd. "Your granddaughter has grown up fast; she knows her own mind; has developed magical abilities; and most strange of all, I believe somehow she has become a high elf."

Touchwood with a shaking hand brought the mug to his lips and downed it in one. Dafydd, understanding his distress, went over to him and laid a comforting hand on his shoulder.

"Look old chap. I know it is a lot to take in, but we need to get ready. We are at war; whether we want it or not. We are all relying on you, old friend, to 'charge' the weapons so they can kill off those diabolical dark elf councillors."

Dafydd looked over at the remaining treasures, still on the floor of the mess hall, then eyed the gigantic cauldron of the Dagda.

"And I feel very strongly, that we can't risk taking the cauldron of regeneration and rebirth, to Tech Duinn in case it is captured. We will need to hide it somewhere in your community Touchwood."

Touchwood nodded his head in acknowledgment and took a great sigh. It was all he could do at the moment.

2

When Victoria returned to the mess hall looking for food, she first strode over to Touchwood, who was still deep in thought and still sat at a table. As he looked up, he thought, was it his imagination but had she actually grown taller as well? Victoria loomed over him. She still seemed intimidating. The war paint was very convincing.

Trying not to make it obvious, Touchwood looked coyly at her ears. Yes, they had grown elf like. Elongated and pointed towards the top.

"Grandpapa, I want to apologise for startling you earlier," began Victoria. Her voice seemed to have changed too. It was more confident now, much deeper, with more resonance.

"The warrior in me, seemed to just take over at that point, and came rushing out. Rumanadil told me, I need to be able to control the warrior's rage, and to never direct it at a friend. It is against the warrior's code of honour. He told me I need to apologise." As she said this, she bent down on one knee and laid her bow across her arms, offering it to him. "You hold my life in your hands."

"My dear child," said Touchwood as he stood up. "How you have grown. It is me who needs to apologise. I have been blind to your growth. I have tried to hold you back. But what I see now is a wonderful thing."

He stood up, and went over to the treasures that still lay on the mess hall floor. Picking up the Ring of Eluned, he turned again to Victoria, "I want you to have this, it will protect you," he held it in the palm of his hand. As he looked at it, he realised that it really was too small for any male warrior.

"What does it do, Grandpapa?"

"It is the Stone and Ring of Eluned, one of the legendary thirteen Treasures of Britain, thought to be lost for all time. It has magical properties."

Victoria took it from his hand and slipped it onto her first finger of her left hand. It was a perfect fit. The colour of the green emerald stone matched her eyes.

"Its beautiful Grandpapa. Thank you so much."

"It can make you invisible and thus undetectable. It may save your life when you go hunting dark elves."

Victoria suddenly realise the implications of this. That he had accepted her as a warrior and had consented to her going to Tech Duinn with the other warriors. Overcome, she threw her arms about his neck and kissed him on the cheek.

Touchwood, hardly able to hold back a tear, tenderly said to her, "Here, I will tell you how it works. The ring will make its wearer invisible when the ring is twisted round the finger, hiding the stone inside the wearer's fist. You should try it before you go."

Her excitement bubbling over, and unable to contain it any longer, she did a little victory dance right there in the mess hall. Then she simply disappeared.

"Victoria!" exclaimed Touchwood.

Silence.

"Victoria, are you still with us?" Touchwood was sounding extremely worried now. He had no idea what actual powers the ring had. He cursed himself for not testing it first. For all he knew, it could have transported her to a dark elf prison!

But then suddenly she reappeared again, right where she was before.

"Just messing with you Grandpapa," Victoria giggled. "Seems to work fine. I could see and hear everything you did, but the funny thing was I could still see myself. So I wasn't sure it had worked properly. However, clearly you couldn't see me. But Grandpapa, you forgot to tell me how to reappear again, silly. But I figured it out. I just twisted the ring so the gem stone was visible again."

Touchwood was so relieved that he gave her a big hug again. But Victoria squirmed out of his embrace and said, "You know, Grandpapa, I'm famished. I'm going to get something from the food synthesiser thingie."

Touchwood shouted after her. "Make sure it's some proper food, not just ice cream. Warriors need their strength."

"Sorry to intervene, old chap," said Dafydd. "But we need your services again to charge all the weapons that are to go with the task force to Tech Duinn."

He looked round at Finnbar. "Can you help me and Touchwood to round up all the weapons? We can place them here with the others.

3

Finnbar, Dafydd and Touchwood had gathered all the various weapons that were to be used on the raid to Tech Duinn. They had been placed in a pile in the mess hall. The Dagdas cauldron was dragged to one side, as this was to be hidden somewhere in Rath Grain; at this point Touchwood had no idea where.

Then, in a ceremony that everyone attended, Touchwood had charged the weapons 'so that none can stand against them'. Just as he had done before. Only this time, he had charged them all at the same time. Rumanadil also had felt it important that everyone swear a warrior's oath of allegiance to the cause of the war council. This caused a few murmurings, as some felt they were not warriors. But in the end, everyone had sworn allegiance. Touchwood noticed also that none of the weapons were made of iron: swords and knives were bronze, bolts and arrow tips were flint.

The strike team had now become Victoria, Brad, Rumandil, and Finnbar. Dafydd had rethought and decided that a human needed to carry Núada's Sword of Light, so he gave it to Brad to bear. Rumanadil already had his charged cross bow & bolts, so now reached for the curved Arabian sword. Next Victoria reached for her Yew bow and arrows. She already had the Ring of Invisibility - The Stone and Ring of Eluned.

Lastly, Finnbar reached for the newly forged bronze spear. He had fitted the yew wood shaft, so had taken quite a liking to it. Then Dafydd reached inside his cloak. He had almost forgotten that he still had Arthur's cloak of invisibility, the one that Goibniu had given him to escape the dark elf prison. He considered for a moment, but then handed it to Finnbar. "This may help you in Tech Duinn. Promise you will share it with the others."

Finnbar shook him by the hand and nodded his assent. "I thank you brother Dafydd."

Touchwood looked down at the mess hall floor. All the weapons had been distributed except the Knife of Llawfrodedd. Solemnly he bent down, picked up the knife and weighing it in his hand considering. It was well made, more of a dagger really, with a very sharp point and two sharp edges. It was small enough to be concealed in clothing and could be secretly produced if in close contact fighting.

He eyed Victoria and walking over to her, laid the dagger across his palm holding it out saying, "For you brave maiden, keep this well hidden. It could come in handy if you get captured."

Solemly Victoria accepted the blade, meeting his eyes unwaveringly. The warrior in her knew just how useful such a weapon could be in close contact fighting.

4

Going back a bit to the time when Touchwood had slept for twenty-four hours in his own rooms. And Victoria had entered the Void craft mess hall by herself to find no one about. Remembering she had fallen asleep and had had her encounter with the light being. Afterwards, she had awoken with a scream on her lips, only to find herself alone in the mess hall. The table covered in water and all her clothes and hair were soaking wet.

With the vision of the light being, still burning in her mind, she had stood up disorientated and puzzled by what had happened, but quickly realised she really did need to change her soaking clothes. So wondering what the void craft might have to offer, she dared to leave the mess hall. Searching the corridors, she found many small sleeping rooms with bunk beds four to a room. But no change of clothes. But in one of the bunk rooms, she found a strange being.

He was crouched in a corner of the room, sat on the floor, with his hands clasped over his head. He looked like he was expecting the ceiling to come crashing down on him. Her heart melted, and the healer in her kicked in. She slowly went over to him, and crouched down in front of him, gently placing her hands on his shoulders.

Immediately, his head shot up in a start, his eyes met hers. She could see there was madness there, but also terror. Immediately, she recognised who it was.

She had encountered him in the otherworld when Touchwood had taken her there. It was Grandpapa's friend and druid brother Adge. He had seemed sane enough then, but now she knew there was something very wrong. But she had had no experience treating such problems.

There had been a moment of recognition in his eyes, but then they had become unfocused and dim. He began trembling and sweat was forming on his brow. Victoria felt so sorry for this miserable creature and vowed to help him somehow. Raking her brains for an answer, she realised she needed help. Star would know what to do. Yes, Star, that was who she needed to contact now.

Leaving poor Adge for the moment, she went searching again for some dry clothes and a place she could lie down, meditate and journey to her mentor Star.

.

Chapter 22

The Battle

1

Dafydd and Morgana stood beside the enormous bronze cauldron in the community garden of Rath Grain. Touchwood had gone on ahead to see if he could find a suitable hiding place for the Tuatha treasure. They watched as the glowing void craft rose into the night sky, gradually getting smaller and smaller as it floated towards the summit of Sliabh an Iarainn. Then it seemed to wink out as though it had never been.

Dafydd didn't envy the occupants of the craft, or their mission. He had had firsthand experience of how ruthless and cruel the dark elves and their grey guards could be. But he kept silent about that, instead asking Morgana if she, in her long life, had had any experience using the magical properties of the Dagdas cauldron.

"Not as such, no. Its exact location was always a closely guarded secret. However, there were many rumours that it was located in the Brú na Bóinne, but no one could say where. There were also many of our tribe who professed to seeing the Drui Masters use it after a battle; warriors wounded in battle could be immersed in it, and they would emerge whole and restored. In some tales, the cauldron could even bring the dead back to life.

"Of course, I was a mere child in those days and didn't pay much attention to such things. And then later, when the Tuatha tribe transcended to the otherworld, it was hidden away in a secret location, said to be: 'In darkest depths. Where no ordinary man may set foot.'"

Dafydd nodded. He remembered those exact words from 'The Song of Merlin' that he had discovered combing through the ancient documents held by the St. Johns Hospitallers. It had been in ogham script in a very old Brythonic language, and coded in cryptic poetic language. It had stumped him for quite some time, but with Touchwood's help, they had eventually discovered 'the Crystal Cave', the hiding place of the Tuatha treasures, along with many other magical tools. And, of course, this very cauldron he was now standing beside.

Touchwood suddenly reappeared out of the darkness. Breathless, he took a moment to catch it before declaring between pants, "I have been all over Rath Grain... initially I wanted to put it inside the house but it is too big to get through the doors... I thought of the cave nearby, that I have used for ritual, but the passageways are too narrow... in short... the only place it will fit is the turf shed. Not very elegant, I know, for such a treasure, but we can cover it with turf and I have some old iron cartwheel rims to put over it. That should keep the grey elves away if they come snooping. I reckon it will be safe there until the winter."

"Don't expect me to go near those iron rings," Morgana replied with a look of distaste.

2

In the very heart of Tech Duinn, the dark elves' realm, stood the mighty castle that belonged to the former King Indech. Its black basalt walls sculpted to give the appearance of melting lava that had suddenly cooled while dripping down its sides. It stood in a vast area of fetid marshland and sulphurous pools. Over head blue-black clouds formed grotesque shapes as they scudded across the oppressive sky.

Rumanadil had landed the void craft in the large underground hangar area dug out of the bedrock beneath the castle. Previously, when Dafydd and Rumanadil had escaped their prison, they had made their way under the cloak of invisibility to the cavernous hanger which had accommodated dozens of void craft. Avoiding the grey elf guards, they had stolen the first one they had come to.

Now, when they emerged from their void craft, they found the hanger empty. Rumanadil, although surprised, blessed his luck that they had landed unseen. This stroke of luck had also raised more than a few concerns for Brad too, but his disciplined soldier's mind had focused on their mission to assassinate all the dark elf councillors before they elected a new king.

Rumanadil had led the way, as he was the most familiar with the layout of the castle. He led the strike team through a warren of tunnels, always ascending, making their way to the throne room. Rumanadil suspected this was the most likely place for the king's councillors to be gathered. However, the tunnels were strangely empty as well. This fact kept nagging at Rumanadil's mind as he wondered why this was so.

The tunnels had widened now as they had entered the castle proper, and he knew the throne room was not far away. When suddenly round the corner marched a squad of grey soldiers. Both parties were surprised by this encounter, but Rumanadil quickly lowered to one knee, and raising his cross bow, fired several bolts in quick succession.

Victoria immediately followed him, raised her bow and let fly several flint tipped arrows. The Greys in the front line of the squad squealed like pigs as they clutched their chests and fell to the ground like felled trees.

But the Greys behind surged forwards trampling over their colleagues. There were too many of them, and they quickly gained ground in between the strike team's reloads. Brad raised Núada's Sword of Light in readiness for the inevitable clash. Finnbar too raised his new bronze spear, ready to thrust.

But suddenly, from behind the strike team came a bloodcurdling battle cry, which struck fear into the hearts of each one of them, for they felt for certain they were now surrounded back and front.

Finnbar felt his bowels turn to water, but before he could turn to look, a large naked man, with a shaved head, pushed past him, grabbed the hilt of Rumanadil's curved Arabian sword and charged towards the remaining grey guards.

The naked man, was covered head to toe, in blue painted spirals and zigzag patterns. His long red beard, splattered with blue paint parted, and the large mouth opened to produce the most unearthly noise imaginable. With the Arabian sword raised, he descended on the grey guards before any of them realised what was happening. Victoria watched in horror as two Greys died, their heads split from crown to jaw bone. Swiftly turning, the blue painted man swung his sword cleaving sculls as if he were scything wheat.

Brad, quickly recovering from the surprise, joined the fray, raising Núada's Sword of Light, slashed out with his blade and felt it bite into the chest of a Grey. Two Greys broke off from the fray and charged towards the remaining task force. A blade scythed the air by Finnbar's head, -- ducking he stabbed out with his spear, his initial fear over taken by a battle rage that came from the very core of his being. The Grey, vomited blood in a red spray, and fell to the floor with a gurgled scream. Another Grey descended on Victoria, who backed up, till she was pressed hard against the corridor wall. Too late and too close to raise her bow, her terrified eyes, fixed on the approaching Grey. She fumbled for the Knife of Llawfrodedd tucked into her belt, but she was too slow: the grey guard had already raised his sword and was about to strike. Suddenly, his chest exploded in a fountain of blood, a barbed bolt protruding from the gore.

With not a second to lose, Rumanadil had fired his crossbow at point blank range into the Grey's back. Victoria, splattered with blood and gore, watched as the Grey tumbled to the floor in a heap. She looked up to see Rumanadil's imposing form clutching his crossbow. Briefly, their eyes met, and he slightly inclined his head, acknowledging a friend.

Victoria panted out a breath in relief. Her long blond hair, braided in a warrior's plait. A wide band of paint blackened her eyes, with two red finger width bands from bottom lip to chin. Shock turned to relief. Her handsome face, now splattered with blood, broke out in a wide smile, displaying her white teeth and her piercing green eyes, all relayed a deep felt gratitude verging on adoration.

It was all Rumanadil needed to spur him on. Quickly turning, he set the crossbow string and reached for a new bolt from his case, in readiness to lose another bolt. Inspired by this, Victoria quickly notched her bow and let fly. The arrow striking the back of a Grey who was about to decapitate the blue painted man; who she now recognised to be her Grandpapas, druid brother, Adge.

But Adge had been disarmed and was surrounded by four grey guards, who now realising that the strike forces weapons could destroy spirit beings, had taken Adges 'charged' Arabian sword. The Grey struck by Victoria's arrow staggered momentarily, but with the arrow still sticking out of his left shoulder, raised Adges 'charged' Arabian sword and thrust sideways into Adge's broad neck. He fell to his knees, spurting blood from the severed artery in his neck.

Brad and Finnbar rounded on the remaining four Greys that surrounded Adge. Brad's Sword of Light chopped at the Grey's arm, still clutching the Arabian sword, severing it clean off the shoulder. Victoria loosed another arrow, hitting her target in the gut. Finnbar dispatched another Gray with the new bronze spear. Rumanadil loosed several bolts into the remaining Greys. But one still remained standing, arrows and bolts sticking from his arms and legs. He looked about him, somehow surprised to see all his colleagues dead about his feet.

Victoria notched another arrow, and with her battle cry spewing from her lips, let fly another arrow, hitting the remaining Grey squarely in the heart. Victoria would never forget the look of loathing and hate in the eyes cast towards her, as the Grey fell backwards like the felling of a giant tree.

The battle over, Victoria ran to Adge's side, checking to see if she could find any signs of life. With Brad, Rumandil and Finnbar looking on, Adge slowly opened his eyes and regarded Victoria's concerned face. He smiled up at her then rasped, "Thank you, brave elf, for your help in giving me the perfect death."

His head fell limp to one side and Adge was no more.

3

Inside Touchwood's kitchen, the wood stove had eventually caught, and the pine wood kindling was roaring up the chimney. It was a chilly evening, and the kitchen was feeling damp from lack of use. Touchwood had no idea how long had passed in the physical world, while he had been coming and going from the void craft. But he suspected it had been several weeks.

Morgana leaned silently against the back wall. She seemed subdued, turning inward. Perhaps she was feeling the effect of losing the energy field of the void craft.

"Pity we didn't think to synthesise some bottles of whiskey, while we were on the void craft. Would have come in very hand round about now," bemoaned

Dafydd.

Touchwood, still fussing with his wood stove, threw on some larger logs and nodded in agreement. Then said pointedly, "Yes. And it's a pity someone polished off my last bottle of sloe gin! Otherwise we could have had that."

Touchwood stood up, stretching his back. Then walked over to the workbench, feeling the tea pot there. It was stone cold. Picking up a griddle cake from the plate that was still there, he tapped it on the workbench; it was hard as stone.

"You know Dafydd, I think we have been gone quite some time. Remember those griddle cakes Ruby brought in for us? It only seems a couple of days ago, but they are rock hard."

Dafydd stepped over to the bench, "And the cheese has a film of blue mould over the surface. It must be several weeks, at least."

Yes, at least. Look, you and Morgana stay here and tend the stove. The kettle on top still has some water in it. I will go into the community kitchen to see if Ruby has some bits for us to eat and some fresh tea.

4

It had been the middle of the night when Touchwood, Dafydd, and Morgana had left the Void craft with the cauldron. They had considered it the best time, less chance of anyone seeing the void craft take off. So Touchwood had not been surprised when he entered the refractory to find it deserted and dark. Everyone in the community was up early tending to animals and the vegetable gardens before the heat of the day came.

On his way to the pantry, Touchwood didn't notice that the proofing box for the overnight rising of the bread was empty and turned off. Nore did he notice that all the days pots and dishes were only halfway through the washing process, as if they had been abandoned in a hurry.

In the pantry, Touchwood tut-tutted to himself when he couldn't find any bread or even any griddle cakes. And there weren't even any leftovers from the evening meal. Something that he usually survived off, because he often didn't keep regular hours. But he did find some smoked hams hanging from a rail at the back, which he sliced off some slivers with a sharp knife on to a plate. Then, rummaging in a dusty corner right at the back, he found a covered box on the floor. Inside, he found some bottles with labels attached, stating:

Not for general consumption
Medicinal purposes only
Mrs Ruby Polards Tonic Wine

Touchwood chuckled to himself, 'The cunning old crow. Ruby has a secret stash of wine.' Feeling only slightly guilty, he removed a bottle, knowing he would see her right the next time he saw her.

Chapter 23

The Throne Room

1

In the gilded throne room of King Indech, the king's dead body had been removed. None of the king's councillors could agree what to do with it as they had never encountered one before; this being the spirit realm. They knew it would just remain as it was, indefinitely. However, the only thing they could agree on was that the body must be removed from sight.

In the end, the Greys had been ordered to remove the body and dispose of it how they saw fit. The spiteful greys had fed it to the castle hunting dogs.

The seven councillors could not agree either, on which of them would be elected as a new king. Instead, they had arranged for the massive throne, to be put in storage, and a long conference table placed on the dais, with three chairs on either side, and a seventh on the head. The Right Honourable Nightheart, had elected himself the chair of the committee and was now sitting at the head of the table.

All the councillors had become very fearful, now that they had found out that not only had the God Pan been released from entombment in the Oak, but two of their most important prisoners, had somehow escaped, right under the noses of the grey guards. They were convinced now that the humans must be planning some sort of invasion of their realm. With this very much on their minds, they had posted a dozen grey guards inside the door of the throne room to protect them at all times. And another dozen greys took patrol along the corridors near the throne room.

2

The four members of the strike team had disposed of the dozen Greys patrolling the corridors. And were now looking down at the dead body of their team mate Adge. Each giving a moment of silence, honouring a fallen soldier.

Brad said at last, "Sounds like he went out the way he wanted - fighting."

Each one of them nodded in agreement, but then Finnbar asked, "But what did he mean Victoria, when he said 'Thank you for your help?' You were nowhere near him."

"No," replied Victoria. "But before we came here, I found him suffering in the void craft. My spirit guide told me he had PTSD - posttraumatic stress disorder, she called it, and recommended I treat him with the secretions of the venom glands of the Natterjack toad. She said it was a chemical called DMT or bufoviridine. I made up a small bottle of the secretions and told Adge to take it in small doses, to help him feel better."

"I reckon," remarked Finnbar, "he took the entire bottle at once. It turned him into a berserker!"

3

As Touchwood entered his rooms with his scanty haul of food and wine, Morgana and Dafydd were deep in conversation.

"...There is a big difference between the clairvoyant consciousness of the ancients and the objective consciousness of modern humans," proclaimed Morgana. "I had forgotten that when the fay blood is diluted, the sight comes to you unreliable and incomplete."

"Yes, I cannot help but agree with you," remarked Dafydd. "Morgana, mankind has strayed so badly from the golden years of Atlantis, when the race of men honed and improved upon their clairvoyant gifts so well, that they became a spiritually advanced, hyper-human race. Such a waste that it was destroyed. Do you know what happened?"

Touchwood silently entered his room and, not wanting to interrupt Morgana, placed the food platter and wine quietly on the workbench.

"Many prophetesses predicted the end times. Some priestesses and their confidants knew and were prepared. Before the final days, many had boarded ships and followed the trading routes to other lands that we traded with, for we were a seafaring race and had mapped the whole globe. West, east and south we went. To every coast there was around the great Atlantis ocean.

But it wasn't until much later that we discovered that, 'The Hidden Ones,' the priests that wore the Black robes, also knew of the coming of the great comet. And when it came, they worked their magic secretly to divert it away from our home islands. But their meddling only made matters worse. The great comet became subject to massive opposing forces. The momentum of the rock and the power of the Black robes caused the comet to break up in the atmosphere. Many fragments were diverted to the great ice, causing it to melt, creating catastrophic floods. Which poured into the Atlantis ocean flooding west, east and south every coastal town there was, around the great Atlantis ocean. The very places our people had fled to avoid the comet."

Uncle Dafydd had been staring out the window at the stars in the sky, while Morgana had been talking. He had a faraway look as he spoke now, "And the third angel sounded his trumpet... and a great star, blazing like a torch, fell from the sky... the name of the star is Wormwood."

Touchwood knew that Dafydd had quoted some ancient text, he had memorised. A prediction perhaps, or an account. Non the less, it caused a chill to flow up his spine.

Dafydd turned now from the window and spoke directly to Morgana, "I had no idea the course of the comet was diverted. How did you survive then," asked Dafydd?

"Of course, I wasn't born in the nation of the Y's, you know. Nor was I a part of the new explosion of births that came when those few evacuated the homeland fleeing south, west, and east. Many of those were killed by the Tsunamis, the giant waves caused by earthquakes and volcanic eruptions under the sea, that followed the fall.

But by some miracle, some did survive. Once the Great Ice receded and the flood waters settled to regular tides, my descendants migrated north to Ireland. The 'new dawn generation', they called them. When they all felt they had found a new motherland, and the call was to procreate as much as possible, to increase our numbers after the disastrous losses incurred, when our nation was submerged.

"But of course, we were forbidden to mate with the indigenous population. Everybody agreed it was important to keep our 'blue blood' pure. And not to water it down with the blood of the natives. Even at the cost of mating with our own mothers or siblings.

"This, of course, was the cause of our second downfall. Although at the time nobody realised it. It was only much later that we came to realise our mistake. But in those early days, they found that our new land was barren; births didn't come easy for us. And those few born rarely survived to maturity.

"The elder counsel realised this was because the fertile dragon energy, was weak in this new land. So a great building project, was set into motion to rebuild the energy accumulators, like the ones we had in the old homeland. Great megaliths were set up as Orgone accumulators, directing and amplifying the fertile dragon energies. The hunter gatherer natives were employed in the building works. In exchange, we educated them in efficient agriculture, animal husbandry and the many things necessary for civilisation; although we forbade them writing."

"I was one of those born because the dragon energies began to flow again. But it was already too late. This in-breeding, in an effort to keep our blood pure - only weakened us. Seeing this, some of our young people rebelled and took it upon themselves to mate with the indigenous population. The elder council feared that we, as a great nation, would soon be lost and integrated into the indigenous population. So it was, that the elders decided that the entire Tuatha race should transcend permanently to Tír na nÓg, via the gateways of the stone circles." Morgana stopped talking. Instead stared into a dark corner, seeming to forget anyone else was there.

Touchwood decided to brave an interruption, "Dafydd I have managed to find some food for us and this," as he held up the bottle of Tonic Wine.

Dafydd's eyes lit up at the sight, "Ho ho, Touchwood, you spoil us".

Dafydd picked up a sliver of smoked ham, declaring it delicious. Then took the bottle from Touchwood and inspected the label. Touchwood went to a cupboard on the wall and brought out three glasses, offering one to Morgana. But she just continued to stare, lost in the past, ignoring him. Touchwood shrugged his shoulders and walked over to Dafydd. "What do you think Dafydd? Do you want to chance it?"

"Beggars can't be choosers Touchwood," he said, holding out the bottle. "We need a corkscrew."

"Ah yes," said Touchwood as he went to a drawer in the bench and fished about, looking for one. Eventually, holding up a rather unusual twisted piece of wood.

"Ah yes, here we are. I found a gnarled, twisted knotty section of a grapevine, and thought I would convert it to a corkscrew. Stained to a deep brown, I rather like it. Quirky don't you think?"

"Yes fascinating. But more to the point, does it work?

Touchwood showed him that it did, and poured some of the deep red liquid into two of the glasses. He risked a sideways glance toward Morgana, to see if she was interested, but she still seemed lost in her own world.

Dafydd held up his glass for a toast. "To a successful raid," he proposed as he clinked his glass against Touchwood's.

"To the end of the dark elves," Touchwood replied and sipped his glass. Both he and Dafydd balked at the taste, and lowered their glasses in unison.

"What has she done to this, asked Touchwood?

"Its definitely fortified with gin," said Dafydd, grimacing.

"But these herbs in it don't taste good at all," complained Touchwood.

"Well, it did say tonic wine." They both laughed but continued drinking all the same.

4

Victoria twisted the Ring of Eluned round her finger, instantly becoming invisible. Even so, she slowly and silently crept round the corner and entered the king's throne chamber. She didn't want to alert anyone to her presence. She had volunteered to do a reconnaissance of the throne room using her ring of invisibility. Now she could plainly see the seven councillors deep in conversation sat round the conference table. A line of grey guards stood a few feet inside the doorway.

With her back to the wall, she could circumnavigate the guards and get close to the councillors. She was tempted there and then, to raise her bow and take out a few of the nasty dark elves. But there were too many for her to handle single-handedly. Looking about the vast throne room with all its gaudy gilded tapestries and ornaments, she noticed, high up on a wall was a balcony which contained a mighty organ with massive pipes reaching up to the ceiling.

There were no steps leading up to it, so she figured there must be an entrance to it from behind the organ. If she could find the stairway leading up to it, she would have a clear line of sight to the guards and the councillors.

The councillors were engaged in a heated argument with each other in their own dark elvish language. It reminded her of the gurgling that drains sometimes made in her cottage when they were blocked. She screwed her petite nose up in disgust. Looking up at the organ balcony again, a plan formed in her mind. She must report what she had seen and discuss it with the others.

Chapter 24

Last Stand

1

Victoria and Rumanadil had found the small winding stairway, which led up to the high balcony above the throne room. The pipes of the enormous organ loomed up above them. Victoria peeped over the stone balcony rail, down at the scene below. The councillors were still arguing with each other in their gurgling language. The line of a dozen grey guards stood guarding the massive doors, which remained open so that no one could enter unseen.

The plan was for Finnbar and Brad to enter the throne room, secreted under Aurthur's cloak of invisibility, and make their way towards the councillors, unseen by the guards.

Victoria and Rumanadil in the balcony, were to be ready with long Bow and cross bow to pick off the guards, while Finnbar and Brad took out the councillors. It was a risky plan and relied on split second timing. The signal to start firing was to come from

Finnbar, who would shout as he thrust his spear when they had got into position close to the councillors.

Victoria and Rumanadil were waiting on the balcony platform, however it was a small cramped space intended only for one elf sitting down, and Rumanadil was a large elf. Victoria had her long bow notched and ready to fire. Rumanadil was pulling the string, to set his crossbow. As he strained, his fingers slipped, still greasy with gore, and he stepped back a little, to keep balance but as he did, he bumped poor Victoria backwards onto the keys of the organ; she sat on several keys at once. Suddenly the pipe organ emanated a deafening, discordant sound from the huge wind pipes. The ominous discord reverberated from the walls of the throne room, alerting everybody to their presence.

Finnbar and Brad, still under the cloak of invisibility, were not in place yet, still only halfway along the enormous throne room. Surprised by the thunderous sound of the pipe organ, Brad's heart almost stopped. Finnbar, thinking quickly, threw the cloak to the floor, the element of surprise now gone. He raised his bronze spear as he charged at the conference table, impaling Sauron Darkweaver through his back. The spearhead bursting out of his front, spewed blood and gore across the table. Brad, recovering from the initial shock, ran at the table, decapitating one of the dark elf advisors.

The Grey guards at the door, alerted by the pipe organ, looked up at the balcony in unison, to see Rumanadil aiming his crossbow directly at them. One Grey, thinking quickly, ran for the door, clearly intending to seek out the spiral staircase to the organ booth. But Rumanadil let fly his bolt, catching him squarely in the heart. Victoria had found her feet again. Notching an arrow, caught one grey through his eye and into his brain. He fell backwards, screaming.

Meanwhile, the carnage at the conference table continued. Brad swinging Núada's Sword of Light like a farmhand scything hay. Finnbar, careful to keep clear of Brad's blade, tackled the farside of the table. But the councillors were up and running now, so Finnbar cast his spear at Sir Gloomwhisper as he ran for the far door. He fell with the spear still sticking out of his back.

Fortunatly Finnbar had had the foresight to claim the curved Arabian sword that Adge had taken. He pulled it from his belt now, and chopped at Sauron Darkweaver's neck, blood spurting from the severed artery there.

High up in the balcony, Victoria and Rumanadil were working in harmony now; taking out grey guards as they ran the length of the throne room, attempting to protect the Dark elf councillors. But one fast running Grey had made it to the side of the Right Honourable Nightheart, and was standing on guard, sword raised ready to protect his ruler.

Brad had dispatched all the councillors on his side of the table. Looking round for more, he spotted the Right Honourable Nightheart pressed against a wall, protected by his grey guard. Brad decided on the spot that this was the obvious leader of the committee, so realised it was a priority to take him out. Quickly looking over to see if Finnbar needed aid, however, he seemed to have the situation well in hand. So Brad sprung across the table and leapt towards the Right Honourable Nightheart.

Meanwhile, Victoria and Rumanadil had been

working their way through the running grey guards, till there was only one left. The one guarding the Right Honourable Nightheart. Finnbar's curved Arabian sword slashed down, cutting the last advisor's belly from sternum to groin. His intestines spilling to the ground like a string of pork sausages.

All eyes turned now to the last stand between Brad and the grey guard, that was protecting his ruler. The grey seemed more accomplished with his sword than the others. As blades clashed in a fury of sparks, Brad, growing tired, now realised he was bested by the Grey swordsman, and was losing this duel.

Finnbar, seeing this, called to encourage him, "Brad, you must call upon the power of Núada's Sword of Light to aid you."

Upon hearing this, Brad summoned the last of his warrior's fire, in an attempt to raise the magical power inherent in Núada's Sword of Light; that he held in his right hand. The sword with two edges which stood for honour and justice: 'the truth against the world'. The sword used by the legendary King Arthur to win against the marauding hordes, attacking his land. The sword imbued with the magical power that makes the keeper insuperable and impossible to defeat. As he swung the sword to defend himself, he could feel it vibrating in his hand. Then he noticed a nimbus glow forming along the length of the blade. The sword seemed to take on a life of its own, besting the grey at every thrust and parry.

The wicked, winning grin of the Grey, suddenly fell from his face as he realised something had changed. He noticed for the first time the glow of his opponent's sword. And now, as the sword seemed to best him at every turn, it seemed to sing, emitting a resonant hum, like the gentle strumming of a harp.

Brad too heard his sword singing; the melody was both haunting and beautiful. As it sliced through the air, the sound was a symphony of metallic whispers, each swing producing a distinct note, harmonising with his own movements.

The mystical singing, seemed to strike fear into the heart of the Grey, who started to back-step at every thrust. The singing of the sword, reaching a crescendo now, and as if seemingly of its own accord, the sword made a powerful sweep down. The enemy's eyes widened in a final, shocked expression, before his head was split from crown to jaw bone. Blood and brains sprayed in a gruesome arc, and the two halves of his head fell apart, lifeless.

For a long moment, everyone stood still; silently stunned by the incredible spectacle. The Right Honourable Nightheart, now stood alone amongst his enemies. But quickly recovering his wits, proclaimed as he stepped forwards, congenially splaying his arms wide, "Gentlemen, gentlemen, a most commendable victory. But surely we can now come to some mutually satisfactory arrangement."

Brad, still stunned, looked up from the dead grey at his feet. Finnbar stepped to his side, the curved Arabian sword in his hand ready. But Nightheart quickened his pace towards Brad. Reaching inside his regal cloak, produced a long dagger.

But before he could raise it, an arrow flew from the balcony, thudding squarely into his heart. It was quickly followed by a bolt, straight through his eye into his brain. Victoria, with another arrow notched and ready, let fly and hit Nightheart as he fell backwards. The first arrow split asunder as the second hit a perfect gold. The Right Honourable Nightheart fell to the ground and was no more.

2

"They have transmitted the power of their ideas through something that is eternal," stated Dafydd. "They created a force, and projected it to the future."

Dafydd and Touchwood were sitting beside the glowing wood stove in Touchwood's kitchen; slowly sipping their tonic wine. The conversation had moved on to the aftermath, of the apocalyptic destruction, that the comet had wrought on the planet. And how the ancient survivors of the Atlantean nation, knowing they were a dying civilisation, had sought to preserve some of their hard earned sacred science for future generations.

"And that force is the questions it challenges you to ask," added Touchwood.

"Absolutely. I have no doubt that the ancients knew the human mind to perfection," stated Dafydd. "This is how their initiates were trained, through ritual and riddles, that were asked by the elders; and that the initiate had to solve.

"Just look at you and me. We have been faced with riddles to gain what we sought. Remember the velum scroll formula?"

Touchwood nodded silently, then looked up from his glass. "The one you gave me for Adge to solve?"

"Yes. It was a riddle coded with cryptic poetry," Dafydd continued. "Something you had to solve to gain what you needed. That riddle was very old and had been remembered and passed on for millennia. It was taught to me as a young apprentice, so long ago now, I don't care to contemplate it. I reluctantly wrote it down only because of the unique circumstances.

"Then, there was the 'Pat-a-cake' riddle that Adge's spirit guide had given him. After he solved it, it allowed him to transcend to the otherworld."

"And of course, the Song of Merlin," added Touchwood.

Dafydd nodded. "They knew that they could initiate people, far ahead in the future, into their way of thinking; that of the magician. Even though they couldn't be there themselves. That is why they created things like the Pyramids, the Sphinx, Göbekli Tepe, Machu Picchu, and Sacsayhuamán in Peru. They beg us to question their impossibility, and there are many other long-lasting structures like them.

"They are riddles. At first, they don't make any sense, but they draw you in, and if you have the right mindset, they cause you to ask questions. Those questions lead to more questions, until you have solved the riddle and learnt some of their secrets." Dafydd shook his head in mock disbelief. "We are in the hands of real magicians here. Real magicians know that with the right symbols and the right questions, they can lead you to initiate yourself. Provided you are a person with the right mindset."

"They were sowing a seed," Touchwood whispered to himself in wonder. "This is what Candra, the Rhennish girl, who surely had Fay blood, had said to me when I was a young man, all those years ago. She had said to me that she had planted a seed, in what she hoped was a fertile mind, and had left; knowing it would grow in its own way.

"And in his own way, this is what Hamish the Scottish fisherman had done, before that even. He too, had claimed Fay blood; born of a Selkie maid. He had sown a seed of doubt in my mind, about my chosen life path, at that time. And set me on a path to seek enlightenment."

"Yes. You could look at it like that," confirmed Dafydd. "They were magicians that were sowing the power of ideas. They knew how to set ideas growing and developing in people's minds. When it enters a fertile mind, it goes deep into the subconscious and grows of its own accord. Once there, you can't resist it."

"So, in a way, " stated Touchwood. "Those long lasting megaliths, like the pyramids, are like a batch of 'seed ideas', from a golden age. That are scattered throughout the world, perfectly preserved for millennia; waiting for the right conditions to occur. Then, when the time is right. When civilisation has regrown again, producing minds mature and wise enough to ask the right questions. Those seed ideas, enter those fertile minds, and start to bloom into a tree of knowledge."

Dafydd looked at Touchwood with a delighted grin on his face. The look of a mentor, who had guided and nurtured a student for years, and had finally graduated.

He raised his glass. Touchwood did likewise. Dafydd clinking his glass, declared, "To you Touchwood, I knew you would make it in the end, boy."

3

Beltane had come around again and Star, along with several of her fellow priestesses, attended the ceremonies with barely restrained excitement. The May Queen had been crowned; the young priests had competed in their tournaments; and the midday feast was a delight. All had gone well and now all the participants had gathered about the may pole ready for the blessing from the horned God.

Helios Arkonephus, the Draoi Magician from the sun temple, raised his arms high in salutation, calling out the sacred names of the horned god. His voice was trained and powerful, reverberating off the stones of the circle. When he had finished his invocation, he slowly lowered his arms, and as he did, the leaves on all the trees of the grove started stirring in a wind. Gently at first, but then there was a powerful rushing of sudden winds, causing the tree branches to creak and sway. An icy shiver ran down Star's back, and then she saw him. A dark shadow at the edge of the grove, the silhouette of a crown of horns.

"He has come!" proclaimed the Draoi Magician, smiling, as he raised his arms in welcome.

But the wind only increased again, thrusting floods of air through the grove. Star felt her cloak flapping with it, and her hair blew about, covering her face. With clawed fingers, she pulled it out of her eyes. She could hear muted murmurings from the people about her.

Suddenly there was a tremendous flapping of wings, and a deafening screeching of birds, as thousands of starlings took to the air. Forming black clouds of living creatures, that swooped and glided in perfect synchronism. A symphony of motion, moving all together, producing strange and impossible, organic shapes.

Star gazed up at them, between her fluttering bronze tresses, as the birds performed nature's dance across the midday sun. Puzzled, she thought, they don't normally perform this wonder in the middle of the day! But then something changed. Star watched in horror as the birds, now seemed genuinely terrified, swooping and shifting faster and faster. The pleasing organic shapes, now became jagged and out of sync. A frenzied swirling rush of frightened birds, haphazardly clashing into each other, as, one by one, they fell dead to the ground, at the feet of the puzzled spectators.

The Draoi Master, let his hands drop to his sides, as he looked questioningly at the priests that surrounded him; who only looked back with puzzled faces. Helios Arkonephus then looked back towards the horned one, who still stood unmoving, in the shadows at the edge of the grove.

Determined not to be phased by the unexpected events, the Draoi Master called out again, "Oh, horned one, do you not come to bless the happy couples before the Great Marriage?"

But the God remained silent at the edge of the grove. Helios Arkonephus looked again to his priests for support. But every last one of them was now staring, openmouthed, up to the sky. Slowly, Helios followed their gaze. As a chill flowed down his back, now he could see what distracted them. For the sun's disc was partially obscured at the edge, by a black crescent shadow.

"An eclipse! Helios exclaimed. "But this was not predicted".

Helios Arkonephus turned to his chief astronomer, who was now kneeling on the ground, with his charts spread out before him. He was agitated, franticly shuffling through the charts and scrolls.

The Draoi Master impatiently waited a few moments, then asked, "Well?"

The chief astronomer, a weaselly little man, continued to consult his charts a few moments longer. But eventually, he looked up at Helios and just shrugged apologetically.

The Draoi Masters' face became the colour of a thundercloud, as he looked up at the sky again. Now the sun's face was almost completely obscured by the eclipse. In the twilight, some of the brightest stars were becoming visible. Then, a panicked murmur was set up by the crowds of people at the ceremony; for now, a new cosmic wonder had become visible. In the darkened sky could be seen a huge comet, whose fiery tail could be seen trailing across the sky.

Then, as Star watched in amazement, the sky suddenly lit up in an explosion brighter than the midday sun. When it died down, she could see there were now several comets falling in unison. Her heart stopped, for now she realised that this was the vision she had seen in the mirror pool. In horror, she watched as one of the comet fragments descended lower and lower. As it approached the horizon, she could see that it was headed straight for the island of Atlantis!

The Draoi Master had been watching the comet in horror too, unable to utter a word. But then, as it lowered towards the island, he managed to utter in a terrified whisper, "...Wormwood!"

The massive comet struck the volcano at the centre of the island, causing an apocalyptic explosion of blinding light. Everybody screamed at once, and started running. But Star still stood paralysed, by the realisation that she had seen all this before; by the gift of her 'sight'.

Blaze ran up to her, grabbing her hand and pulled on it, shouting, "Don't just stand there, we must run for the harbour." Star, in a daze, ran with Blaze down towards the harbour; and the hope of escape.

But only nineteen seconds after the comet impact, the powerful shock wave from the impacting comet, hit them all like an atomic blast, vaporising every living thing on the islands.

Chapter 25

Sweet & Sour

1

The atmosphere inside the void ship was electric. Rumanadil had coaxed the food synthesiser to create some Elven Champagne and was filling everybody's glass to the brim. Victoria, never having tasted anything close to Champagne before, declared it tickled her nose too much and made her sneeze. She preferred to pour it over her chocolate ice cream.

Finnbar was demonstrating to everyone, how an Irish jig should be performed, but he was already on his third bottle of Champagne, and was getting the dance so badly wrong that everyone was in hysterics. He eventually collapsed on to the floor, exhausted, but no one was inclined to help him up.

Brad took the opportunity to raise another toast, "To the sweet taste of victory," he crowed. Everyone lifted their glass repeating in chorus, downing their Champagne. All except Victoria, who, after spooning some ice cream into her mouth, admitted thoughtfully.

"You know, I really didn't think we would be able to do it. There seemed to be so many of those ugly grey thingies running around."

Rumanadil remarked, "There were an awful lot more of them last time I was there. I'm curious to know where they could have got to."

Finnbar, still on the floor, unsteadily sat up and said, "But we did beat them. We all worked together and killed off all those dark elf councillors."

"And we know that Dafydd had killed off their king," said Brad with a slur. "And... and we must have killed off a couple of dozen greys between us."

"Those greys seemed pretty stupid. Without their councillors to guide them, I doubt we will be seeing any more of them anytime soon," added Finnbar, still on the floor.

Victoria stopped spooning ice cream, and tilting her head thoughtfully remarked, "It's a shame about poor Adge, though. Grandpapa would have loved to have seen him again."

"But at least he went the way he wanted - fighting. I can relate to that. And not many get to die twice either," said Brad with an ironic smirk.

"Personally, I can't wait to tell Touchwood and Dafydd we were victorious," said Rumanadil.

Victoria replied, "Let's not forget Morgana."

2

Deep beneath the dark elves' castle, forgotten by all, lurked Dr Feanor Darkbrood. Now at last, resting in his secret laboratory off the large underground hangar area, which had accommodated the dozens of void craft. He was not interested in the querulous intricacies of court politics that the other councillors engaged in. He didn't want the dubious honour of being the High King of the dark elves.

His passion was science; and, more particularly, genetic engineering. The recently deceased king Indech had, long ago, commissioned him to solve the over-riding problem that the Dark elves had. They had grown weary of immortality; they had grown weary of the otherworld; and longed to walk on the physical earth, procreate, and have children.

Dr Feanor Darkbrood, had plaintively explained to King Indech, that they lived in the otherworld and were only creatures of spirit. They had given up their physical bodies millennia ago when they transcended to the otherworld. To live on the physical plane, they would need a physical body to link to. This had not deterred King Indech, however, who had only decreed that Dr Feanor Darkbrood make some physical bodies for them to occupy.

Thus 'The Genesis Project' had been born. It had become Dr Darkbrood's brainchild. However, the task had proved easier said than done. And had involved centuries of our human years, of experimentation. Initialy Dr Darkbrood's early experiments in genetic engineering had spawned creatures that were born deformed, with no visible ears, and enormous eyes that wrapped around the sides of their heads. They were much shorter than the dark elves and had a lighter skin - a greyish appearance. They were also born with piebald hair all over their bodies. However, they were of low intelligence, easily manipulated and proved to be excellent servants. This result pleased King Indech and with his blessing, they had become a lower cast, a slave race, under the leadership of the dark elves.

However, King Indech found the piebald hair distasteful to his eyes, so had insisted their hair be shaved off all over. And as slaves, they had to go naked. These 'Grey Elves' had become known simply as 'Greys'.

Although successful, this result had still not solved the problem of living on the physical plane. But in time, Dr Darkbrood had figured out a way for a dark elf spirit, to 'takeover' a physical body on the earth plane. But they could only do it in a very brief window; just after the human spirit leaves its earthly body, when the physical body dies. Then, the Elven spirit can simply 'walk-in' to the earthly body and take it over.

Dr Darkbrood's early experiments had begun at about the time that humans called the medieval period, and involved new born humans, who had died in the cot. With the help of an army of Greys, secretly, under cover of darkness, when most humans slept, a grey elf spirit body would sneaked into the human household, seeking the dead child and 'walked-in,' and taken over, while the body was still warm.

The poor human parents had awoken to find their babies changed. And were even more distressed when other people had labelled their babies 'Changeling's'. In the medieval period, this was happening all over Europe.

However, some people, suspecting it was the work of the Fae, called them 'fairy children', for they displayed unusual behaviour, and would most often appear sickly, and would not grow in size like a normal child. And would often have notable strange physical characteristics, not unlike the grey elf inside.

This state of affairs had persisted for many human centuries, in the hope that, given time, some changelings would adapt to the physical plane and live long enough to be useful. Unfortunately, this had not proved to be the case. The dark elves loosing heart that they would ever walk the physical plain again.

It wasn't until what humans called the 'technological age,' that things began to change for the better; Dr Darkbrood discovered he could blend advanced human technology with Elven magic. The result was the proto type Void crafts.

This breakthrough enabled Dr Darkbrood and the Greys, to travel to the physical plane and stay for longer periods. They could kidnap suitable humans, bring them into the void craft, which were kitted out with advanced laboratories. Now Dr Darkbrood spent years studying human physiology and experimenting with genetic engineering. Eventually he created an elf-human hybrid foetus, that could grow and survive a long and healthy life.

With the promise from Dr Darkbrood that success was only a matter of time, king Indech, who was alive at the time, had implemented the second part of his plan; to rid the physical plane of humans altogether. Using dark elf magic, they had manipulated the Earth's Elemental forces to intensify global warming, which would severely disrupt human civilisation. They also had stifled the power of the nature god Pan by entombing him in a tree.

The result of all this was the polar ice caps melting, causing a huge rise in sea levels. As mankind's twenty-first century civilisation collapsed, the foolish humans had completed the rest of the work themselves. The oil wars had instigated a holocaust, eradicating the remaining humans on earth. Only small pockets of isolated tribes and people able to live off the land, had survived.

It was at this point that a small band of humans, (Dafydd and Touchwood), had discovered the dark elves' plan and fought back. King Indech had been assassinated using the Gae Assail, one of the four treasures belonging to the ancient race of the Tuatha de Danann. Touchwood and Uncle Dafydd had discovered these hidden in the crystal cave.

However, this turn of events had only caused the evil king's councillors to accelerate their invasion plans. Efforts to breed Elf-human hybrids intensified. Dr Darkbrood already had vast nurseries, filled with incubators containing the tiny foul creatures. The incensed king's councillors had pressed Dr Darkbrood to speed up the process any way he could.

So, even before the human strike team, led by Rumanadil, had left in their stolen Void craft, on a mission to assassinate the king's councillors. Dr Darkbrood was herding the goblin like, elf-human hybrids into the Void crafts, led by an army of greys.

As the strike team travelled to the otherworld. The invasion force of void crafts were travelling from the otherworld to the earth plain. As Victoria, Brad, Rumandil, and Finnbar were battling with the remaining grey guards and assassinating the king's councillors. The Goblin invasion force had landed on the earth plane and sought out any humans they could find.

3

A golden dawn edged up over the eastern rim of the magic mountain of Sliabh an Iarainn. The new leaves of March made the orchards of Rath Grain glow a glorious green, and the morning resounded with a joyous birdsong. A warm breeze coursed through the trees and the gently swaying branches played a delightful rushing music.

Suddenly, in the west, there was a quick movement in the sky. Something like a shooting star, but somehow different; as it remained steady in the sky and did not burn out quickly, as shooting stars usually did.

Instead, the tiny pinpoint of light moved steadily across the sky. As it grew larger, it appeared to be much lower in the sky. Eventually it hovered over the gardens of Rath Grain, just hanging there like a balloon bobbing in the breeze; the thing had a metallic silvery glow.

Suddenly, four smaller balls of light appeared beside it, which gradually descended till they touched the earth of the garden. Which caused silent explosions of light, radiating in all directions; then was gone.

"Grandpapa is going to be so excited when we tell him we got rid of all those ugly dark elf thingies for him," exclaimed Victoria, as she stepped from the shadow under the trees into the dazzling March sunshine. Her blond hair, still braided in a warrior's plait, her lithe body adorned only by a wide plaited leather band about her chest; and soft leather leggins. The black war paint about her eyes now smudged and splattered with blood.

Brad stepping into the dazzling sunlight beside her, shielded his squinting eyes said," I'm sure he will be over the Moon. But I'm surprise that there is no one working in the gardens. The sun is already up, there is usually several people out and about by now tending the animals and checking the vegetables."

Victoria frowned as she looked about the gardens, confirming Brad's observation. The strike team had deliberately landed their Void craft in the garden of Rath Grain during daylight. So jubilant were they that they felt there was no need to be cautious anymore. They wanted everybody in the community to know they had accomplished their mission. Victoria had agreed that there was no point in hiding anything from the Rath Grain community now. They needed to know what had been going on and now needed to understand that they had been saved from imminent disaster.

Finnbar and Rumanadil stepped up beside them. Rumanadil said, "Where is everybody Victoria? Thought you said the entire community would be out here to give us a hero's welcome!"

Victoria, looking a little concerned now, replied, "It does seem a little odd. I wonder where they could be."

She strode purposefully towards the little cottage doorway that led into Touchwood's rooms. The others tagged on behind her. She found the little door with the heart-shaped window was left ajar. Cautiously she called out, "Grandpapa!"

No answer.

She walked into the corridor, and found that the door to Touchwood's kitchen was wide open too. Something that never happened. Cautiously, she peered round the door.

Brad, Finnbar and Rumanadil had remained outside,

not quite sure what to do. Suddenly, there was a horrific scream from inside. Brad reacting quickly, rushed through the door to see if Victoria was being attacked. He found her just inside Touchwood's doorway, crouched over a body on the floor. Her whole body shaking and wracked with sobs.

"Grandpapa!" Victoria cried. "Oh, Grandpapa, what have they done to you?"

Brad crouched down beside her. Touchwood's body lay on the floor, surrounded by a pool of congealed blood. Three arrows sticking out of his chest.

Victoria was beside herself now, muttering his name between sods and kissing his dead face. Finnbar and Rumanadil, now at the doorway, looked on with impotent horror.

Brad placed his fingers on Touchwood's neck, feeling for a pulse. Then looked up at Finnbar with a hopeless expression and shook his head, confirming the worst.

Rumanadil, however, was staring into the shadows at the far end of the room. He stepped forwards carefully, avoiding the figures on the floor. In the shadowy gloom besides the cold wood stove, he bent and discovered another body. A large bloody gash in his chest, and his grey face confirmed he had met the same fate as Touchwood.

"Dafydd?" Rumanadil whispered as he gently slapped his face in the hope of reviving his friend. But the lifeless head only lolled to one side. Rumanadil checked for a pulse on his exposed neck. But the body was as dead and cold as the wood stove beside him.

Rumanadil looked up to see Finnbar looking his way, "Is that…?"

"Dafydd," Rumanadil nodded. "He has gone as well."

Finnbar was stunned at the deaths of Touchwood and Dafydd. But he was also a man of action, "I will go and find the other community members and tell them what has happened here; we will need help with the bodies to prepare them for burial."

But even though he searched high and low, there was no one inside the main house. So Finnbar went outside and looked in all the various eco dwellings that were part of Rath Grain community. But he drew a blank there as well. No one seemed to be there. But he did notice, that all about the community grounds, there was evidence of a hasty departure, and jobs half finished with gardening tools left strewn on the ground. The animals had been neglected too. Chickens were running wild over the vegetable gardens; the goats looked like they needed milking, their udders fit to burst. He would need to tell Victoria of this, so she could relive the poor animals of their milk.

On returning to Touchwood's kitchen, he found that the bodies had been laid side by side and covered in an unused sheet. Victoria was sitting on a hardback chair, quietly sobbing. Brad stood beside her, holding her head comforting the young girl.

Finnbar told the others what he had found outside. Rumanadil, shaking his head, declared, "I like not what we have found here, this does not bold well." Secretly, he suspected that the Greys were responsible for this turn of events. And this would explain why there were only very few Greys in King Indech's castle. But he had kept these thoughts to himself. He didn't want to alarm the others till he was certain he was correct.

Chapter 26

Elf Ears

1

Everyone had forgotten about Morgana. She had, of course, been left behind at Rath Grain with Touchwood and Dafydd, while the strike team had gone off on their mission to Tech Duinn and King Indech's castle.

While they waited for the return of the strike team, Touchwood and Dafydd had been in good spirits, toasting beside the hot stove and now that they had found some wine to drink. However, Morgana was feeling the effects of losing the energy field of the void craft. As a spirit being who normally resided in the otherworld, she could visit the physical plane only for limited periods. It needed large amounts of magical energy to stay there, and hers was depleting fast.

While Touchwood and Dafydd, in their physical bodies, were talking excitedly about all manner of philosophical and metaphysical subjects, Morgana had sunk to the floor and leaned against the cottage wall for support. She had turned silently inward, attempting to save her energy. She had been contemplating using the last of it to transport to the Dolmen up on the mountain to recharge, when the kitchen door burst open and two hideous creatures had marched in.

They were about the same size and naked like the Greys, but their skin was a sickly green. She noticed they had pointed ears, but instead of elegantly pointing upwards close to the head, like an elf; they were much bigger, sticking out and pointing downwards. Their mouths were larger too, filled with wickedly pointed teeth. But worst of all were their deep-set eyes. Tiny red points filled with menace, stared out of a black socket.

The first one had a small bow, set and notched with an arrow, which he let fly as Touchwood ran towards the intruder. It was at this point that Morgana blinked out like a light and, using the last of her magical energy, transported to the Dolmen.

2

At the Dolmen up on the mountain, Morgana had materialised and sat gasping like a fish out of water. While she charged herself with the earth energies present in the megalithic structure, she realised she had left it far too long before charging.

She berated herself that she had barely made it to the dolmen. But she wouldn't admit it to anybody, that she had been shaken and surprised, by the sudden intrusion of those goblin creatures. She had never seen their like before. However, they did remind her somehow of the Greys, which she had encountered many times in her long existence in the otherworld. She had learnt it was best to avoid those malicious beings. But these new creatures were hideous, and she wondered where they had come from.

Morgana had lain beside the Dolmen, replenishing her magical energy for a long time. Eventually she had fallen asleep, so exhausted and depleted was she. However, after some time of sleeping, she began to search with her inner eye, for the life force energy of Touchwood and Dafydd. Even though they were mere humans, she had to admit to herself, she had begun to grow quite close to them. But nowhere in the community could she find even a glimmer of human life force.

Thinking that perhaps they may have fled away from the cottage, she extended her psychic search to a wider area. Gradually, she became aware of physical humans on the edges of her search area. Narrowing her psychic search for human life-force, to pinpoint accuracy, she found there was a small group huddled together in an underground cave. Her inner eye homed in on one, whose life force energy was strongest.

Yes, Morgana thought, that one has the sight, she has Fay blood. Because of this, she was able to see through the human eyes of Ruby; and hear what was being said.

"But Ruby, where did those hideous creatures come from?"

"I don't know Emily, but I have been having very strange dreams of late, with those very same creatures in them. They were horrible nightmares."

"They were more than nightmares Ruby. They were very real," declared Emily. "They killed my poor husband Samuel. And everybody else in our community. Me and Forge barely got away with our lives."

"We are so grateful to you Emily, for coming to warn us about those creatures. You must have run like the wind," said Ivy, a Rath Grain community member.

"We did Ivy. But we would never have made it without my son Forge helping me. I'm sure he near carried me most of the way." Nervous laughter followed this. Everyone huddled in the cave together, were trying to keep their spirits up. However, Forge had lowered his head, his face deep red, not enjoying the attention.

Morgana withdrew her far-vision. And considered what she could do with this new information. She had to admit she was concerned about this developing situation. But convinced herself that she was vulnerable in this depleted state, and needed quite some time to recharge if she was ever to have to face those terrible goblins alone.

3

Now, back in Touchwood's kitchen, the two bodies were still laying on the floor covered by a sheet. Victoria, not wanting to face anyone or anything, had retired to her granpapas bed up in the roof space above the stove. She had pulled the covers over her head, and could smell his familiar scent on the sheets. Her grandpapa was the only blood family she had, and now he was gone; it was all too much to bear.

Brad and Finnbar, being practical men, were discussing where they should bury the dead bodies. Rumanadil, leaning against the cottage wall opposite the window, was still contemplating the possibility, that if it was the Greys who had committed these murders, where were they now? Would they come back? Perhaps they should post a guard outside in case they did. And where was the rest of the community? Finnbar had said he had found no more bodies in the community grounds. And, for that matter, where was Morgana? She was supposed to be here protecting Touchwood and Dafydd.

It was at that precise moment that Morgana had silently materialised in the dark corner beside the cold stove. After eavesdropping on the humans huddled in the cave, she had returned to the dolmen to continue recharging her magical energy. It had been some time later that she had detected an Elfen presence that she knew very well. Her lover had returned to the hovel, the humans called Rath Grain.

"Did you miss me, Rumanadil?" Morgana crooned. She had silently materialised directly into Touchwood's kitchen and sidled besides Rumanadil, who was still deep in thought.

Rumanadil, startled, turned to her, "Ye Gods Morgana, where have you been? I was beginning to think the Greys had somehow killed you too."

"They were not Greys Rumanadil, that came here. They were some other disgusting goblin-like creature."

By this time, Brad and Finnbar had heard Morgana's voice and stood up, alert and angry. Finnbar cried out, "Where have you been Morgana? Do you know what happened here? Touchwood and Dafydd have been murdered."

Morgana, feeling threatened by the angry men, thought carefully before answering, "I went searching for the other community members."

She paused slyly, checking for reaction to this piece of information. Seeing everyone's interest, she continued. "Have no fear. They are safe and hiding in a cave nearby."

But then, seeing them relaxing their guard a little, she thrust like a knife, "Have you tried reviving them yet?" she accused. Casually waving a hand toward the bodies under the sheet.

"What mean you? Revive? They are stone dead," asked Finnbar, puzzled.

"The Cauldron of Cyrridfen, of course. Fool!" Morgana said cuttingly. But seeing no reaction from him laid it out, "The Cauldron? One of the treasures? The magical cauldron, able to resurrect the dead! Oh, this is hopeless. The man is an idiot."

Rumanadil came to Finnbar's aid, "Of course, the one Touchwood brought back from the crystal cave. We had it on the void craft. But where is it now?"

Morgana gave a great sigh, exasperated, "They stored it in some filthy shed full of the dirt they burn in the stove. But don't ask me to go near it. They covered it with iron."

"That sounds like it could be the turf shed," chipped in Brad. "I know where it is. Follow me."

4

She was rising to the surface of deep water, her lungs about to burst. Thrusting her legs harder and harder in a panic to reach the sunlight above. She needed to reach the air before she drowned…

Victoria awoke suddenly.

Her whole body jolted in a violent awakening. Gasping for air, she sat bolt upright in the bed, the awful dream still vivid in her mind.

She had been there. She had seen the comet falling. The blinding flash as it struck the distant island. She had been inside Star's mind as Blaze took her hand and ran. Running harder than she had ever done in her whole life.

Victoria could feel the panic in Star, and the other people running beside her. She felt the pain from the scorching heat, as the super-heated airburst hit, gnawing at her flesh. Yet still her body involuntarily continued running downhill, as a series of titanic shockwaves, washed over her with unbelievable intensity. Shaking the scorched flesh from her bones, and thrusting her ruined body back up the hill, to mix with all the other bodies; tossed about like rag dolls in a hurricane.

Victoria, still gasping for air, shook her head, trying to shake away the intensity of the vision-dream, that she had just endured. But was it a dream?

5

Brad, Finnbar and Rumanadil had dragged the precious cauldron out of the turf shed. But of course, when they tried to bring it inside, it would not fit through the cottage door. Feeling threatened that those murderous Goblins could return at anytime, and see them if they stayed outside. Brad thought it best if they put the cauldron in the workshop, as it had a double door big enough to admit a horse-drawn cart.

Once it was installed in the middle of the workshop, they proceeded to bring the dead bodies in, and laid them beside the magnificent bronze cauldron.

"Now what do we do?" asked Finnbar.

"I know not. I do not know that sort of magic," said

Rumanadil.

"Perhaps Morgana would know," said Brad.

As they opened the door to Touchwood's kitchen, they could hear soft singing.

Morgana had climbed upto the platform, and was comforting Victoria, her head on Morgana's lap while she stroked her hair softly; singing a soothing lullaby in the high Elven language.

Morgana had responded to the horrific scream that had come from the bed up above her. And did what only a mother could do.

6

Soothed and healed by Morgana's healing hands, and feeling a deep bond developing between them. Victoria had opened up, and told Morgana all about Star, her spirit guide and the magical training in herb lore, and healing she had been receiving from her in dream-visions. Consequently, she had said; it had been all the more horrific for her to witness Stars' death, by the fallout from the wrecking comet.

Morgana had brought Victoria's head down to her lap. While she softly stroked her hair, she gently tucked the wayward strands behind her ears.

"Do you know Victoria, you are turning into a high elf? You already have our handsome Elven ears," Morgana said while she continued to stroke her blond hair. Then, softly, she began humming an elven lullaby.

Suddenly she stopped and gently laughed, "Did you know that Dafydd and I were lovers when he was younger?" she shook her head fondly remembering those days, long ago. "He would probably come up with some scientific theory about your dreams, calling it quantum entanglement or some other long scientific term. Yet Star lived in the ancient homeland of Y's before it was lost so long ago. Perhaps then he would call it temporal entanglement," she laughed again, but this time there was more mirth in it.

"Human scientists seem to feel the need to explain everything with such long words," she continued. "Instead of just admitting that these things, are simply just 'magic' at work. The magic, I believe, of the Great Mother herself. The living entity we all live upon and depend upon for our very existence. All the creatures of the earth plane, as well as we in the otherworld, and all the other spirit realms."

Suddenly, Morgana stopped stroking Victoria's head and declared, "You're pregnant, Victoria. Did you know?"

Victoria had been sleepily charmed by Morgana's mesmeric humming, and stroking, but now she lifted her head, looking at Morgana questioningly.

"How did you know?" Victoria sat up now, looking earnestly into Morgana's eyes. "I had suspected I was. But that's impossible."

Then she thought again. "There was a boy I was with, but that was over a year ago."

Victoria paused again, trying to think, then continued unsurely, "There was also an elven boy I was with, in the otherworld recently. He was so beautiful, I could not help myself. But that's Impossible. Surely I could not be pregnant from him. Could I?"

She looked at Morgana for reassurance. But Morgana just smiled, and nodded her head. "It's not an uncommon occurrence. Especially in the old days, when humans were more aligned with the spirit world."

Tears flowed down Victoria's cheeks. She didn't know whether to be happy or sad or, simply be amazed. Such conflicting emotions flowed through her.

Morgana reached out, placing her hands on either side of Victoria's head. "My darling girl," she said as she drew her down to her lap again and continued to sing the ancient Elven lullaby.

7

Now Morgana stood in the centre of the community workshop, her hands open wide in the stance of invocation, before the magnificent bronze cauldron.

Brad and Finnbar, not wanting to incur her wrath by interrupting Morgana, while singing her lullaby to Victoria up on the bed platform. Had left it to Rumanadil to inform her that the cauldron was in position and ready for Morgana's magic. Yet even he had been over cautious as he approached, for he too had noticed previously the close bond developing; Morgana and Victoria had seemed more like mother and daughter now.

However, after but a little time for them to ready themselves, Victoria and Morgana had slowly made their way to the workshop.

In the centre was the cauldron. It was a magnificent piece of ancient craftsmanship. The burnished bronze had intricate designs etched into its sides, with interweaving knots and animals, crescent moons, and zigzags. All around its rim were inlaid large pearls. Two enormous handles grafted to the sides looked to be reworked torc's, the twisted metal wire design made of bronze, copper, silver, and gold.

Victoria, bravely trying to stifle her sobs and standing beside Brad for support, watched as Finnbar and Rumanadil took the first of the bodies and lowered it feet first into the cauldron.

Chapter 27

The Magical

Cauldron

1

Bang, bang, bang! A loud knocking sound like someone banging on a door. But no, it was the beating of a massive drum, the rhythms reverberating all about him.

Suddenly he could see, like someone turned on a light. Now he could see that he was travelling down some sort of long tunnel that swung left and right like a snake. But he wasn't walking, he was flying. He wasn't aware of any limbs or even any body; just his essence, faster and faster he flew.

Touchwood, for now he realised this was who he was, gradually became aware of visions projected on the tunnel walls as he passed. Visions of his life: here a goblin with a malicious grin firing an arrow at him; there, the crystal cave full of wondrous treasures; now, a mysterious Void craft landing in his garden.

On and on it went, for he had lived a long life; the quest for the missing syrinx; brother Adge visiting him as a shade; the time he and Adge took the velum scroll potion; meeting Uncle Dafydd for the first time; the first meeting of the lovely Hazel, his High Priestess; the Cat Tribe dancing round a standing stone in the rain.

The visions came, going back in time. All those lovely memories, going back through his entire life. Every significant moment was there. For a brief moment, he thought that he could discern a pattern forming. But then it was gone, and he was suddenly out of the tunnel and in a world of blinding light.

Instinctively, Touchwood raised his hands to his eyes to protect them. It somehow surprised him that he had hands, and yes, he had a body too. Then the intensity of the light slowly diminished, and he began to discern a shape before him. It was a round globe with green and brown landmasses, and deep-blue oceans, and white swirling clouds. Planet earth as he had seen it portrayed in many books. Then suddenly, the globe morphed into a forest floor with succulent fruit trees growing all about. He could feel the texture of the soft, spongy mosses under his bare feet. A warm breeze struck up, on it was a strong fragrance of ripening fruit. The air too, seemed filled with an enchanting bird song.

But then he noticed a beautiful woman standing amongst the trees. Her appearance was a breathtaking embodiment of nature itself. Her hair cascades in waves of lush greenery, interwoven with vibrant flowers and delicate vines. Each strand seems to shimmer with life. Her skin has the rich, warm tones of the fertile soil, and it seems to glow with an inner light.

Somehow, he knows she is the spirit, the very embodiment of the Earth, the Earth Goddess - Gaia. Her presence was both awe-inspiring and comforting.

Gaia's attire was woven from the finest elements of nature: a gown made of soft moss, adorned with petals and leaves whose colours shift and change as she moves towards him. Around her wrists and ankles, she wears bracelets of twining ivy, and blooming buds. She moves with the grace of a flowing river. Her eyes were deep set and ancient, like pools of clear water, yet holding the wisdom of the ages, and the mysteries of the earth.

Those eyes fix on him now, and suddenly he can see the terrifying power of the being. He steps back a pace as an icy shiver runs down his back. The power in those eyes is like staring into the bubbling magma chamber of a volcano.

Gaia's voice, is like the rushing of a powerful wind, through the leaves of a mighty tree, as she speaks accusingly, "Every worm, every insect, every animal is working for the ecological wellbeing of the planet. Every fish, every bird is moving in harmony with the 'Music of the Spheres', each playing their part, inaudibly singing their own keynote, which is part of a greater chord, and thus in harmony with our environment.

"You humans claim to be the most intelligent species on earth. Yet only humans are working against this harmony. You are more like the dark elves than you would like to believe. Do you really think you can change that?"

This condemnation of his species took him aback; this mortally wounded him. Yet he knew, deep down, she spoke the truth.

But he bravely spoke up, "But you can't compare us to the dark elves."

"Why not? At least they have worked for millennia to return to the physical world. They have craved for it. Realising the limitations of the otherworld, they may now fully appreciate living on the physical plain. Can your human kind say the same?"

Poor Touchwood was at a loss at how to answer this. He hung his head in shame, and desperation. But Gaia had not finished with him.

"Living on the physical plain, being the supreme species, is a privilege, not a right. I could decide that the elves are a better candidate than humans for this role.

"But you would never do that, would you? Destroy human kind?" Touchwood whined.

"Over the millennia, human civilisation has risen and been found wanting many times in the past. Each time I have destroyed them almost completely. And allowed them to prosper and rise again; hoping that this time they would remember their place as custodians. But alas, their memories are short. Perhaps now is the time to give the Elves a turn. They could do no worse than you humans."

In desperation, Touchwood wrung his hands. He had a sense that somehow this was a nodal point in time, a significant pivotal event in human evolution. What he said now to this Goddess could determine the fate of humankind forever.

He knew this was too big for mere mental capacity alone. He must tune in, and channel his higher self. Breathing deeply like he had never done before, he just let the words flow from him:

"Once I dreamed of a world, where once again, creatures as arrogant and lovely as the High Elves roamed the earth and shared it with humans. And one where humanity, once more spirit-walked in the Otherworld. Each race shares with the other its wisdom, knowledge, and experience. A world were high elves and humans, could balance each other out. A world where mankind and high elves, were so busy with one another that neither could subvert all nature to themselves."

Gaia was silent for a long moment, which, in this place, seemed like an eternity, yet only a fleeting second.

Then Gaia smiled, and it was like the crepuscular rays radiating from a hole in the clouds upon a winter's day. She moved towards him again and as she gestures, flowers bloom at her feet. She touched him on the shoulder, and her touch was as gentle as a summer breeze. "Go Touchwood. I will help you make your dream for the world."

2

Victoria watched as the dead body of her grandpapa was slowly lowered into the Cauldron of Rebirth. The gloom of the workshop reflected in the faces of her comrades in arms.

Over the past few months, Victoria's young mind had witnessed so many terrible, and unlikely things, as well as amazingly wondrous things; that she had begun to think that anything was possible.

But her heavy heart, after seeing the terrible sight of her grandpapas desecrated body, could not believe that it could be revived. Surely this was against the laws of nature. A nature that she had begun to revere, and respect through her mentor Star, and her herb lore teachings.

This thought reminded her too, of the terrible vision she had seen while asleep in the loft bed above the stove. In it she had witnessed not only the death of her mentor Star, but of all the people she knew on that sacred island.

It was confusing, for she had come to see Star as a close friend; the sister that she had never had. A person she could confide in, and talk about anything that was on her mind. And now she was dead too. The two people that she cared about most had died at about the same time. She felt like her poor heart was torn into a thousand pieces.

Her misery was complete, as she watched the familiar face of her grandpapa disappear below the edge of the cauldron. Morgana's incantations had ceased at that point, and there was a pregnant silence of expectation that flooded through the small group who witnessed the ceremony.

The silence continued, into what seemed like to Victoria, an eternal silence. Eventually, though, there was a shuffling of feet, as a low murmur passed round the group.

Finnbar was the first to leave. Followed by Brad. Then Morgana and Rumanadil, left together. Victoria was alone with the bronze cauldron. She looked at it; beautiful but inert.

She hadn't believed that it would work. It would be too much to expect. She forced her feet to step around the enormous cauldron. She was just about the go through the workshop door, when a flash of light behind her, so bright that the reflection off the door almost blinded her. A searing heat scorched the skin of her back, for a moment, then was gone.

As she turned, the light from the cauldron gradually diminished, until white fiery flames appeared to be coming from it. The flames steadily increased until they leapt up to the workshop roof, dazzling her, and filling the whole place with their intense light. However, before long, the flames diminished, and she could see a figure moving within them.

Eventually the flames died down all together, and there remained a human figure which glowed with its own light. For a moment she thought it may be Luminara, the light being she had seen in the otherworld, come to visit her again. But no, this was a naked young man shining with a nimbus glow. He had long dark hair, tied in a warrior's knot, his face youthful and clean shaven. The young man all but leapt out of the cauldron, and stood before her in his full nakedness.

Looking at her intensely, he cried, "Victoria?"

It was all too much for her. The warrior she had been, crumbled into the frightened young girl she was inside.

She screamed. And kept on screaming, till Brad came rushing in, and pulled her to his muscular chest, where she crumpled in a torrent of sobs and tears.

Brad looked over her shoulders at the glowing young man, wondering who this stranger could be; yet there was something familiar about him.

"Don't you know me Brad, even after I have been among you such a long time?"

The voice of the glowing young man was not familiar to Brad, but Victoria turned in his arms and faced the stranger, uttering, "Grandpapa?"

3

They had all felt the safest place to be was the void craft. No one knew if those murderous goblins would come back, to finish off any survivors they had missed. Brad had found the young Touchwood some clothes to wear. He had felt that Victoria had seen her grandpapa murdered, then resurrected all in one day, and that was enough to bear; without seeing him walking about naked.

Now the young Touchwoods warrior persona was complete. Wearing dark elf warrior garb, made him look for all the world like some ancient Celtic warrior. Once they were gathered in the void craft mess hall, Brad, remembering from his army training, knew that chocolate may help improve someone's mood, and even improve cognitive function: it would certainly make them smile. So Brad, still concerned for Victoria's welfare, had synthesised some seventy per cent dark chocolate, and had given it to her, saying it was medicinal.

However, Victoria, clutching onto Brad's arm, had devoured the chocolate bar, like some ravenous animal. Having grown up in this isolated community, she had never tasted pure chocolate before, and found it infinitely better, than the synthesised chocolate ice cream she had tried previously. As she ate, she occasionally made furtive glances over towards Touchwood; who had stopped glowing now. She still had a hard time processing the fact that he was now a young man, even though her eyes told her it was true. It had been a miracle, everyone said so, but it would take some time to adjust to it.

Finnbar, still finding the resurrection hard to believe, had none the less explained to Touchwood, all that had happened on their mission to the dark Elves realm of Tech Duinn.

Morgana and Rumanadil had earlier also returned to the void craft, but upon hearing familiar voices in the mess hall, had entered to see the young Touchwood standing in the centre. Morgana looked this young man up and down candidly. Dressed in his warrior's garb, it stirred something akin to lust in her.

But Morgana, immediately recognised him for who he was, and was not overly surprised at what she saw. She had grown up hearing countless reports about the magical cauldron's effective ability to revive the dead.

Touchwood, aware of her gaze, turned to Morgana. Seeing her amorous stare, smiled, but said, "Morgana, who were those vile creatures that shot me down. Surely they are from the otherworld."

Morgana walked over to him, a glint in her eye. "I have never seen them before this. However, they remind me of the Greys. But I suspect from what I have heard, that they are something spawned by the dark elves as an invasion force. Your people said they had ransacked one of the other communities on this mountain, killing everyone there."

"My people?" Touchwood cried, "You have seen them? Are they alive?"

"Only through 'far sight'. They seemed safe, hidden in a cave close by. I advise leaving them there for the time being. We don't know when those goblins will return."

Touchwood nodded his assent. Then sudden realisation rushed through him, "And Uncle Dafydd, is he, alright?"

Brad and Rumanadil lowered their eyes, not wanting to break the news to him, but Morgana spoke up, "He suffered the same fate as you Touchwood. He awaits the cauldron."

"But we must get him to it immediately. There is no time to lose. Those goblins could return at any minute."

Morgana, moving closer, looking him in the eye, placed a hand gently on Touchwood's muscular shoulder and said quietly, "I will need time to recharge my magical energy, if I am to attempt another resurrection so soon. The cauldron cannot work by itself Touchwood, but needs an accomplished magician to gather and direct the necessary power."

Touchwood was caught off guard by Morgana's amorous advances towards him, unsure of how he felt about it.

But then smiling at her said, "Of course, when you are ready."

Chapter 28

The Lost

Chronicles

1

Several weeks passed, and the goblin creatures had not returned to Rath Grain. However, this had created very mixed feelings within the void craft. Even though there was relief that they hadn't returned, no one could really relax, and everyone remained on high alert, preparing for their potential return.

The war council continued to meet regularly, making plans for how they would defend themselves, and assigning tasks to each member. Early on, Victoria had voiced her concern for the animals, and wanted to go outside to tend them. Touchwood had allowed it on condition that Brad worked with her, and they had an armed guard.

Brad and Victoria by now had both discarded their warrior's garb, and returned them back to the void craft store. Reverting to their usual clothing that they wore about the smallholding. Victoria wore her usual baggy blue denim dungarees, and the funky woollen hat that had a long tail and a small woollen tassel at the end. Brad wore a patched army shirt, and a coarsely woven woollen kilt and bare legs.

So a regular routine was established. Every day, Victoria and Brad had gone out from the safety of the void craft to attend to the animals under armed guard. Even though they had ample army rations on the void craft, and of course, the food synthesiser, Victoria and Brad felt it important, to try to salvage the ruins of the vegetable gardens, as well as attend to the animals. The fresh farm produce they brought back was very welcome to those community members who had been used to an organic, vegetable-based diet.

2

When Morgana felt sufficiently recovered, an attempt was made to revive Dafydd in the mystical cauldron. The young Touchwood had however, become ever cautious and watchful for a return of those malicious goblin invaders. He was armed with a crossbow and busy watching over his granddaughter whilst she worked in the gardens.

Towards lunchtime, Rumanadil had slowly emerged from the workshop, and had told Touchwood, "We lowered Dafydd's body into the cauldron, as we did with you Touchwood. Morgana did the same incantations as before. But, though we waited a long time, no light or flames came from it. When we cautiously approached the cauldron, and looked in, it was empty. The body of Dafydd had gone. Disappeared to who knows where."

Although this news saddened Touchwood greatly, he suspected he knew what had happened. Dafydd had met the Earth Goddess, just as he had. But Dafydd as an Emrys had served the Goddess all his very long life, perhaps five hundred years or more. Dafydd had belonged to the old world, the old order of things. And perhaps between them they had decided that Dafydd's spirit should at last be rewarded, and move on to the next realm - the Summerland.

3

As time wore on, Finnbar had become restless, wanting to return to the Purple Mountains of Killarney, to look for any survivors of his own community. The other traders had left long before the invasion, in the boat they had arrived on.

Then early one sunny morning, Finnbar, while on guard duty, had noticed a fishing boat approaching the gravelly beach, that had formed all-round the island. As he watched, fascinated, it landed on the makeshift wharf. He decided on the spot, to go and check if they had any news from the other islands. He called to the others who were attending the gardens what he had seen; intrigued, Victoria and Brad followed him down to the wharf.

Amongst the fishing boat crew was Victoria's friend Cockle, the fisherman's son from the nearby island of Sidhe-Mor. He had a strange tale to tell. He reported that some weeks ago they had been invaded by strange green creatures, who had killed several people on his island. But the burley fishermen had been armed with large fishing knives, boat hooks and fishing nets, and had managed to capture one of the strange creatures. The others had run away and flown off in a glowing orb, like a shooting star.

Thinking that the strange creature had emerged from the ocean's depths, the fishermen had kept the creature in the net, and submerged it in the sea so it could be in its natural habitat. However, when they checked it again the next day, the thing had drowned. Cockle said that no one on any of the nearby islands had seen any more of the creatures since then.

This news was well received by all on the void craft, for it demonstrated that the goblin creatures could be killed by natural means, and were just as vulnerable as any creature on the earth plain.

Finnbar had left Sliabh an Iarainn on the little fishing boat, with the promise that they could take him to a larger boat, bound for islands in the south. Touchwood sadly waved him off, wondering if he would ever see him again. But he was encouraged by Cockle's news, and decided it was time to find the remnants of his own community.

After gathering some food supplies from Rath Grain, for he felt their own supplies must surely be running low; Touchwood had set off. Morgana had told Touchwood what she had seen with her far sight, so he had a good idea where they might be. He had found them hidden in a nearby cave. The one that many years before, Touchwood and his High Priestess Hazel had performed their shamanic rituals in. But of course, the community members were unaware of this.

They were in a sorry state, and devoured all the food Touchwood had brought, within minutes. With the news from Cockle, Touchwood had deemed it safe for them to return to Rath Grain. But, of course, they would still have to set an armed guard when people went outside.

It would be hard to describe the consternation, and amazement mixed with relief of the Rath Grain community members when confronted with the void craft. It took quite a lot of persuasion by Victoria, Brad and Touchwood that they would be safest on board; as the goblin creatures could return anytime. Eventually though, they had settled into this new and exciting life aboard the void craft.

As the weeks and months passed by, Victoria's baggy denim dungarees could no longer hide the round bump, that had developed where her flat tummy used to be. And more and more Victoria, and Morgana could be seen chatting intimately with each other. Touchwood had noticed Victoria's condition, and approached Morgana about this. She confirmed that Victoria was indeed pregnant, but not from an earthly boy.

After seeing so many strange, and terrible things these last years, Touchwood went away shaking his head, delighted that, amongst it all, something wonderful was blossoming.

There was still no sign or news of the goblin creatures' return. Caution and fear were replaced by puzzlement. What were those creatures that had attacked? Where had they come from? And where were they now?

But gradually, life at Rath Grain returned to some semblance of normality. However, armed guards were still posted just in case. But crops were still planted, and animals tended. The young Touchwood became an avid farmer again, using his youthful muscles to fetch and carry and dig and plant.

4

One autumn day Finnbar returned with a crew of traders. Their wares were, as usual, very well received, but more so was the news they brought. Finnbar confirmed, that the goblin creatures had indeed attacked several of the islands in the south and west. Although they had killed many settlers, several of the creatures had been killed also, using normal hunting bows or spears.

"They clearly have weaknesses," Finnbar said. "Perhaps we could defeat them if they returned."

But Finnbar reported too that after their initial attacks, no one on the many islands he had visited had seen them again.

"It was a mystery to be sure," Finnbar had said.

But stranger still, and Finnbar was particularly keen to tell this to Victoria, was the news about a development no one expected. It seemed that many children were being born with long Elven ears, something like Victorias. And stranger still, these young people seemed to exhibit uncanny psychic powers. He also noticed, and commented on Victoria's now very large belly, saying perhaps you too may give birth to this new type of human-elf hybrid.

Even though it had been several months since the first attack, the war council still met regularly. On one such occasion, it had been decided that Rumanadil and Morgana, should return to the otherworld, and seek out the High Elven Queen to tell her all they knew about the dark elves; if she didn't already know. There was concern that the remaining dark elves could rise up again if left to their own devices. While they were depleted and disorganised, it was deemed that it would be the best time to deal with them.

And so it was. An army of High Elves descended on Tech Duinn, and the dark elf castle. It was there they discovered many dark elves hiding away in dark corners, including Dr Darkbrood.

However, the High Queen, not wanting to kill fellow elves, no matter how far into the destructive side they had fallen, had deemed that all the dark elves be rounded up, and imprisoned in their own dungeons. Their gaolers, it was decreed, would be the Greys, who the Queen knew hated their masters. And left it up to the Greys to feed and water their prisoners; if they had a mind to.

5

On a chilly February morning, just as the sun was rising, Victoria became a mother; giving birth to an Imbolc child. The baby girl, born with a crop of blond hair and tiny Elven ears, was as beautiful as her mother. Ruby, who was the midwife, presented the new baby to the young Touchwood, who was delighted and so proud of Victoria, even though technically it made him a great grandfather.

During the winter months of her pregnancy, she had told Touchwood all about her connection to Star, the priestess of the moon, and about the herbal teachings she had been receiving from her. And even about the Elven boy, she had met in the otherworld and how she had miraculously conceived through him.

It was several weeks later, just close to dawn, that Victoria had rushed into Touchwood's bedroom, rudely awakening him, to tell him that she had had the most amazing vision while sleeping. She had been visited by Star again, who proclaimed with some urgency, that she was distressed that she had lost all her log books on herb lore, and her journals on temple life, and the way of life in her homeland; when it was destroyed by the comet.

Now she had found her way back to Victoria. She desperately didn't want all that knowledge to be lost forever. She wanted to dictate it to Victoria, and for her to write down all her lost chronicles, so that it could be used to reform the new society, that Victoria and all her people were starting to create.

6

The Void craft remained in the community garden, accumulating and concentrating the mysterious magical energy, that it gathered from the earth itself. And because these energies have beneficial powers to all living things, this increased the fertility of the land all about it, including the animals and the humans living on it. Rath Grain became an oasis of green fertility, everyone living there thrived and became youthful.

But as we know, the void craft was a two-way portal linking the earth plain to the otherworld, consequently Rumanadil and Morgana became regular visitors to Rath Grain community. On one such visit, they were sitting with Touchwood, and Victoria on the outside decking, enjoying the sunshine, and overlooking the orchards. Morgana was delighted with Victoria's new baby, and sat with the little girl on her knee cooing at her like a proud grandmother.

Meanwhile, Rumanadil sat with Touchwood, and told

him that the High Elven Queen had been informed about his part in the rescue of the Great God Pan, and the finding of the lost Syrinx. And also the vital part played by him in the demise of the dark elves.

Rumanadil, now the Elven Queen's ambassador to the earth plane, officially informed Touchwood, that the Elven Queen wanted to award him a special commendation. And said he would be welcome to visit the High Elven Queen in her otherworldly palace, any time that he chose.

This pleased Touchwood no end, and said he would be delighted to oblige the Queen and would come as soon as the spring planting had finished.

Rumanadil then turned to him and said when you do come to the Elven palace, the Queen will present to you the special commendation. You must know Touchwood, that this is a very great honour, for she intends to grant you three wishes.

Touchwood, in his turn, looked about him at the apple blossom on the trees in the orchard, and the visiting elves from the otherworld, and at his granddaughter with her new baby on her knee, and said that all he had ever wished for had already come about.

The End

Epilogue

But what happened to the Goblin hybrids?

Well, it was like this. During the climate change years, the malicious magic of the dark elves had transformed the planet into a landscape of extremes; the Earth becoming a shadow of its former self. The once-mighty glaciers and polar ice caps had all but vanished, causing sea levels to rise and swallow up all low-lying land. This included major coastal cities. Billions of humans had died; human civilisation was in ruins. Then the battle for resources had begun. The oil wars had all but brought the remaining humans to the brink of extinction.

And so it was, that the recently deceased King Indech Lord of Chaos, had got his wish, albeit posthumously. The over-riding desire of the Dark elves to walk on the physical earth plain, procreate, and have children looked close to coming about.

With advanced technology in the form of the void craft, and a ruthless determination to claim Earth as their own, Dr Darkbrood's brainchild, the genetically mutated elf-human hybrid's had scoured the earth, and had already killed many humans. They looked set to achieving their goals.

But there were only fifty void craft, and the king had rushed Dr Darkbrood towards the end, so a mere five hundred goblin creatures had been spawned. The Earth was a big place and the human survivors were spread about, miles apart, in small pockets here and there. Indigenous tribes were hidden away in thick jungles or isolated islands. The survivalist, self-sufficient communities were usually far from the ruined cities.

As the days turned into weeks. And the weeks turned to months. The invasion force of goblin creatures had only covered a small fraction of the earth. Word had spread fast among the human survivors. Many had hidden away in caves. Others had already been prepared for the inevitable end of the human civilisation, and had built underground fall-out shelters, in which they could survive for months, perhaps years.

High up in the polar wastes of northern Canada, the melting glaciers of Baffin Island had revealed a hidden world beneath the ice. One that was both fascinating and potentially dangerous. Rugged rocky surfaces, newly formed lakes, ancient plants and exposed soil, that had not seen daylight for at least 115,000 years.

Soil exposed by the retreating ice is often nutrient-rich, having been shielded from erosion and weathering for millennia. This can lead to a burst of plant growth, as seeds and spores that have lain dormant in the ice begin to germinate. However, this newly exposed soil can also harbour ancient microorganisms, including bacteria and viruses that have been trapped in the ice for thousands of years.

Bacillus anthracis, the bacterium that causes anthrax, are incredibly resilient and can survive in a dormant state almost indefinitely. Reindeer are particularly susceptible to anthrax because they graze on vegetation close to the ground, where anthrax spores can be present in the soil. Anthrax can be fatal for reindeer and most animals. When animals ingest or inhale these spores, they can develop severe symptoms and die quickly.

Now our gaze turns to one such area of mud, and earth that had recently been revealed. Entombed within it lays the remains of a herd of reindeer that had been snap-frozen, subjected to some ancient and sudden, extreme freezing event which preserved their bodies almost instantaneously, preventing decomposition.

As we watch, an invading void ship containing a squad of the goblin hybrid creatures, glides over the area, then suddenly stops and hovers above the frozen herd.

The goblin squadron had stopped to investigate, their physical bodies now subjected to what all bodies need; the need for sustenance, the need to eat.

However, being spawned in a lab, and their growth artificially accelerated, they had not experienced such feelings and desires before. Consequently, they were by now feeling ravenous. Their animal instincts told them that the reindeer carcases strewn below were food; and they intended to eat it.

The goblin creatures, never having been taught any different, had eaten the defrosting reindeer meat raw. Once their voracious appetites had been sated, they loaded the rest of the carcases onto their void craft, and flew off to the agreed rendezvous site to meet with all the other invading goblins. They were going to have a feast. They would be hailed as heros for providing such an abundance of food for all their comrades.

About the Author

Corin Thistlewood has lived an eclectic life. He began his career as a successful aerospace engineer. However he had a deeply spiritual side as well, so followed his passion for Metaphysics & personal development. This eventually led him to qualify in several Alternative therapies including Shiatsu, Shamanic healing & Transpersonal hypnotherapy before opening the Australian College of Druidry, which was given the moniker 'the real-life Hogwarts by the media. Corin now resides in South-west England, where he has become a full-time author. His literary works delve into captivating realms, blending elements of Shamanism, Celtic spirituality, and hypnotherapy.

www.corin-thistlewood.ueniweb.com
Blog: https://corin-thistlewood.ueniweb.com/blog#space
Facebook: Corin Thistlewood: Novelist | Facebook

If you have enjoyed 'Atlantis: The Lost Chronicles', you may be interested in the pre-story of this book which is explored in the trilogy 'The Touchwood Chronicles.' In it, the author relates the early life of Touchwood and how he came to establish the self-sufficient community of Rath Grain. And how he was drawn into the realms of magic and the Otherworld with the aid of the mysterious alchemist, Uncle Dafydd. These books tell how the young Touchwood, through his spirit guide the Oak King, is gifted the power to mind meld with animals. How the climate crisis came about, and how the rising waters transformed Ireland into a series of isolated islands.